# A Week with Fiona Wonder

## A Novel

Kelly Huddleston

Published by Open Books 2013

ISBN: 0615722822
ISBN-13: 978-0615722825

*For David, my catcher*

# CONTENTS

# SUNDAY

*T*he Assistant Marketing Director at *Almost There Magazine* called at ten-thirty this morning to talk to me about what's going to happen next week. I mean my week with Fiona Wonder, the movie star. Except when she called I wasn't anywhere near the telephone. I was at the bottom of the hill outside our apartment building lying flat on my back with my hands underneath my head and staring up at the sky, contemplative and dreamy I guess you could call my state of mind, thinking about nothing really worth thinking about, only how glad I was that it was summer and how big and blue the sky looked, and also what was behind it.

What I mean is just because my eyes couldn't see behind all the blue of the sky didn't mean that what was behind it wasn't there. So what I did was this: I imagined taking Mom's nametag—I chose the BONANZA BURGER nametag, a shiny orange button with her name written on it in fat loopy cursive rather than the nametag for Waffle Falafel, a white rectangle with her name misspelled on it in solid black capital letters—and with the sharp point of the metal clasp I poked a hole into the blue.

Through the hole I saw the next layer; I saw a pinprick of space.

Except what I really wanted to see was less sky and more space. So I imagined taking a pair of scissors from Nikki's hair station at Clippers, and with the point of the scissors I dug into the hole I'd punctured with the nametag pin. I snipped at the blue until the sky split in half. The two halves drew open like an old-time movie theater curtain until eventually they fluttered away completely. What was left was space. Deep black space. I saw all the planets in the solar system and then, way far out there, the end of the galaxy and the beginning of the next, and then the end of that galaxy and the beginning of the next; and everywhere I saw ribbons and folds of every color imaginable, and millions upon millions of twinkling white hot stars, most of them fixed in place just like the glow-in-the-dark stars glued onto the ceiling above my bed that Mom bought on sale at CostMart, but a few of the stars fell and spun and exploded and fizzled into the blackness. And it went on forever, and it was so endless that it was like looking at everything.

So, as I said, I was thinking about nothing really worth thinking about. Still, it was nice, you know, to just lie there feeling the cool wet grass on the backs of my arms and legs. I felt an ant crawl under my shirt and start to work its way up my stomach. I was in such a mellow mood that it didn't even bother me.

Then the sun went dark, like an eclipse. The eclipse turned out to be Mom's head. From where I lay, and from where she stood, it looked like her head was put on backwards. Mom looked down at me, her mouth where her eyes should have been, and her lips the wrong way, and her nose turned round so I could see right into her nostrils. Behind Mom's head the two blue halves of sky fluttered back together until there was just a seam of space left where I had snipped open the sky with Nikki's scissors. That's when I saw a woman's hand zipper the seam that closed the universe.

It was Mrs. Redding's hand. I recognized it from the pink, perfectly manicured nails and the plain gold wedding band she wore on her ring finger. I had watched Mrs. Redding's hand perform the exact same movement last Wednesday morning after I had spent the night at the Redding's house, only with a zipper on the back of my best friend Valerie's skirt.

"Why are you lying there on the grass like that?" Mom wanted to know.

An airplane moved across the sky, its vapor trails reminding me of the lines made by the green felt pens that my English teacher, Ms. Starburn, uses to underline metaphors in books. I watched the airplane enter one of Mom's ears, disappear inside her head, then reappear from her other ear.

"Mercy—" Mom said, saying my name, but then she stopped. A second later she started to breathe hard. I knew what was coming next. She was going to have an asthma attack.


The last time Mom had an asthma attack was on the morning after Junior Prom. But at least that time it wasn't as bad as the time before that. The time before that she ended up in the hospital Emergency Room.

The day after Junior Prom I was still in bed when I heard her come home from her graveyard shift at Waffle Falafel. Mom has two waitressing jobs. She is a waitress at BONANZA BURGER, a chain restaurant inside Heritage Shopping Mall where you build your own burger and get unlimited steak fries. She works there from six pm until ten or eleven pm. Then she works at Waffle Falafel, which has its own building and is located on the perimeter of one of the mall parking lots. She works there from midnight until six am, except Thursdays. That's Mom's one night off from serving both burgers and falafel waffles.

Usually she is home by six-fifteen—six thirty at the latest. On the morning after Junior Prom, however, she arrived home at five minutes after nine. I remember the exact time because I looked at the clock when I heard the door open. Instead of going straight to her bedroom as she usually does, she went instead into the bathroom.

I checked to see if my best friend, Valerie, had woken up. She hadn't. She lay in a sleeping bag on the floor next to my bed, her thick red hair in a tangled mess all over the pillow that she'd brought with her, and her mouth wide open, snoring. Valerie's entire right hand was not visible. That's because it rested inside an opened, jumbo size bag of potato chips. Her huge stomach expanded and deflated with her breathing. The snoring stopped momentarily, interrupted by a loud snort, then picked up again with the same rhythm and loudness as before. I watched her left foot twitch. Then her right hand spasm. It went flying and ended up on top of her chest, the cellophane glove of the potato chip bag still firmly in place. It looked like she was about to recite the pledge of allegiance.

The night before, while most of our classmates attended Junior Prom, Valerie had ordered and paid for an extra large Hawaiian pizza. She'd eaten, except for the two slices that I ate, an entire pie. She drank a quart of fruit punch that she'd brought with her from home. The bag of potato chips, as well as a bag of Jelly Squiggles, had emerged from her over night bag about ten minutes before ten o'clock, the same time that Heritage Shopping Mall closes and that Mom stops serving at BONANZA BURGER.

Sitting next to me on my bed, Valerie alternated eating chips and squiggles. She told me that she thought my mom was nice looking in an average sort of way—that she's not too skinny and she's not too fat, she's not too tall and she's not too short. She's not movie star beautiful like Fiona Wonder, or classically beautiful like her own mother, but at least she didn't look like our English teacher Ms. Starburn, with her weird square shaped glasses, or like Nikki, my mom's best friend, who Valerie thinks looks like a ferret. "She looks like a lot of other mothers out there," Valerie said.

In her own way I think Mom is beautiful, but I think everyone is beautiful in their own way.

"She'd look better if she didn't wear her hair in that big greasy-looking ponytail all the time," Valerie said. "And it might help if she bought some perfume to hide her smell," she added.

"What do you mean?" I asked. "I think she smells fine."

Valerie huffed. "She smells like her work: grease and fried onions and dirty mop water and hamburger meat and disinfectant and powdered sugar... And, the ever-so-faint scent of tip money, too!"

"That's not nice," I said.

"Your mom has been a waitress forever, hasn't she?" Valerie said.

I just nodded my head and looked out my bedroom window at the shopping mall.

Heritage Mall is an eight-minute walk from our apartment building. From my bedroom window I can see the entire south side rooftop and part of the giant skylight in the middle of the enclosure. Sometimes at night, after Mom's gone to work, I turn off the light in my bedroom and sit on my bed and look out the window at the bright rectangle of light that comes from the skylight. I think about all the people walking around inside the mall, and about Mom serving burgers and never-ending baskets of steak fries at BONANZA BURGER, and about Nikki, too, who cuts hair on the upper floor of the mall at the chain hair styling salon, Clippers. Thinking about all the people inside the mall doesn't make me feel happy or sad; it makes me feel, in some unexplainable and wonderful way, that we are all connected to each other.

One time last year I tried to explain it—this idea that we're all connected—to Ms. Starburn. It was during fifth period, the hour I spent with her during junior year inside the English teachers' room working as her teaching assistant. As usual, we were sitting across from each other at an old lunchroom table. I had just finished grading a multiple choice quiz on Chapter 11 of *Word Power Made Easy*, and Ms. Starburn had just finished reading an essay about the various metaphors found in John Irving's *A Prayer for Owen Meany*.

It's really obvious that Ms. Starburn loves words. Last year in class we spent a lot of time searching through whatever novel we were reading for metaphors and allegories and similes. It was fun—like hunting for Easter eggs or digging for lost treasures. Ms. Starburn always uses one of her green felt marking pens to underline metaphors, but I still use a pencil in case I make a mistake and need to erase something.

The day I tried to explain to her how I thought we were all connected, Ms. Starburn at first seemed startled, then less startled and more surprised, then not surprised at all but really, really happy, like I had just presented her with a big golden nugget that I had magically produced from my backpack.

It's funny because that same day after school I tried to explain it to Valerie. We were sitting at her kitchen table, pretending to do our social studies homework, drinking sodas and eating chips. Actually, now that I think about it, it was more Valerie than I who plowed her way through the chips along with a plate of homemade cowboy cookies that Mrs. Redding had laid out for Jeremy, Valerie's big brother, and his friends from football practice.

Valerie's mom, Mrs. Redding, had her back to us. She was silently cutting stalks of flowers over the sink. They were purple tulips from the garden. She was using a pair of garden scissors with rubber handles, not like the scissors Nikki uses to cut hair at Clippers. I could hear the thud of each stem as it hit the basin.

Valerie is right about her mother: She is beautiful. She

is very tall and slender, and she has thick red hair and big gray eyes and perfect pale skin that actually looks like porcelain. In a way she reminds me of a corpse laid out in an open casket, she's so pale and perfect and silent. In any case, Mrs. Redding finished cutting all the stems of the flowers. She placed them in a tall glass vase then turned from the sink to the kitchen nook where Valerie and I sat on matching wooden bar stools. Her eyes found and held mine, then flicked away. I don't know why exactly, but the way she looked at me made me want to stop talking about how I thought we were all connected to one another.

It was Senior Prom that really mattered, not Junior Prom, and everyone knew it, too—that's what Valerie had said on the night of Junior Prom, as she sat next to me on my bed before tilting her head and dropping an iridescent squiggle into her mouth. She took a huge swig of fruit punch straight from the bottle. Then she belched.

I had a moment of déjà vu. All her eating and swigging and belching reminded me of the night of another dance— the Winter Ball during Christmas vacation that her parents had attended at the city's art museum. I had spent the night at Valerie's house that night, too. Now here we were more than six months later—Valerie, the girl with everything except the one thing that she really wanted, and me, the girl without anything except the truth.

The truth was that I had been asked to the Junior Prom. I told the boy no because of Valerie. If Valerie had known that I had been asked, and more specifically if she had known just who had asked me, and if I had said yes to him instead of no, then it would have meant that she would have suffered deeply. You see, regarding Junior Prom and my refusal of the invitation by the boy who'd asked me to go, I looked beyond myself and my feelings and looked instead at Valerie and what it would have meant to her. I mean, I tried to look at the whole picture.

The next morning, while Valerie lay snoring with her hand inside a potato chip bag on top of her chest, I heard

Mom start to wheeze inside the bathroom. Valerie didn't move a muscle as I got out of bed, tiptoed across the room, opened the door and made my way down the hallway to the bathroom.

She hadn't closed the door all the way. Without her knowing that I was on the other side of the door, I saw Mom sitting on the edge of the bathtub, not only wheezing but crying too. She still had on her waitress uniform. The front of it was soiled red with a gigantic ketchup stain—an entire bottle's worth of it, it looked like, caked dry, the color of blood.

The way that she wheezed and coughed, I could tell that she was having a full-blown asthma attack. I wanted to push open the door, to ask her what had happened, to tell her to calm down, to make her take a dose of her rescue asthma inhaler, but something held me back.

I felt like I was a witness to something that wasn't real, to something that wasn't actually happening. It was almost like I wasn't me at all, but rather Mom watching a movie with Fiona Wonder in it. By far Fiona Wonder is Mom's favorite actress. She owns all her movies on DVD. Any chance she gets she watches one—no matter how many times she has seen it. She slips in a DVD, sits or lies on the couch, and stares at the television, wordless and almost hypnotized. Movies aren't based on real things, and yet to Mom they seem real. A lot of times I think that they seem more real to her than real life. And that's just how I felt watching Mom.

The attack came and went. Slowly, Mom stood up from the bathtub. She wasn't too steady on her feet. She had stopped crying, at least. Without looking at herself in the mirror she started to undress. The ketchup stained uniform fell in a rumbled pile to the floor. In her underpants and nylons, she picked up the uniform and looked down at it. She started to cry all over again.

"Stop it!" she told herself in an unforgiving tone of voice that doesn't usually sound like Mom at all. She said to herself: "It's over. It's done. So just *stop*!"

Her hands worked through the material, slowly at first then more frantically. She was looking for her nametag, of course. The one with her name misspelled. If she loses it then the cost of it is deducted from her pay. Ditto with her nametag for BONANZA BURGER. The ketchup stained uniform, I already knew, was ruined. I'd wash it later that morning, but the stain had already set. She wouldn't be able to wear it again. Luckily, she had an extra uniform, identical to the other, hanging in her closet.

When she found the nametag within the folds of stained material it took her forever to unclasp the needle on the back of it. That was because her hands were shaking. She dropped the uniform to the floor again. She worked at clasping the needle back into its tiny notch. When she set it on the edge of the bathroom sink it immediately dropped to the floor. Slowly, Mom crouched down to pick it up.

That's when I saw it—the small white bag, not big enough to place an orange inside, on the floor. Block letters written on its side read: COLEANNE'S JEWELLERY & FRAGRANCE DEPARTMENT.

Of course I had no way of knowing then what was inside the bag—Fiona Wonder's Shooting Star Bracelet and the receipt that came with it. For all intents and purposes, it was the receipt that really mattered; it was the receipt that won me a week with Fiona Wonder, the movie star. On the back of the receipt was a sixteen-digit number that later that day Mom sent, along with my name and our address, to the contest that she found in *Almost There Magazine*. Out of all the Shooting Star Bracelets that were bought, and all the millions of receipts that came with those bracelets, and all the gazillion sixteen-digit numbers that were sent to the contest in *Almost There Magazine*, it was Mom who sent in the winning number— 0188236908826738—and won me an entire week with Fiona Wonder, the movie star.

Just where Mom had gotten the money to buy the bracelet in the first place was another story altogether—a story so incredible that when Mom finally spilled the beans and told me—well, it was like I wasn't me but Mom, sitting on the couch, staring at the television, wordless and hypnotized, watching a Fiona Wonder movie. All over again it was like looking at Mom through the crack in the bathroom door, knowing that she didn't know I was watching her, knowing that I was a witness to something that was real yet all the same didn't seem real at all. Like looking at the beam of yellow light coming from the skylight of the mall and having the feeling that we are all connected to each other and knowing it so simply, and so plainly, as I explained it to Ms. Starburn, yet not knowing it at all later that day when I tried to explain it to Valerie and her mother, who had turned from the kitchen sink to look at me as if I really didn't belong there, or even belong on Earth, as if I were some sort of alien. Like saying no when I really wanted to say yes to the boy who'd asked me to Junior Prom because I didn't want to hurt my best friend's feelings. Like looking up at the sky—seeing everything and nothing all at the same time.

$The$ Assistant Marketing Director," Mom said to me at the bottom of the hill outside our apartment building. Her hands fluttered at her sides. She stopped to try to breathe. "The Assistant Marketing Director at *Almost There Magazine* is on the telephone. She wants to talk to you about your week with—" But she didn't—couldn't—finish her sentence because she wasn't getting enough oxygen to her lungs.

I sat up, wheeled my butt in a circle on the grass, and looked up at her.

"Mom," I said, "where's your asthma inhaler?"

She waved her hands at me as if the fact that she couldn't breathe was no big deal. That's when I saw the red blotches bloom on both her cheeks.

"Mom, where's your inhaler?" I repeated.

I don't know why I even asked her. I knew exactly where it was—in the chipped blue dish on the dressing table in her bedroom where she keeps her nametags.

I stood up quickly, so quickly I almost bumped heads with her. I took another look at Mom then started running up the hill to our apartment building. It seemed to take forever to climb that hill. It was like one of those dreams where I'm running as fast as I can yet at the same time not moving at all. When I reached the top of the hill I had to stop for a minute to catch my own breath. Below me, on the freeway, there were less cars than usual, but only because it was Sunday morning. Most people, I figured, were still at home or at church. It would pick up again starting at noon. For one thing, Pacy's Department Store was having a big sale—50% off everything! For another thing, Fiona Wonder's new movie, *The Immortals*, had opened on Friday and was playing in the mall theater opposite BONANZA BURGER.

Still trying to catch my breath, I turned away from the freeway. At the bottom of the other side of the hill I saw Mom. She looked so small and fragile and alone standing there with her back to me. I watched her put her arms over her head, something she always does when she's having an asthma attack. I started running again. In my mind I could see her rescue asthma inhaler next to the two nametags inside the chipped blue dish on top of her dresser. Mom takes one inhaler twice in the morning and twice at night every day; the other inhaler is much stronger, more expensive, and only used when she gets an asthma attack. We call it the rescue inhaler. That's the one I was on my way to get.

The first thing I saw when I rounded the corner to the front of the apartment building was Nikki's car—a two-door Daihatsu that leaks oil and smells like hairspray and is almost as old as I am. As usual, Nikki had parked it in our designated parking space. We never use it, the designated parking space, because Mom doesn't have a car. I looked up the flight of stairs to the top floor where our apartment is located and saw a cloud of cigarette smoke.

"Nikki!" I shouted.

"What?" Nikki's voice shouted back to me.

"Go ahead inside!"

I ran up three flights of stairs as fast as I could. As I rounded the landing I saw Nikki leaning against our door, lighting a cigarette using the burning tip of the one she'd just smoked.

"Hey, M," she said.

That's what Nikki calls me: M. She's not the only one who doesn't call me by my real name. It doesn't seem to matter how many times Valcrie corrects her mother; Mrs. Redding always calls me "Marcy".

"How come you're running like that?" she wanted to know.

"Mom's having an asthma attack," I said, panting.

As usual she had her gigantic black leather purse with her and had changed the color of her hair again. It was jet black—an improvement, I thought, from last week's choice: black and brown and white all mixed together, like a raccoon's hide. She'd cut it, too. The length was shorter and spikier than usual. The ends stood up sharply. It looked pretty severe, but then again almost everything about Nikki is severe. Her body looks like an arrow; she's so skinny except for her big head and that short spiky hair sticking up from the top of it.

Nikki and Mom have been best friends since forever— since before I was born; since high school. I have a feeling that deep down, underneath all the passing years, Nikki has and will always be the way she is—too hard—and Mom has been and will always be the way she is—too soft—and that's why after all these years they're still best friends. Because they're such opposites, they even each other out.

"Nikki, move away from the door. I need to get

inside."

She didn't move. Instead she stubbed out the cigarette on the right heel of her cowboy boot then flicked the butt over the side of the railing. She knew how much I hated it when she did that. She stood leaning against the door, blocking my entrance.

"Guess why I can't let myself inside?" she said. "Go ahead, guess."

"Nikki, I don't want to guess. I need to get inside. Mom is outside at the bottom of the hill and she's having an—"

"Then don't guess. I'll tell you why. Because of them."

She meant her boyfriend Kurt's children, Brandi and Tucker. Brandi is ten and Tucker is eight. One time I met them, or at least I met the top halves of their bodies as they sat inside Kurt's cement truck. It was on a Saturday. They live with their mom Alicia but spend every weekend with Kurt, who recently moved in with Nikki after he lost his job at Pullman's Cement, Builders & Contractors, Ltd. I remember that Kurt and his kids were on their way to the zoo, but first they were dropping off Nikki at our apartment.

Nikki didn't go to the zoo with them that day because Nikki can't stand them. It's because, I think, they represent a part of Kurt's life that happened before her. Nikki calls Kurt's kids "baggage" and Kurt's ex-wife *that woman. That woman*, otherwise known as Alicia, works as a stylist at Clippers too, although not at the same location where Nikki works inside Heritage Shopping Mall but about fifteen minutes north of the mall in a strip mall called Patriot Plaza. One time I asked Nikki, while we were walking from the parking lot at Patriot Plaza toward the entrance of CostMart Supermarket, if she thought it was weird that her boyfriend's ex-wife not only had the same profession as she but also worked at the same chain hair salon. Nikki just looked at me like I was crazy. "There are a lot of hairdressers and a lot of Clippers in the world,"

Nikki said matter-of-factly.

It's not often she says something remotely right-on-the-money like that. Nationwide there are 2,029 Clippers Hair Salons. That's even more than all Waffle Falafels (1,500) and BONANZA BURGERS (505) combined. I know this because last year I looked it up online on one of the computers in the school library.

Someday, Nikki says, she wants to own her own Clippers, except I don't know how that's ever going to happen. It says right on the Clippers corporate web site that anyone who applies to own one has to have at least fifty thousand dollars up front and three hundred thousand dollars more in the bank. Maybe that's not a lot of money to some people, but it sure is to Nikki. One time I asked her how much money she makes and she told me: eight dollars and eighty-four cents an hour plus tips. It is way more money than Mom makes at both of her waitressing jobs combined, not including tips, of course, but it still sure isn't enough to buy a Clippers of her own.

It would be really great, I think, if she could just open her own salon. Snippy Nikki or Snip Nik—either would be a good name for her salon, I think. Nikki could have her own place with her own chairs, her own mirrors, her own scissors, and her own customers. She could be her own boss instead of working for a corporation.

One time, when I was spending the night at Valerie's house, Val told me that she and her mother had *almost* gotten haircuts at Nikki's Clippers. Mrs. Redding made Valerie go first. It wasn't Nikki that *almost* cut Valerie's hair but another stylist. The stylist had already washed Valerie's hair and had gotten her into the chair and was about to get out the scissors when suddenly Mrs. Redding changed her mind. It was because she remembered that Jeremy, Valerie's brother, had told her about pictures of razor burned heads and lopsided haircuts posted on the Clippers Facebook page. They'd left the salon immediately, Valerie wet-headed, without explanation.

"Nikki, please move!" I said.

She frowned at me. "Don't you want to know what they did with my key?"

"No, Nikki, I—"

"Yesterday, while I was still at work, those kids, Brandi and Tucker, drank all my diet soda. Tucker spilled some on the card that Kurt made for me. The one on which he'd written, I'M SORRY. He made it for me because of the big fight that we had last week, the one where I told him that he doesn't do a thing all day long but sit in front of the TV, drinking beer and feeling sorry for himself. Do you remember me telling you about the fight?"

Of course I remembered. Last Thursday night, which also happens to be Mom's one and only night off, it was all we'd heard about from Nikki after we'd gotten back from doing our weekly grocery shopping at CostMart. I had helped Mom put away the groceries then the three of us ate chicken lo mein, eggrolls and sweet and sour pork right out of takeaway boxes, drank root beer sodas and watched, or at least tried to watch, the movie *Sunny Sunshine Girl*.

Fiona Wonder stars in it; it is part of Mom's extensive Fiona Wonder DVD collection. Mom pretended to listen to what Nikki was saying about Kurt, but I could tell that she was really focused on the film and, more specifically, who starred in it. When it comes down to it, it's Mom who loves all the movies. It's really Mom who thinks Fiona Wonder is the greatest.

"When I got home I was real nice about it," Nikki continued. "I didn't yell at them; I just said that maybe in the future they shouldn't drink my diet soda without asking me first. I said it'd be better, actually, if they didn't take anything at all from my fridge until I said it was okay. I asked them nicely to turn off the TV and clean up the living room, because that's where they sleep, you know, on the fold-out bed in the sofa, when they spend the weekends with us, and it was starting to look like a real pigsty. Except, did they listen to me?"

I opened my mouth.

"No, they did not," Nikki told me before I could say anything. "Kurt left to watch a baseball game at his friend's house, and I went to take a bath, and that's when Brandi, the little brat, decided to go through my purse. Guess what she and her snotty little brother did."

It was not a question.

"They buried my hairbrush, some rubber bands and a new set of shears in the backyard. They threw my cigarettes down the toilet, which clogged. They took my keys, dropped them down the drain, and turned on the garbage disposal."

I kept looking at the door, thinking about Mom.

"There was other stuff in my purse, too. Stuff that I bought. Stuff that was mine. It was my stuff and they stole it. They took it and hid it and they won't tell me where it is and it's my stuff and they are—" she said slowly, like she always does when she thinks what she has to say is of supreme importance and that I can only comprehend exactly what she is saying if she speaks in slow motion "the worst—little—bratty—horrible—monsters—that—I—have—ever—"

"Nikki, cut it out!" I said, finally losing patience. As gently as possible I shoved her out of the way, put my key into the lock, and flung open the door.

In the kitchen I saw the telephone off the hook, the receiver on top of the table.

"The phone's off the hook," Nikki said, following me inside and noticing it immediately.

I didn't answer her; I ran straight to Mom's room.

Instead of the rescue asthma inhaler in the sky blue dish next to Mom's two nametags, I found the Fiona Wonder Shooting Star Bracelet.

*I* don't know why but I couldn't stop looking at it. For all the fuss—the telephone calls back and forth between the

Assistant Marketing Director and Mom, the long complicated legal documents that both she and I had to sign well over two months ago now, and the newspaper and local television media that came to interview me three different times about winning the week with a movie star—it's actually a very simple piece of jewelry.

The Fiona Wonder Shooting Star Bracelet is shaped like a star with clear crystals glued onto the points. The star is connected to a silver bangle that can adjust to just about any size wrist, including Valerie's, who tried it on along with Mom and Nikki after Mom bought it. The first time that I asked her about it, Mom said it was inappropriate to ask where she'd gotten the money to purchase the bracelet.

"You didn't let Nikki—you know," I had asked Mom.

"Oh, Mercy, for heaven's sake, no."

"Good," I said.

Nikki is a kleptomaniac. That means she can't stop stealing. At her hair station at Clippers there are all these glittery gold dolphin stickers stuck onto the mirror—stickers I saw her steal one day from the thrift store on Madison Street. Like everyone else, Nikki pays her rent and buys groceries. Because she has a car, she buys gas. Even though she needs fifty thousand dollars in cash and three hundred thousand more in the bank to even consider buying her own Clippers, she'd never consider robbing a bank or holding up a gas station. I guess that's a good thing. The point is that it's never big things or things she really needs that she steals, but rather just junk like lighters and key chains and stickers.

"You didn't use any of your money stash, did you?" I kept bugging Mom.

Mom keeps four money funds, one for rent, phone and electricity, one for food, one for rainy days that she mostly uses to buy movie tickets, and one for medical expenses that mostly pay for Mom's two asthma inhalers. The funds stay safe in the third drawer of her dresser in four different colored socks without matches.

"I took just a little money from the rainy day fund," she told me, but she'd given herself away when she bit down hard on a fingernail. About two minutes later, after she'd figured out that I wasn't going to leave her alone until she told me where she got the rest of the money for the bracelet, she sighed and said, "If you really want to know, then I'll tell you. But just so you know, I think knowing all the particulars about it takes away some of the magic."

I just waited until she finally decided to spill the beans.

*I*t's like something out of a Fiona Wonder movie. The only difference, I suppose, is that Mom's story is fact, not fiction. The fact that it actually happened along with the fact that the bracelet that she ended up buying had the sixteen-digit winning number attached to it is more than just incredible—it's actually wondrous. At least that's what I think.

It was on the night of the Junior Prom—the same night that Valerie stayed at my place, ate pizza and chips and Jelly Squiggles, and fell asleep with her hand inside a potato chip bag. Mom was well into her graveyard shift at Waffle Falafel. It started out slow, then picked up a little, then got slow again. That was okay with Mom, who was alone that night because the other waitress that works the graveyard shift with Mom simply hadn't bothered to show up. That happens sometimes. When it happens, and the manager of the restaurant finds out about it, he always fires the person—no matter what the reason.

Luckily, the manager wasn't there that night. He'd left a note for Mom saying that at around nine o'clock that night, while she was still waitressing at BONANZA BURGER, he'd eaten a double stack of cherry chocolate pancakes and had developed, quite rapidly, intensely bad stomach cramps. He wasn't coming back until tomorrow. Except for the two line cooks in the kitchen, she was on her own. It was an uneventful night—that's the way that Mom described it to me.

The sun crept up over the horizon. Mom sat down at the counter, having some coffee, taking a break. She was looking through a magazine, too. It was a copy of *Almost There Magazine*. Mom thumbed through it, turning pages, and then she saw it—the advertisement for the Fiona Wonder Shooting Star Bracelet. She saw that if you bought the bracelet and kept the receipt and turned in the receipt to the magazine that you'd get a chance to spend an entire week with Fiona Wonder herself.

The sun shone through the plate glass windows. It was blinding. Mom put her hand over her forehead. She squinted. Even though it hurt her eyes she kept looking outside.

The door swung open, breaking the silence, and in they walked—the ballroom dancers. He wore a tuxedo with ducktails and shiny black shoes. His black hair looked wet, slicked back. He looked like a sleek, wet seal. His partner had on a sequined dress with feathers. She was the spitting image, Mom thought, of Fiona Wonder. Her entire face glowed so nicely, exuding pure beauty and grace and elegance—that's how Mom described her to me. Something else too: her face shone a warmth and kindness that made Mom feel good. That's because it was something that couldn't be faked, or acted, but was just there, alive and real and unshakable.

Like you, Mom, I remember thinking to myself at the time, but I hadn't opened my mouth. I hadn't told her that.

"They were stunning together," Mom said to me, "like two graceful swans. They were like Fred Astaire and Ginger Rogers. They sat together in a booth and held hands."

Mom said she felt a little excited, and queasy at the same time, because walking to their table felt like walking right into a movie scene.

"Welcome to Waffle Falafel," she'd greeted them. "May

I take your order?"

They both smiled warmly. It made Mom feel good inside—those two warm smiles. They started talking—but not to tell her what they wanted to eat. They told her instead that they'd just won the State Ballroom Dancing Competition, and that they'd received the highest marks for all the dances—the Waltz, the Quick Step, the Tango and the Paso Doble.

Mom stood in front of the table, listening to them and watching them, a pitcher of ice water in her hand. She was in total awe of them.

They thought after winning the competition that they'd feel exhausted, but as it turned out they were the exact opposite of exhausted. Instead they felt exhilarated. The dance competition had ended hours ago, and still they didn't feel tired. They felt hungry. They wanted two orders of strawberry waffles and strong black coffee.

By that time it was a quarter till six in the morning. It wasn't long now until the end of Mom's graveyard shift. She served the strawberry waffles and coffee. After she set the plates before them she started to walk away, but they asked her to sit with them. So that's what Mom did. If the manager had been there, then she wouldn't have done it, because he would have yelled at her. He might even have fired her. But he wasn't there. Nobody was there. She was all by herself, with the dancers. She could do what she wanted. They seemed so full of life, and it made her feel happy and full of life too just to be there with them as the sun shone its first rays of light through the window.

They ate the waffles and drank the coffee. Afterwards she took away the empty plates and cups. Then she came back to the table and asked them if they wanted anything else.

"We're fine," they said. "Thank you."

She started to turn away—she didn't know what came over her exactly—but she turned back. Shyly, she asked, "Would you mind terribly showing me one of the dances?"

Of course we will, they told her.

So Mom moved some of the chairs and tables out of the way. She stood back. They told her to sit at their table while they showed her one of the dances. "Oh, no, I couldn't," she said. When they insisted, when they made her sit, she laughed. She watched them do the Waltz, right there in the middle of the empty restaurant. She thought it was the sweetest thing imaginable.

The clock on the wall ticked over to six o'clock. Her shift had ended. She could leave now. She could come home and rest.

The ballroom dancers paid their bill to her at the cash register near the front counter—that's the way that she remembers it. She watched them as they walked, hand in hand, out of the restaurant into the parking lot. It wasn't until they drove away in their car that she noticed that they hadn't factored in a tip. It didn't matter to her, she decided immediately. They'd given her a boost—that's the way that Mom had put it to me. They'd given her a lift that was worth more than any tip could ever buy.

The morning shift waitresses and line cooks had shown up by then. All Mom had to do before leaving the restaurant was clean the table where the ballroom dancers had eaten. She got a fresh wet cloth and a spray bottle full of disinfectant. She'd already taken away the plates and cups. As she prepared to squeeze the trigger of the spray bottle she saw it. She placed both the cloth and the bottle on the table and took a big breath. They had left her a one hundred and fifty-dollar tip.

It was just the right amount of money, of course, to buy me what turned out to be the contest-winning Fiona Wonder Shooting Star Bracelet.

When I asked her where the dance competition had been held, that maybe next year we could go to the competition, and that maybe we might even see the generous couple there next year, Mom had answered by saying that she thought it was a great idea, that she'd like that.

"So where was the competition held? Did they say? I asked again.

She was quiet for a long time. Then it was like a light went on in her head. "The competition was held downtown, in the art museum's events room. You know the place, the one where your friend Valerie's parents went last Christmas for the annual Christmas Ball."

"And what about the ketchup stain?" I asked. "How did that happen?"

"Oh, that," she said. "I don't really remember. I guess it just *happened*."

*I* heard the front door open and shut, some muffled voices, then really loudly: "Hello, ma'am? Are you still there? Hello, ma'am?"

It was Mom's voice. I turned away from the bracelet inside the sky blue dish. For a moment I was in awe of her—I mean the fact that without using her asthma inhaler she had recovered from the asthma attack and managed to climb to the top of the hill, walk around the apartment building, past Nikki's two-door Diahatsu, and up three flights of stairs to our apartment. But then my feeling of awe passed and I felt weighed down with the reason *why* she'd done it.

I walked out of her bedroom, down the hallway and into the kitchen. There she was, all red in the face and doubled over from exhaustion. Nikki stood beside her, her big black purse still flung over her shoulder. The knuckles of Mom's right hand, I noticed, were bone white. That's because she was gripping the phone so hard.

"Mom," I said, but she waved her hand at me to be quiet.

"Mom," I said, not giving up. "How come I found the Shooting Star Bracelet in the dish instead of your rescue inhaler?"

"It's no big deal," Mom said, her hand gripping the telephone still pressed to her ear. "Really, I swear! I must have left it at work last night."

"You left it at work?" I said.

Alarmed, Nikki looked at me, then at Mom. "You climbed all the way up that hill and up three flights of stairs while you were having an asthma attack? What's the matter with you? Are you crazy? Are you trying to—?"

"Would both of you please be quiet!" Mom shouted.

Nikki and I looked at each other. Mom never shouts or makes demands. That's usually Nikki's department—and now that I think about it, it is also my friend Valerie's.

"Hello, ma'am?" Mom said again into the receiver. "Hello, ma'am?" She looked at me with tears in her eyes. "There's nobody there," she said. "She hung up."

"Don't worry about it," Nikki told her. "She'll call back."

"But what if she doesn't call back?"

"Don't be stupid," Nikki said.

"But what if she thinks we don't care about the contest because we didn't pick up the phone in time? What if she decides to pick somebody else to spend a week with Fiona Wonder?"

"Don't be retarded," Nikki said. She unclenched Mom's hand from the phone and placed it back in the cradle. "You know it doesn't work that way. M won the contest, not somebody else."

"I know," Mom said, "but you never know..."

"One missed phone call isn't going to change the contest results."

"I don't know," Mom repeated. "I just don't know."

"This woman at *Almost There Magazine*," Nikki said, "probably just got another call and had to take it. She'll call back, you'll see. And when she does, M will be right here to talk to her."

"No, Nikki, I won't," I protested. "I promised Valerie I'd go to the mall with her today."

Nikki dumped her huge black leather purse on top of the kitchen table. "I thought the three of *us* were going to the mall today, before your mother's shift, to see that movie—what's it called?"

"*The Immortals*," Mom said.

"Yeah, that's right," Nikki said. "I thought we were going to see the four o'clock show."

"Actually, it's four-thirty," Mom corrected. "I wish it were at four o'clock," she added. "That way I could see the entire film. Because my shift at BONANZA BURGER starts at six o'clock, I'll have to leave early. I won't be able to see the end of the film." She looked deeply sad about this.

"I remember that we were going to see the movie," I said to them both, "but last night Valerie called to ask me if I'd go to the mall with her today. She and her mom are supposed to pick me up at noon." I looked at the clock. "That's just ten minutes from now. If you want, I can meet you outside the movie theater at four-thirty. I promise I won't forget. Is that okay?"

"Sure," Mom said.

"And Valerie asked me if I could stay at her house on Friday night. Is that okay with you?"

This time she decided to protest. "But you leave for California early Sunday morning. When are you going to have time to get ready for your trip?"

I shrugged. "On Saturday afternoon; that's plenty of time."

"Well..." Mom started.

"Well, I don't care one way or another," Nikki interrupted, "just as long as you don't miss my birthday party tomorrow night. But I bet you already forgot. That would be so typical of you," she added.

I turned to look at her. "Of course I haven't forgotten about your birthday party," I said.

Nikki unzipped her purse and started looking through it for her cigarettes.

About a month before her birthday Nikki had started talking about her birthday. Even though her birthday was on a Monday, she'd said, we could wait until Mom's night off on Thursday to celebrate. But Mom got the feeling that she really didn't want to wait to celebrate her birthday until three days after the fact, so Mom suggested that Nikki and Kurt and I, and anyone else, which turned out to be no one other than, by default, Kurt's kids, to have dinner at BONANZA BURGER. Afterwards, if we felt like it, we could have dessert at Waffle Falafel.

So Nikki's birthday party is going to be at BONANZA BURGER. We have a reservation for seven o'clock tomorrow night. The hostess, a girl in the same grade as Valerie and me, already promised Mom that she'd keep one of Mom's tables open for us. "At least that way," Mom said, "I can help celebrate Nikki's birthday by waiting on you."

Mom can't wait for Nikki to open her present from us. She thinks she's going to be *super* surprised and *super* happy with what we decided to give her. Those are Mom's words, not mine.

Nikki's present from us is a practice head. I didn't even know that practice heads existed until Mom showed me pictures of them on the Internet. What you do with it is practice cutting hair. The practice head that Mom chose is made out of 100% human hair, has the same facial features as Fiona Wonder, or at least that's what Mom says, and even has its own name—"Mandy".

She found it on eBay. It cost $48.00 dollars, including shipping and handling. Mom paid for it with her credit card. When it arrived in the mail, we immediately wrapped it in shiny white paper, because that's all we had in the apartment, and hid it underneath my bed. Three days later, when the phone got turned off for an entire week because Mom had used the money for Nikki's present instead of paying the bill, Mom said she wasn't sorry, that Nikki was her best friend and that she deserved a nice present—just like I had deserved the Fiona Wonder Shooting Star Bracelet.

"Well, I guess it's okay," Mom finally decided. "I mean about you spending the night at your friend's house on Friday night. Just as long as you make sure you give yourself enough time to get ready for your trip on Sunday morning," she added.

Nikki looked at me. "This Valerie person... This is the fat kid you're talking about, isn't it?"

I frowned at her. "She's my friend."

"How come you always stay the night at her place but she never stays the night over here?" Nikki wanted to know. "Is it because her mother won't let her?"

I felt put on the spot: "I don't know... She's stayed the night here," I said at last.

"Twice," Mom confirmed.

"Twice?" Nikki questioned. "You seem to be there almost every weekend."

"That's not really true," I said.

"Come off it, M," Nikki said. "You're over there all the time, especially since school let out for the summer. And you were there most of Christmas vacation, too."

"No, Nikki, that's not right. I only stayed there once during Christmas vacation. It was on the same night that Valerie's parents went to the annual Christmas Holiday Ball at the art museum."

Mom nodded, agreeing.

"All the same," Nikki said, "you sure spend a lot of time over there. It's like you want to live there or something," she continued. "It's like you'd rather be there than here with your mom. And with me," she added.

"Oh, Nikki," I said, sighing, "that's not true, and you know it."

Her face turned as hard as a rock. "In case you haven't noticed, M, your friend Mallory—"

"Her name is Valerie."

"Whatever... She has the body of a walrus, and she

smells like one too!"

I didn't try to hide my exasperation.

"And that mother of hers! What's her name?"

"Mrs. Redding," I said.

"Lady," Mom said. "Her name is Lady."

Nikki snorted. "Yeah, that's right. Lady Redding. What a piece of work that one is!" Nikki plunged her arm, almost to the elbow, inside her gigantic bag. She seemed desperate to find her cigarettes. "I remember one time she and her daughter the walrus—"

"Please don't call her that," I interrupted. "It's not nice."

But she just kept talking—"came into Clippers without an appointment—just walk-ins. Nothing special: just a trim for each of them; that's what she told Andrea. I was busy with a highlight, and Jenny was busy with a perm, and Tanya was home sick with a migraine, so it was Andrea who ended up with them. The *walrus* went first. That lady called Lady just stood there in her stupid white coat and big black sunglasses, all high and mighty and watching Andrea wash her fat kid's head. Then, when it was time to actually cut some of that flaming red hair, she said she had changed her mind. She didn't give any reason, but she acted like she had decided that Andrea wasn't good enough to cut their hair. She didn't offer to pay for the shampoo. She just walked out with her daughter waddling, wet hair and all, behind her. That'd never happened to Andrea before. She was so upset that for the rest of the day she ran to the bathroom between cuts because she couldn't stop crying."

I bit my lip, wordless.

"Where the hell *are* they?" Nikki practically shouted as she turned her purse upside down and dumped the contents onto the kitchen table.

In the middle of the pile of stuff was an unopened box of elbow macaroni.

Mom and I just looked at one another.

Nikki's face went bright red. As fast as she could, she stuffed the box of macaroni back inside her purse.

"I—" she started to say, but just then we heard the sound of a car horn outside.

I opened the door, walked out and peered over the edge of the balcony. Three flights down in the parking lot, Mrs. Redding's pearl-colored Mercedes-Benz Wagon was parked next to Nikki's Daihatsu. In the passenger seat I saw Valerie, or at least I saw Valerie's thighs and crotch and lap. I could see she was wearing black 'skinny' jeans (even though it was at least ninety degrees outside) and the tight pink top that her mother hates because she says it draws attention to Valerie's "problem area". What she's talking about, of course, is Valerie's belly fat.

With the window already rolled down, Valerie stuck practically half her body out the window, craned her neck to look at me on the balcony, and shouted, "Mercy Swimmer!"

"Valerie Redding!" I shouted back, and waved.

For as long as I can remember, we've always greeted each other by shouting out each other's names. I don't know why we do it; it just feels good. It feels like Valerie devoting all her energy to me, and me devoting all my energy to Valerie, if only for one brief moment.

In the driver's seat, Mrs. Redding's long slender hand pressed down hard on the center of the wheel, blowing the horn again. She was waiting for me to come downstairs so she could drive us to Heritage Shopping Mall.


_V_alerie has anger issues. That's what a psychologist had determined after she'd repeatedly smashed the front end of her brand new, bright red convertible into the back end of Robin Bell's pickup truck in the parking lot of a Quick-E-Mart. The incident had occurred two miles south of the high school, just one week before the end of our junior year and two weeks after Junior Prom.

What happened was this: Valerie was standing in front of a Slushee machine filling a jumbo size cup with raspberry flavored ice. Robin walked past her with a group of his friends—two from the high school baseball team, on which he plays catcher, and three from the astronomy club, of which he is a member. The way Valerie describes it, he said to her, "What's up, Red?"

Three minutes later, after Valerie had paid for her Slushee, and while Robin and his friends were still inside the minimart, she started plowing—BAM! Reverse, stop, back into drive, speed up, BAM!, repeated times five, according to the police report (or seven, according to Valerie)—the front end of her car into the back end of his truck.

It was Valerie's father who'd convinced Robin's parents not to press charges. In return for not getting either insurance company involved, Dr. Redding paid all the damages to Robin's truck, took away Valerie's drivers license and car (or what was left of it) and promised to find her some "help".

At the time Valerie thought all this was unfair, but to tell the truth I think she got off easy. It would have worked out much different, I have a feeling, if Valerie's parents and Robin's parents did not go to the same country club. Not only that, but a couple of years ago Valerie's father, Dr. Redding, had diagnosed Robin's grandfather with lung cancer, or emphysema, or a combination of both, I'm not sure, but I do know that it had something to do with his lungs because that's Dr. Redding's specialty: he's a pulmonologist. Just like the doctor on a TV show that Mom used to watch before it was cancelled, Dr. Redding works in a private practice with six other doctors including a psychologist, Dr. Antoinette Zuwansky. I know her name because that's who Valerie began seeing after she plowed repeatedly into Robin's pickup truck.

The last six Tuesdays, ever since summer break started,

I've been at the private practice from 10:30 to 11:30, because that's when Valerie has her therapy appointment. That first Tuesday Valerie asked me to come with her, and I've been going with her ever since. I don't mind. It's really nice inside, or at least the waiting room is really nice. It is air-conditioned. There are all sorts of pictures on the walls, a big maroon-colored sofa and two matching chairs (all of which I know are comfortable because I've alternated sitting on each of them), a big glass-top table with lots of magazines neatly displayed in a fan shape on top of it, a water cooler in one corner of the room and a flat screen TV in another.

If there's one thing that overwhelms the room, then it's the reception area. It's in the shape of a half circle, looks like it's made out of chrome, and just about the same size and height as Nikki's Daihatsu. It's all a bit overdone, if you ask me, but that's just my opinion. To the right of the desk is a single door that leads to the examining rooms and private offices. The door is made entirely out of frosted glass. I've never actually seen any of the other doctors, just the shapes of their bodies behind the door. I'm not allowed back there because I'm not a patient.

Last Tuesday, about fifteen minutes into Valerie's therapy session, as I sat on one of the chairs inside the waiting room, the glass door opened, and guess who appeared: Dr. Redding. He didn't have on a white coat. No stethoscope around his neck. He was wearing moccasins, ironed blue jeans and a tucked-in shirt. There was a red smudge that looked like blood near the corner of his mouth, but I'm sure it was just ketchup.

To tell the truth, he didn't look much like a doctor. He was holding a whole bunch of papers that he gave to the receptionist, a woman in her early sixties named Jeannette Jenkins who Valerie thinks smells like mothballs. In a low voice, he started talking to Jeannette about something that had to do with numbers. He told her to make sure to tell him right away, whether or not he had a patient with him, when the accountant returned his call.

"Hello, Dr. Redding," I said to him.

He looked up, surprised. Even though we'd already met countless times, I could tell that it took him several seconds to register who I was. He didn't say hello, only nodded his head and resumed talking to Jeannette.

That's normal. Dr. Redding never seems to have much to say—and not just to me. During all the years I've known him I can remember only a handful of times when he spoke more than a few words. I wonder if he's ever had an actual conversation with his daughter Valerie, or with his son Jeremy, or his wife. Once, at night when I couldn't fall asleep, I tried to picture Dr. Redding and Mrs. Redding engaged in a deep conversation about life and love and happiness and hopes and dreams and disappointment, but for some reason I just couldn't picture it.

Those are the types of conversations that my mom and my dad had, I hope, before he was killed, when I was just two and a half years old, in a pole climbing contest. Dad was a lineman for the power company. To this day, Mom still hasn't thrown out his toe spikes. Dad was good at his job. He was fast at climbing utility polls, which are really just logs. I guess that's why he thought he could win the poll climbing contest at the county fair. Out of ten contestants, Dad was the first to reach the top of the ninety-foot-tall poll. The fact that he knew he had reached the top of the poll first, which meant that he'd won first place, and which also meant that he'd won the five hundred-dollar prize—I think that's what killed Dad. I mean, thinking about all that money that he'd won and being number one, I think it made Dad lose his balance.

"Is your dad super shy or something?" I remember once asking Valerie about her father. "Is that why he hardly ever says anything?"

She looked at me like I was crazy.

"If you want to talk to my father," she informed me matter-of-factly, "you have to pay him a minimum of one

31

hundred and fifty dollars an hour."

*H*ello, Marcy," Mrs. Redding said to me as soon as I had closed the backdoor of her pearl-colored Mercedes-Benz Wagon. She drove out of the parking lot and onto Bird Road.

"For the millionth time, Mother, her name is Mercy," Valerie said from the passenger seat.

Mrs. Redding just kept driving. From Bird Road she took the on ramp to the freeway. In the rearview mirror I thought she glanced back at me, but there was no way to tell for sure because she had on her big black sunglasses.

"Valerie, for the last time, the air conditioner is on. Roll up the window."

Valerie didn't say anything. A minute later I heard the *shoosh* sound of the window rolling up.

"Thank you," Mrs. Redding said.

"You're welcome," Valerie answered back, but it came out sarcastic.

The car smelled like hot leather and Avon Skin So Soft. Mrs. Redding's hands, I thought, looked especially slim and white on the steering wheel. She signaled, crossed lanes, and took the off ramp to Heritage Avenue. One left turn later the Mercedes-Benz Wagon was outside the entrance to Coleanne's Department Store. Mrs. Redding always used to park on the other side of the mall, outside Time & Luxingham, but last month it closed, although the way it happened—out of the blue, without any prior notice—made it seem more like it had simply disappeared, as if one night a giant hand had reached inside Heritage Shopping Mall's most expensive department store and took out all the merchandise and locked the outside doors and over the indoor entrance drew down a huge metal gate.

Even though it was her favorite department store Mrs. Redding didn't seem upset when it closed. She simply started parking on the other side of the mall, outside Coleanne's. She figured, I guess, that it wasn't such a big deal considering there are still three more big department stores inside Heritage. Just as she did outside Time & Luxingham, Mrs. Redding circles the parking lot at least once before choosing where to park. Even though it was Sunday, there weren't many cars parked outside Coleanne's. Mrs. Redding found a spot in row B, space #12.

"I'm coming inside, too, but not for long," Mrs. Redding announced. She turned off the engine, reached for her purse and looked at Valerie. "Your father needs a new pair of shorts, I'm going to return that blender that you insisted I buy so you could make fruit smoothies but never used, and I need to pick up a new water bottle for Jeremy at Sporty's."

"Thanks for the information."

"Also," Mrs. Redding said, after a pause, "I'm going to return that dress that you bought at—what's that place called again?"

"Moods," Valerie said. "And, no you're not. I happen to like that dress. That's why I bought it."

"Valerie, like most of the clothing that you buy from that shop, it doesn't fit you."

"Yes, it does."

"No, it does not. It looks like sausage casing. Anyway, you've only worn it once since you bought it. It's been hanging inside your closet for more than a month."

"YOU ARE NOT TAKING IT BACK. IT IS MY DRESS. I BOUGHT IT WITH MY ALLOWANCE MONEY," Valerie said on the verge of shouting.

Mrs. Redding gripped the steering wheel. In the passenger seat, Valerie sat with her arms crossed over her middle. A minute went by, then another. From where I sat I couldn't help but notice that it was difficult to tell them apart. Even though Valerie has her father's face and body—short, round like an apple, lots of freckles—the back of Valerie's head looks identical to Mrs. Redding's. They have the same hair—thick, long and silky, and the same color red as an Irish Setter.

From behind her sunglasses Mrs. Redding looked at her daughter, then looked away and unzipped her purse. "After I finish my errands here, I think I'll see if I can get my nails done at that salon over at Patriot Plaza. Or maybe I'll go for a swim at the country club. I don't know. I haven't decided yet. What time do you girls want me to pick you up?"

"I don't know," Valerie said. "Four-something."

Mrs. Redding sighed deeply. "Four-something is not specific. Tell me exactly, please, what time you want me to pick you up. I am not interested in a repeat performance of last weekend. In case you've forgotten, I waited over half an hour for you."

"That's because you were half an hour early."

"I specifically remember you saying to pick you up at three-thirty."

"Yeah, well, you need to check your hearing, because I said four o'clock."

"Valerie," Mrs. Redding said, but then she stopped. She stared straight ahead. Just what she was looking at—the back end of the car in front of us, or the front doors to Coleanne's—I wasn't sure.

"Fine, Mother. Pick us up at *exactly* four o'clock," Valerie said finally.

"Um, except..." I started to say.

I think they had both forgotten that I was sitting in the back seat. At the same time they turned to look at me.

I cleared my throat. "Except," I told them, "I promised my mom and Nikki that I would meet them outside the movie theater at four-thirty."

"What's playing?" Valerie wanted to know.

"*The Immortals*," I told her. "Fiona Wonder is in it. That's why my mom wants to see it."

Valerie made a face. "The movie guy in the paper gave

it two thumbs-up, which always means that it's long and boring."

Mrs. Redding turned around in her seat. With a flick of her wrist she flipped down the sun visor. Another flick, and she had flipped open the mirror on the inside of the visor. From her purse she took out a tube of lipstick. "Fiona Wonder," she said. "Isn't that the movie star with whom you're going to spend next weekend?"

Valerie answered for me. "I already told you it was, Mother."

"I wasn't asking you, Valerie."

We were all quiet for a minute.

"Yes, Mrs. Redding, it is," I answered. "It's actually for an entire week, not just a weekend."

Valerie snorted. "She'll probably make you cook breakfast and walk the dog and water the plants. I bet she's a real elitist. All celebrities are like that."

Mrs. Redding looked at herself in the mirror and started to apply lipstick. "Have you ever been on an airplane?"

It took me a minute to realize that she was actually asking me a question. "No."

"To California?"

"No."

"Have you ever been outside the state, Marcy?"

"No, Mrs. Redding."

"Then, how fortunate for you to win the contest."

Another snort came from Valerie. "I've been to California at least six times."

"Seven, actually," Mrs. Redding said. She recapped the lipstick and placed it back inside her purse then flipped the sun visor back in place.

"All I remember about it, no matter how many times I go," Valerie said, "is Disneyland and the Hollywood sign and freeways and smog."

"There is a lot of pollution in Los Angeles," Mrs. Redding said, agreeing.

"Daddy would have so many patients if we moved there. Remember, he said that once?"

"Yes. He was joking."

"He was sort of joking, Mother. He said he could be a pulmonologist to the stars. He said he'd probably make a fortune."

Mrs. Redding looked down at her nails.

"Okay. What the hell. I'll go see it too," Valerie said to me. "I mean the movie."

I thought about Valerie and Nikki sitting near each other for at least two hours inside a dark movie theater. I decided not to say anything.

Mrs. Redding sighed again. "I don't suppose either of you girls knows what time the movie ends?"

"Um, duh, when it *ends*," Valerie answered.

"This is ridiculous," Mrs. Redding said. "I'm sorry, but I refuse to sit in the parking lot like last time just to wait for you. I am not your personal chauffeur."

"Well, Mother," Valerie said slowly, as if Mrs. Redding were mentally challenged, "give me back my license and buy me a new car and you won't have to wait for me ever again."

"Keep it up, young lady, and you can walk home."

"Ooh," Valerie sang. She waved her hands in front of her like she was scared. "I don't even know why I'm talking to you about it anyway. I mean getting me a new car. I should ask Daddy. It's Daddy who makes all the important decisions in our family."

"Goddamn it, Valerie," Mrs. Redding said, her voice on the verge of cracking.

Before we knew what had happened Mrs. Redding had opened the door, gotten out and slammed the door shut. Flinging her purse over her shoulder, she began walking toward the entrance of Coleanne's.

"*That woman*," Valerie said, staring at her mother.

Mrs. Redding stopped at the entrance and just stood there. Still in the back seat, I craned my body forward.

Even though I could only see the back of her, I could tell that she was contemplating something. Then Mrs. Redding turned round, crossed the parking lot, and marched back to the Wagon.

"Get out of the car, girls," she said. "I have to lock the car."

I looked at Valerie. She didn't move a muscle.

"GET OUT OF THE CAR, GIRLS!" Mrs. Redding shouted.

I heard the sound of the car doors locking after Valerie and I were both outside the car and walking with Mrs. Redding toward the entrance.

"You don't have to worry about what time the movie gets out," Mrs. Redding said as she pushed open the door. "I just remembered I haven't seen a movie in a movie theater for a long time. I think I'll see it too. What's it called again? *The Mortals*?"

But this time Valerie did not correct her.

*H*eritage Shopping Mall is old, Valerie said one time, because it was built more than twenty-five years ago when my mom and Nikki—and Mrs. Redding too, now that I think about it—were about the same age as we are now.

If I remember correctly, Robin Bell was in our sixth grade social studies class. Maybe he's the reason why Valerie wasn't paying attention when we learned that the area where we live used to be high plains full of bison. Then the Europeans came and killed all the Indians. All the land was sold and plowed and developed. If anything is old, then it is the land. Heritage Shopping Mall is a blanket that has been thrown over the land. For the time being, history sleeps.

If Valerie is bad at history, and if the reason she is so bad at it is because she was paying too much attention to Robin, the catcher on the baseball team, the boy in the astronomy club who likes to look at stars through a telescope, then the same could be said about me almost flunking economics last year.

You see, that had to do with a boy too, Randy White. All semester he sat in front of me in economics class. Unlike Valerie with Robin, I did not want to pay attention to Randy. All I wanted to do was to pay attention to the teacher, but what happened instead was that Randy made sure that I only paid attention to him. All throughout class he rammed his body hard onto the back of the chair so that it touched my desk, making my pencil jerk away from my paper, jarring me. Other times he threw bits of paper over his shoulder, landing mostly on top of my desk. Some of the bits of paper hit my face, got in my hair. He tried to trip me once during the middle of class after I had come back from the bathroom. Another time, five minutes before class started, he threw an eraser at me. I ducked just in time; otherwise it would have hit me in the head.

Randy plays pitcher on the baseball team. I know this because last year, before Valerie rammed her car into the back end of Robin's truck, she dragged me to watch all the home games, and a number of the away games too, so that she could watch him—not Randy, but Robin—play catcher.

On the last home game of the season I remember the two boys got in a big fight right on the pitcher's mound after the seventh inning stretch. Valerie practically held her breath as Robin walked slowly to the mound to talk to Randy. During the brief conversation, Randy kept throwing his fist into the pocket of his glove. He shook his head violently. He spat on the ground right in front of Robin's feet.

The next pitch that he threw, I remember, hit the batter. The umpire gave him a warning. On the next pitch he did it again. This time the umpire threw him out of the game. All the people in the stands booed him. As he walked off the mound, Randy said something inaudible in Robin's direction. Then he started laughing.

Behind home plate Robin stood staring straight ahead, waiting for Randy to leave the field.



$V$alerie said she was starving. This was right after we had entered Coleanne's and parted ways with Mrs. Redding. We began walking toward the food court. In the center of the mall, at the water fountain, I stopped to retie my shoelace.

"Hurry up," Valerie said. I could hear the impatience in her voice. "Can't you hear my stomach growling?"

"Nope, I can't hear that," I said, and looked up at the skylight directly above the fountain. The sun shone down on my face. There wasn't a cloud in the sky. Then something strange happened: I wasn't there anymore but back in my bedroom looking out the window at the light coming from the skylight.

Valerie tapped her foot. "Well, I can," she said. "I think there's a high probability of me fainting if I don't eat soon. That actually almost happened once. Who knows—I could have hit my head on the ground, or even split my head open."

A few steps away from the fountain we rode the elevator to the second floor. We walked past Mind, Body & Spirit, eXcite and Clippers. Inside the hair salon, Nikki's station was empty. Nikki doesn't have to work weekends anymore, but only because she and Jeanie, the new manager, get along okay. That's not saying much, however. Managers do not seem to last long at Clippers. The one before Jeanie stayed only two weeks. The one before that stayed longer (two months). Nikki called her the hair Nazi. If I don't miss my guess, then not too long from now she'll be calling Jeanie the same thing.

The problem with being a manager at Clippers is that it's company policy for the manager to time the employees while they cut hair. Every single standard cut is permitted exactly fifteen minutes. If a hair stylist goes over the time limit, their pay is docked. The entire system is stressful for everybody—the manager, the hair stylists and also the customers. The only person that seems to benefit from the system is the owner. During all the years that Nikki has been working as a hair stylist at Clippers, she's only met him once. He actually owns four Clippers—the one where Nikki works, another off Sheridan Boulevard, another on Quincy Street, and the one in Patriot Plaza where Kurt's ex-wife Alicia works. He drives a lemon colored Porsche. His name is Cliff.

"I don't want to eat at BONANZA BURGER," Valerie announced just as we reached the entrance to the food court. Because it's a sit-down restaurant, BONANZA BURGER isn't actually located inside the food court. It's not even on the same level but down the escalator. Opposite it is the movie theater.

I shrugged. "I don't care. My mom isn't there now anyway. Her shift doesn't start until six o'clock."

At HaiSheng, Valerie ordered two egg rolls, a plate of sweet and sour pork and a jumbo size soda. "Anything else?" the boy behind the counter asked us. He was skinny and wore a bright yellow visor and a red apron.

Valerie turned to me. "Aren't you going to order anything?"

"I'm not hungry."

"You're not saying that because you don't have any money, are you?"

"Well," I shrugged. "It's not a big deal."

"You know I don't care about paying. You want some wonton soup? What about chicken lo mein? Just tell me."

"Seriously, Valerie, I'm fine."

"You say that now, but I bet anything you'll want to share some of mine as soon as we sit down. You know how much I'm not into sharing my food with anyone else. No offense."

"Valerie, I swear I'm not hungry."

"Give me one more eggroll," Valerie said to the boy

behind the counter, "and two more packets of sweet and sour sauce."

"Valerie, you don't have to do that."

"I know." She rolled her eyes at me. "If you don't eat it, then I will."

At the cash register the boy stifled a yawn. "That'll be ten dollars and eighty-seven cents."

Except when Valerie handed him the money, he immediately handed back the ten dollar bill. "This money is no good."

"What are you talking about? There's nothing wrong with it." She tried to hand it back to him.

"There's a rip down the middle."

Valerie looked at it, considering. "It's just a little rip," she said finally.

"I'll get in trouble if I accept it."

Valerie blew an errant hair off her face. "I have plenty more," she said, digging inside her wallet for another ten dollar bill.

"You Really Got a Hold on Me" by Smoky Robinson and the Miracles played overhead on the sound system. In the center of the food court we found a table. Valerie swallowed a piece of sweet and sour pork. She sucked hard at the straw coming out of the jumbo size cup of soda. "Did you ask your mom about spending the night at my house on Friday?"

"Yes."

"What did she say?"

"Yes."

"Awesome," Valerie said. "Gretchen is having a party. She only lives five blocks away from me. After my parents fall asleep we can sneak out and walk to her house."

"You mean Gretchen Jones, the cheerleader?" I said. "I didn't realize you were friends with her."

Valerie looked indignant. "I'm friends with her on Facebook. You would be too if you had a computer. That's how I found out about it."

"She invited you to her party on Facebook?"

"She invited her entire friends list. We just have to bring our own beer, but that's not a problem. My father has an entire fridge full of it downstairs in the basement."

I didn't say anything. I was thinking about Valerie repeatedly smashing the front end of her car into the back end of Robin's truck outside the Quick-E-Mart.

I cleared my throat. "Valerie?" I asked hesitantly. "Isn't Gretchen friends with...you-know-who?" I meant Robin, of course.

She set the jumbo size cup on top of the table: "Yeah, so what?"

"So, he'll probably be at the party."

"So *what*?" Valerie said. "It's a free country, isn't it? I got invited to the party too, didn't I?"

"Don't get upset. I just thought—" But I stopped when I noticed her eyes following something over my right shoulder. I turned around just in time to see Mrs. Redding walk past the food court. She was carrying three shopping bags—two new ones from Coleanne's and the other the same one she'd taken out of the back of the Wagon and carried with her inside the mall. Inside it, I knew, was the blender.

Mrs. Redding rounded the glass partition and rode the escalator that led downstairs to BONANZA BURGER and the movie theater. I didn't turn around again until her head had disappeared from view.

Valerie wadded up her napkin into a tiny ball. A moment later her cell phone rang. Taking the phone out of her pocket, she looked at the caller ID screen and made a face. Flipping the phone open, she held it to her ear. "What?" she said into the receiver. She was talking, of course, to her mother. "Not yet. We're at the food court, eating lunch." A pause, then: "Because I was hungry." Listening, she picked at a cuticle. Still listening, she made another face. "Okay," she said. "*Okay*, Mother." She held the phone away from her ear. With her left hand she gave it the finger.

Resuming the conversation, she said, "What are you talking about? Are you positive?" She looked genuinely shocked.

"What's wrong?" I asked as soon as she had ended the call.

"She's lying," Valerie said. "I don't believe her."

"You don't believe her about *what*, Valerie?"

"She said she just walked past Moods. She said it's closed. Just like Time & Luxingham closed. Closed... Like in permanently."

"Oh, wow," I said. "At least seven people worked there. I wonder what will happen to—"

"I can't believe it!" Valerie interrupted me. "That was my favorite shop inside this stupid mall. Now where am I going to find all my clothes? Goddamn it!"

Valerie finished eating the sweet and sour pork. Afterward, I took the plastic tray from the table and dumped all the contents into a wastebasket and placed the tray in the tray holder on top of it. From Cookie Cookie Shop, Valerie bought a giant lemon cookie. We walked out of the food court, rounded the glass partition, and took the escalator down to the first floor. Valerie led the way. I didn't say anything: I knew exactly where we were headed.

Regarding the closure of Moods, Mrs. Redding had not been lying.

Valerie finished eating the cookie. We meandered. Back at the water fountain at the center of the mall we took the elevator back to the second floor. Valerie veered off to enter eXcite. She tried on a dress, then another, then another one after that. None of them fit. Leaving eXcite, we took the elevator back to the first floor.

"Fuck her! I'll wear what I want to wear." By then she was really frustrated, I could tell, and close to tears.

Twenty minutes later Valerie was trying on dresses in a fitting room inside the teen department at Coleanne's. "Valerie!" I said. I was sitting on an uncomfortable chair right outside the fitting room.

"What?" she said.

"I just saw Ms. Starburn! I don't think she saw me. She's walking toward the exit. I should catch up to her and say hello."

"Why would you want to do something like that?" Valerie said from inside the fitting room.

"Because I haven't seen her since school got out."

"Suit yourself. You don't need my permission."

I got up from the chair and started to weave my way through the racks of clothes. It seemed to take forever to reach the aisle in the middle of the store. "Mercy?" I heard Valerie say from inside the fitting room. "MERCY!"

I kept walking. Ahead of me Ms. Starburn made a sharp right turn. It kind of surprised me when she stepped onto the escalator to go down to the basement level. The Garden Center was down there, and the place where they take family pictures.

"Ms. Starburn!" I called out to her. I was about to step onto the escalator when she turned around and looked at me. The look on her face—quite surprised, but not in a good way—made me stop in my tracks. It was only then that I noticed she wasn't carrying any bags. She wasn't even carrying a purse. In her hands was a garden salad. Except why was she carrying it downstairs to the basement?

I opened my mouth to say something, but by then she was almost at the bottom of the escalator. I watched my teacher face forward, step off, and disappear from view.


Why are you standing there like that? Did you see someone you know, Marcy?" It was Mrs. Redding. She was standing right beside me. The bag with the blender, I noticed, had been replaced with a shiny black bag. Printed on the side of the bag was the word, 'Sporty's'. She looked at her watch. "Where's Valerie?"

"She's trying on dresses, Mrs. Redding."

"Oh. Has she found anything that actually fits her?"

I didn't say anything because I didn't know.

"That's what I thought."

We began walking together toward the teen department.

"It's almost four-thirty. Isn't that when the movie starts?"

"Yes, Mrs. Redding."

She rapped hard on the door of the fitting room that Valerie occupied.

"Who is it?" Valerie wanted to know.

"Your mother," Mrs. Redding answered in the exact same tone of voice—suspicious and verging on anger. "Come out. It's almost time for the movie."

A few moments of silence followed. We could hear her breathing in there, heavily. At last the door swung open. Behind her, in the fitting room, I saw a pile of rumpled dresses that she had thrown onto the floor. Mrs. Redding saw them too, I think, but she didn't say anything about the fact that Valerie hadn't taken the time to re-hang the dresses on hangers. I guess she just thought that one of the sales ladies would do it.

"Did you find anything that fit?" she asked Valerie.

It was an unkind thing to say, I thought, considering the answer to the question was more than obvious.

Valerie didn't respond. She just started walking, out of the fitting room and down the aisle toward the exit.

"Why are you so preoccupied with buying a new dress, anyway?" Mrs. Redding wanted to know.

"Just forget it," Valerie said.

I followed behind them, not saying anything, thinking about Ms. Starburn.

*We* found Mom and Nikki standing outside the box office of the movie theater. Nikki had her big purse flung over her shoulder. Mom had on her BONANZA BURGER uniform—black pants without any pockets, white tennis shoes with white laces, and a plain dark blue shirt. Her hair was back in a tight ponytail. A neck ring hung around her neck. Neon orange, the neck ring is the same color as the nametag. Attached to it are fourteen buttons and pins in different shapes and sizes and colors. Every day, before she goes to work, Mom counts all fourteen of them. Just like the nametag, lost pins or buttons means the cost is docked from her paycheck.

Mom smiled and Nikki frowned when they saw me walking toward them with Valerie and Mrs. Redding.

"You're late," Nikki said to me. "Why weren't you here earlier?" She looked genuinely annoyed. "We're missing the previews. You know how much I like them."

"Yes, Nikki," I said. "I know how much you like them."

"It's my fault," Valerie said. "I was looking for a dress but I couldn't find one because my favorite shop closed."

Nikki narrowed her eyes at Valerie. "Which shop?"

Valerie narrowed her eyes back at Nikki: "Moods."

"I guess we need to buy tickets," I said.

"We've already bought three," Mom said.

"I'll buy ours," Mrs. Redding said to Valerie and walked toward the box office. She did not say hello to Mom or Nikki.

"Nikki was right," Mom told me. "She called back."

I looked at her, not realizing what she was talking about.

"The Assistant Marketing Director at *Almost There Magazine*: she called back."

"Oh," I said.

"She wasn't mad or anything. Nikki was right all along."

"That's great, Mom," I said. "Did you find your asthma inhalers?"

Her face fell. "Oh, well, no. But I'm sure I left them at work last night. It's not a big deal, Mercy. I'm sure that I'll find them and—" She looked distressed. "Don't you want to know what the Assistant Marketing Director was calling about?"

"Tell me," I said.

"She was calling to tell you that she's booked your flight to California for next week. Isn't that exciting?"

"Yeah," Valerie chimed in, suddenly. "It's like the news of the century."

But Mom was so excited that I don't think she even heard her. "She needed to have an email address to send all the information about the flight. I didn't know what to say. Thankfully, Nikki was there. Nikki told me to tell her to send the information to Nikki's email. The Assistant Marketing Director said she was going to do it right away. She sounded very nice, but very busy. She must have thought I sounded a little nuts, because I was so out of breath—I mean because I was nervous, Mercy, to talk to her."

Mrs. Redding waved her tickets in the air. She was standing by the entrance to the movie theater. "Hello?" she said. "Are we going inside?"

Mrs. Redding led the way into the movie theater. Valerie followed her, then Nikki, then Mom, then me. Inside the lights had already dimmed. The opening credits had started. Mrs. Redding chose a row of seats in the middle of the theater. Nikki shot a look back at Mom. Usually Nikki chooses where we sit when we go to the movies.

"Mom," I whispered, right after we'd sat down, "guess who I saw inside Coleanne's?"

She didn't answer me.

"Mom," I tried again, "I saw Ms. Starburn. Remember, she's my teacher?"

Mrs. Redding put her fingers to her lips and hushed me.

Everything went black for a moment. Then a sudden flash of light lit up Mom's face; and next to Mom's face, Nikki's; and next to Nikki's, Valerie's; and next to Valerie's,

Mrs. Redding's.

Mom reached for my hand and squeezed it. Then she placed her head close to mine and whispered softly in my ear, so that she didn't disturb anyone else in the theater, so that she didn't offend Mrs. Redding: "When I have to leave for my shift at six, Mercy, you'll stay here and watch the rest of the movie and tell me how it ends, okay? Promise me!"

She looked at me so hopefully, her hand squeezing mine. What else could I do but nod my head.

Relieved, she let go of my hand and sat back in her chair, her face bathed in cinema light. On the screen in front of us Fiona Wonder's face appeared as a big as a planet.

# MONDAY

The first thing I thought about when the telephone woke me up was Mom in her ketchup stained uniform on the day after Junior Prom.

"Hello?" I said into the receiver. I tried to catch my breath. I had just jumped out of bed, run down the hallway and into the kitchen to answer it.

"You sound weird. Are you sick or something? Did you just wake up?"

"Hi, Valerie," I said and collapsed onto one of the kitchen chairs. "Just woke up," I said as I cleared my throat. "What time is it?"

"How should I know?" She sounded offended, as if I had asked her something that was beneath her to answer. "What an awful movie that was yesterday," she said. "You know, Mercy, the more I think about it, the more I feel sorry for you that you have to spend an entire week with Fiona Wonder. She was an okay actress when she was making okay films, but now that she's making all this artsy stuff she's just plain weird. The only movie that I ever liked her in was that one called *Clara's Revenge*."

"You mean the one where she hacks a bunch of people to death with a chainsaw?"

"No," Valerie shot back at me. "You always get movie plots wrong, Mercy. It's like you never pay attention to what's happening. It's with a butcher knife, not a chainsaw. She's studying to be a chef at a culinary school. After she goes bonkers and decides to kill everybody she has easy access to an entire array of sharp utensils. The end of the movie is so gross!" Valerie told me, snorting with laughter. "She gets shot in the head. Then one of the butcher knives falls off a table and lands directly on her skull. Hey, that reminds me: how come your mom left right before the end of the movie?"

"She had to go to work."

I felt bad as soon as I'd said it. I felt bad because I had promised Mom that I would stay behind and watch the end of the movie so that I could tell her what happened. I had stayed to watch the end, but I hadn't paid attention. That always seems to happen whenever I watch movies—specially, for some reason, movies with Fiona Wonder in them.

Valerie said, "Well, my mom said that she thought what your mother did was distracting, not to mention completely rude, to everyone else inside the theater."

I looked at the clock on the stove. It was nine-thirty. "Valerie," I said, "you know you're not supposed to call here until after eleven."

"Oh, yeah; I keep forgetting."

"Next time try to remember," I said. "If the phone wakes up my mom, and she can't get back to sleep, then—"

"*Okay*," Valerie interrupted me. "I already said I was sorry. God! You know, it wouldn't be such a big deal if you had your own cell phone," Valerie told me. "All you'd have to do is switch the phone to vibrating mode while your mom is sleeping. She'd never hear it. You're way overdue to get one anyway. It's like the 1980s inside your apartment. Only one telephone, and in the kitchen, and it's not even wireless."

"Valerie," I began.

"I have a point," she said.

"Yes, you have a point, but next time can you please remember not to call until after eleven? At least until I get a cell phone? Mom's shift at Waffle Falafel doesn't end until six in the morning and—oh, wow!" I said.

"What?" Valerie said.

"Oh, wow," I said again. I couldn't help it. For lack of a better word I felt in a state of wonderment. "Before you called and woke me up I was having the strangest dream," I said, remembering. "I was inside Waffle Falafel where Mom works. At least it looked like Waffle Falafel. It had the same red, white and blue sign outside, the same wooden chairs, the same paper napkins and placemats. And the same specials plastered all over the big plate glass windows."

"Uh-huh," Valerie said. She sounded bored.

"There was this waitress..."

"Uh-huh."

"She was standing with her back to me, pouring something into a glass from a pitcher. At first I thought it was water, but then I looked more closely and saw it wasn't water at all but thousands of those tiny silver foil stars that our sixth grade social studies teacher used to like to stick to the top of our quizzes."

"Mrs. What's-Her-Face?" Valerie said. "I don't remember her doing that."

"Maybe it wasn't her but Ms. Starburn."

"Ms. Starburn? What are you talking about?"

I shook my head. "I don't know," I said finally. "I'm still half asleep. I think I'm confused."

"I'll say!"

"I called out Mom's name," I said. "I mean in my dream I called out Mom's name, because the woman had Mom's legs and Mom's back and Mom's big brown ponytail. She wasn't too skinny and she wasn't too fat, she wasn't too tall and she wasn't too short, just like you said."

"Just like *I* said?" said Valerie. "I don't remember ever saying that."

"I thought it was Mom pouring all those thousands of tiny silver stars from a pitcher, except when she turned around it wasn't Mom. It was Mom's body connected to 'Mandy', the practice head."

"The practice *what*?" said Valerie.

Suddenly I didn't feel so well. "Hang on a minute," I told her. Before she could answer I placed the receiver on top of the kitchen table, walked to the kitchen sink and turned on the tap. Leaning my head forward over the sink, I took several gulps of lukewarm water.

"I've decided I hate summer," Valerie said as soon as I had put the phone back to my ear. "There's nothing to do. Last night my mother actually suggested that I get a job, like at Cookie Cookie Shop or something. But then she shut up when I reminded her that I don't have a car anymore. What am I supposed to do? Walk to the mall?"

"I walk to the mall all the time," I said. "So does my mom."

"Yeah, but that's different. You're only five minutes away. Where I live it's ten."

"At the beginning of summer I tried to find a job," I said.

"That's the other thing," Valerie said. She stopped to yawn. "No one is hiring."

"When I couldn't find anything my mom told me that she was happy. She said I have the rest of my life to work."

Valerie said: "Uh-huh. This summer I'm so happy I decided not to work at my dad's office. What could be more boring than answering phones and making coffee and sitting next to Ms. Mothballs?"

"You mean you could have been working? Like as an office assistant at your dad's office?" I still felt a little shaky. "Why didn't you tell me that your dad was hiring someone? Is the job still open?"

"Oh, well," Valerie said, hesitating, "it wasn't like he really needed someone. It was just so that I could have something to do and get paid and get experience or whatever."

"Oh," I said.

"Like I said before, I'm glad I decided not to do it. Except now I'm so bored I almost wish it was time to go back to school."

"So wait," I said. "I'm still confused. Is your dad still looking for someone to hire? Because if he is then—"

"FOR CHRIST'S SAKE, MERCY, I SAID NO!" Valerie shouted.

I put the phone away from my ear. I guess I expected her to keep shouting. Usually when she starts there is no stopping her.

"It was just for me if I wanted it, okay?"

Tentatively, I put my ear back to the phone. "Oh," I said. "Okay."

Valerie sighed. She sounded extremely frustrated. "About this whole working at my dad's office thing, can we please just drop it?"

"Sure," I said. "No problem."

"Are you positive?"

"Yes," I said. "Positive."

"Good," Valerie said. She sounded relieved. A minute went by, then another. "I am so bored!" she said again finally.

"You can come over if you want," I told her. "We can stay outside until my mom wakes up. Have you ever just lain on your back and looked at the sky? It's actually really awesome."

"Um, yeah, no," said Valerie. "Anyway, there's no one to drive me to your place. My mother went grocery shopping and my dad already left for work and my stupid brother is at a football clinic. Let's do something tonight. This morning, ever since I woke up, I can't stop thinking about hush puppies and popcorn shrimp. Let's go to Blue Shrimp for dinner. It'll be my treat. Afterward we can go bowling."

"I can't," I said.

"What do you mean, you can't?" There was an edge to her voice.

"It's Nikki's birthday. We're going to have a party for her tonight at BONANZA BURGER."

Valerie didn't say anything.

"Val..." I started.

"She's not even your friend; she's your mother's friend."

"I know. But it's her birthday. She invited me. I have to go, Valerie. It would hurt her feelings if I didn't. We can go to Blue Shrimp and bowl tomorrow night."

"Now that I think about it, the last time I went to one of those restaurants the hush puppies were burned and the popcorn shrimp tasted like rubber. What time did you say the party started?"

"It starts at seven. But Valerie—"

"I didn't tell you this, but I was planning to go back to the mall today anyway. So I'll meet you outside BONANZA BURGER at seven. I'll tell my mom she doesn't need to pick me up. I'll just stay the night at your place. I'll see you tonight," Valerie said and hung up.

I placed the receiver back in the cradle, got up from the table and turned on the coffee maker so that hot coffee would be ready for Mom as soon as she woke up. Then I went to open the refrigerator to pour myself a glass of orange juice. Stuck with a magnet in the shape of a lady bug to the fridge door was a piece of paper with a list on it that Mom must have written early that morning after she'd come home from work. It read:

*Milk*
*Tampons*
*Bread*

*Tomatoes*
*Panty Hose*
*Birthday card for Nikki*
~~I~~
*Ticket*
*The End*

I read the list one more time, memorizing it and trying to figure out, and failing, what she meant about the last three entries, and then I walked back down the hallway toward our bedrooms. As usual, the door to Mom's room was closed. I pressed my ear to it and listened. I'm not exactly sure why but when I heard silence on the other end I felt a twinge of panic. Even though I knew I might wake her up I opened the door and tiptoed inside.

Mom lay sleeping with her back toward me. For a minute I just stood in the middle of the room at the foot of the bed, watching her. Mom's hands looked like two small balls of dough, one on top the other, underneath her cheek. Her breathing was slow and deep. Even though she was asleep, I thought she still looked exhausted—like she could have slept for a million years.

From the floor I picked up the Waffle Falafel uniform. In the corner of the room I found the backpack that I had used throughout elementary school and that Mom now brings with her when she goes to work. Crouching in front of it, I first unzipped it then started to unpack it, searching for the BONANZA BURGER uniform so that I could put it, along with the Waffle Falafel uniform, into the washing machine. Out came a pair of nude-colored pantyhose that I immediately wadded into a ball, aimed and threw without missing into the wastebasket beside her bed, an old hairbrush with a hair tie wrapped round the handle of it, a red change purse that Nikki gave Mom last Christmas and which, I knew, contains Mom's state ID card and a twenty-dollar bill that is only supposed to be used in case of emergency, an unopened box of mint flavored tic-tacs, and finally, at the very bottom of the pack, the BONANZA BURGER uniform.

I took both of Mom's uniforms and smoothed them out in front of me on the floor. Usually I can tell what kind of night she'd had just by looking at them. Judging from the state of the Waffle Falafel uniform it looked like Sunday night had been messy. Egg yoke was smeared on the lapel of the shirt, a stain—probably bacon grease—bisected the apron, and a child-size handprint made from powdered sugar shone on the right buttock of the black pants.

I looked at the open closet door. Without even trying, my eyes found the identical Waffle Falafel uniform—the one with the huge ketchup stain on the front of it. I couldn't help it: I thought again about that morning the day after Junior Prom, remembered her misspelled nametag dropping from the sink to the floor. All over again I saw the bag that held the Fiona Wonder Shooting Star Bracelet, and the receipt that came with it and ended up winning me a week with the movie star.

The BONANZA BURGER uniform was in better condition. The only stain I found was a nickel-size spot of grease on the right sleeve. For a moment I closed my eyes and tried to envision the various moments of impact that had made the various stains on Mom's uniforms, but that was impossible. I only hoped that Tide would wash out all the egg and bacon and sugar and grease. I went to stand up but stopped when I saw it—the movie magazine inside the bottom of the backpack. I took it out and looked at it. From the cover Fiona Wonder's face beamed back at me.

I scooped up Mom's uniforms, stood and started to tiptoe back across the room to the door. In her sleep, Mom started to wheeze. I froze. Slowly, I turned my head, looked at her and waited. Still asleep, Mom sighed heavily. The wheezing stopped. I started to walk out of the room, but that's when I remembered the blue dish on top of the dresser. Inside it were Mom's two nametags and the Fiona

Wonder Shooting Star Bracelet, but not her asthma inhalers.

*M*om was still asleep when I left the apartment to walk to CostMart Supermarket. It is a fifteen-minute walk from our building, past Heritage Mall and on the other side of the freeway inside Patriot Plaza, the same strip mall where Kurt's ex-wife Alicia works as a hair stylist at that location's Clippers. Depending on her mood, whenever we're in the parking lot walking toward the entrance of the supermarket, Nikki either pretends Clippers (and a certain person working inside it) does not exist, or points her middle finger in the general direction of the hair salon.

I wish that Mom and I didn't always have to go with Nikki to CostMart. My main concern is her stealing habit. At least she's really good at it (that's what Mom said once). She has a point, I guess. Except the one time at the thrift store on Madison Street when I saw her slip all those glittery gold dolphin stickers inside her pocket, neither Mom nor I has ever seen Nikki shoplift.

Mom would never admit it out loud, but I know that if she had a choice in the matter she wouldn't go with Nikki to CostMart either. That's the thing, though: we really *don't* have a choice. Unless it's only a handful of things we need, like the list Mom made early this morning that I found stuck to the refrigerator door, then it's pretty much impossible not to do our weekly shopping with Nikki, because she has a car and we don't. We used to take the bus, but then last year the city government eliminated the route. On television the mayor called it a budget cut.

Past Heritage Mall I reached the freeway underpass. One time Valerie told me that her mother told her to never walk through it because freeway underpasses are just the kind of places where murderers and rapists and thieves and homeless people lurk. "Don't blame me if you get raped," Valerie had told me when I tried to explain to her that the only others I have ever encountered underneath the freeway are people just like me, passing through to the other side.

With such strong opinions about it, I doubt either Valerie or her mother have ever had to actually walk underneath the freeway. Driving *on* it, now that's another story. Even with Valerie's car smashed and gone, the Redding family owns three more automobiles—Dr. Redding's black Mercedes-Benz, Mrs. Redding's pearl colored Wagon and Jeremy's bright yellow Jeep—plus a three-year-old RV camper that they drove once to California during spring break and has been sitting at the side of their driveway ever since. Not to mention a Harley Davidson motorcycle that Dr. Redding bought for his forty-sixth birthday even though Mrs. Redding had asked him not to because she was worried he'd kill himself.

As it's turned out, there's probably no way Dr. Redding will ever get the chance to kill himself while riding the motorcycle, because he never rides it. Valerie says he's more interested in looking at it anyway, that to him it's just a big shiny toy. I have to admit that it's very shiny. That's because every chance he gets, Valerie told me, he polishes it.

A skinny man on a bicycle sped past me. I stopped walking and looked up at the freeway. That's when it happened again—the same thing that happened yesterday when I looked up at the skylight above the water fountain inside Heritage Mall: my body was still there beneath the overpass, but my mind had gone—this time to a Fiona Wonder movie that Mom and Nikki and I had watched last Thursday night, the one that takes place in 1920s America.

In the movie Fiona Wonder is an aspiring stage actress on her way from her family's farm in Nebraska to Chicago. In the beginning of the film she's onboard a train. That's where I was, too, on the train, sitting on a plush red seat and looking out the window. The country was flying by so fast that it scared me a little. At the same time, though, I felt happy. I felt that it wasn't just Fiona Wonder but all the other people, and me too, traveling *together* in the same direction. I was about to ask one of the other passengers why we no longer had trains like the one in the movie, but then, above me on the freeway, a car blew its horn.

*I*nside CostMart, in the fruit and vegetable section, I lingered over a display of strawberries. Then I looked at the price per basket and walked to the tomatoes. I picked out three slightly bruised tomatoes, bagged and weighed them, then looked at the price. Without even thinking about it I placed one of the tomatoes back in the pile, re-weighed the other two and placed them inside the hand basket that hung over my arm.

In the bread section I found a baguette that smelled delicious. On the shelf below, stacks of square, soft white bread were a dollar cheaper. I inhaled the smell of the baguette one more time, then chose one of the packaged loafs. Rounding the corner to the dairy section I reached for a gallon of whole milk then thought again and reached instead for a half gallon. After I got the eggs I walked the length of the back of the store where I found the cheapest pair of nude-colored nylons. All tampons are expensive, but essential; without looking at the price I placed a box of Multi-Pack Tampax into my basket.

Then something fortunate happened: out of all the birthday cards on the greeting card wall I not only found the perfect birthday card for Nikki, but at half price because it had the tiniest of tears down the center of the card. Nikki wouldn't even notice it, I knew; she'd be too concerned about opening her birthday present. With the extra money that I thought I was going to have to spend on the birthday card, I decided to buy either a basket of strawberries or replace the loaf of packaged white bread with the baguette, which ever turned out cheaper.

Humming along with the music playing over the loud speaker, I made my way back to the fruit and vegetables section. The song was "I am a Rock" by Simon and Garfunkel.

We saw each other at the same time. She was standing at the center of the supermarket in Aisle #10, the drinks and snacks aisle, wearing a pink sleeveless shirt, knee-length white shorts, white tennis shoes, and a gold necklace. Next to her was a shopping cart loaded with stuff. She motioned for me to walk toward her.

"Hi, Mrs. Redding," I said.

"Hello."

She seemed kind of weird—agitated but also sad at the same time. It worried me a little when her perfect posture slouched suddenly. Picking up a jar of Nacho Cheese Sauce, she asked, "Which do you think Valerie would like better, the one with jalapenos or the one without jalapenos?"

I shrugged. "I really couldn't say, Mrs. Redding. Sorry."

She stared blankly at the jars.

I shifted my weight from one foot to the other. "If it helps, one time I remember that Valerie got a pickle stuck in her throat. She was eating a hamburger. I almost had to give her the Heimlich. Maybe you should buy the kind without jalapenos."

Wordlessly, Mrs. Redding took a jar of plain cheese sauce off the shelf and tossed it into the cart. She looked at me, then down at the hand basket that I was carrying, and frowned. "Are you here all by yourself?"

"Yes."

"You walked here, via the underpass?"

"Yes, Mrs. Redding."

"You shouldn't do that. It's dangerous. What's that?" she said pointing at the birthday card.

"It's a birthday card for my mom's friend Nikki. She was there yesterday at the movie."

"I know of whom you are speaking."

I smiled. "Today is her forty-second birthday. We're going to have a party for her tonight at BONANZA BURGER. About an hour ago I talked to Valerie, and she said—"

"Valerie?" Mrs. Redding interrupted me. She looked caught off guard. "You mean *my* Valerie?"

"Yes, Mrs. Redding. She said that she was going to come too, I mean to the birthday party, and then after the party she was going to spend the night at my house."

"You mean your *apartment*."

"That's what I said."

"No. You said house."

"I guess it feels like a house to me because it's where I live. It's my home. But you're right, Mrs. Redding. I guess I should have said apartment."

She pointed again at the birthday card. "Can I read it?"

I took it out of the basket and handed it to her.

"*Never wish you could steal back any of the years of your life,*" Mrs. Redding read with hardly any emotion in her voice. Before opening the card she paused to clear her throat. "*Because, dear friend, you are just as special today as you were yesterday, tomorrow and forever after. Happy Birthday!*"

She closed the card. "That's very nice," she said quietly. It looked like she was about to hand it back to me but instead she held the card close to her chest. She turned toward the shelves. "Are you positive that Valerie wants the kind without jalapenos? You know how she gets if she doesn't get what she wants. It's my fault, I suppose. I spoil her. Then again, maybe it isn't me. Maybe it's all this. I mean, just look at all this," Mrs. Redding said. With Nikki's birthday card she made a great sweeping motion. "Who *needs* all this?" she said and turned to look at me. "Do you know, Mercy?"

"I—" I started, a little startled because for the first time she'd actually said my name, but that's when we both realized a woman pushing a shopping cart loaded with Evian water had stopped walking down the aisle and was standing next to us.

"Lady?" the woman asked tentatively.

I saw her flinch, but just barely. Turning away from me toward the woman, Mrs. Redding resumed her ramrod posture. She smiled brightly. "Joan!" she said.

"Lady!" the woman said back. She sounded relieved. "I thought it was you. Who else has all that gorgeous red hair?"

Mrs. Redding kept smiling, but I could tell that she was a bit uncomfortable.

"I hope I'm not interrupting," Joan said. She looked at me, then back at Mrs. Redding.

Mrs. Redding waved her hand. "Are you kidding? This is just my daughter's friend." Mrs. Redding turned to me. She explained: "This is Joan. Her husband Roger works with Dr. Redding at the practice. Roger is an allergist."

"Hi," I said. "It's nice to meet you."

"Nice to meet you," Joan said. She did not offer to shake hands. She turned back to Mrs. Redding. "I see you're not sneezing anymore. Did the allergy pills work? You know, the ones that I told Roger to give to Rob to give to you?"

"Oh," Mrs. Redding said. She looked a little flustered. "Oh, yes, they did help."

"Great!" Joan said. "I'm glad I thought of suggesting to Roger that he give you some samples. I mean, after I saw you at the annual spring staff picnic... Poor thing, you started up just as Rob turned on the grill for the hamburger patties and didn't stop until he had organized the Frisbee throw. Or was it before the Frisbee throw?"

Mrs. Redding smiled tightly. "I don't remember."

"Well, you looked miserable. What about the rash? Is it gone now?"

"All gone."

"Fantastic! I was beginning to worry when I didn't hear anything from Roger about it."

"Joan, I'm sorry. I told Rob to make sure to tell Roger

that I said thank you for all those samples."

"Oh, I'm sure your husband did and it was my husband who forgot to tell me. You know how men can be."

"Sure," Mrs. Redding said tensely.

I just stood there, listening and thinking.

"Do you need any more?" Joan asked Mrs. Redding. "Because if you do, then I can tell Roger to make sure to tell Rob that—"

"No, thank you. I'm all stocked up."

"Well, you know where to find them if you need them."

"Thanks."

That's when it happened: neither Mrs. Redding nor Joan knew what to say to one another next. An uncomfortable pause followed.

"Mrs. Redding?" I asked.

She looked at me, surprised, as if she had forgotten I was standing there beside her.

"Yes?" she said finally. "What is it?"

"Do you know if Dr. Redding has any extra asthma inhalers? I mean samples?"

I don't know why but she actually looked shocked, like I had just asked her to cut off her right arm and give it to me.

"Excuse me?" she said.

"I don't mean the daily inhaler," I tried to explain, stammering, "but the stronger one, the rescue inhaler. It's the one that my mom uses when she gets an asthma attack and can't breathe."

Mrs. Redding opened her mouth. No words came out.

"Your mother is an asthma sufferer?" Joan asked me.

"Yes, ma'am, since she was a kid."

"And she doesn't have a rescue inhaler?"

"Well, yes, she does usually, it's just..." I stopped to inhale, then exhale, one big breath. "It's just that she lost it. At least I think she lost it. See, the reason I think she lost it is because when she's not working and at home she always keeps it inside a dish on top of her dresser, except it wasn't there yesterday, or this morning. I checked all her pockets, but it wasn't in any of them. It's an expensive inhaler. I mean, for us it's an expensive inhaler, because we don't have any—" But there was something in the way that Mrs. Redding looked at me that made me stop trying to explain the fact that not only did we not have health insurance but Mom wouldn't have enough money in her medicine fund to buy a new rescue inhaler. I cleared my throat and said, "I was just thinking that since Dr. Redding is a lung specialist—"

"A pulmonologist." It was Joan, not Mrs. Redding, who corrected me.

I swallowed, thought about it, decided to continue. "But since Dr. Redding is a pulmonologist," I said to Mrs. Redding, "I was wondering if you could ask him if he has an extra inhaler that my mom could have since I'm pretty sure that she lost hers?"

When Mrs. Redding didn't say anything my arms and legs started to tingle. I cleared my throat again. I really couldn't tell if she was considering my request or if she had simply decided to ignore me.

Joan bit her lip. She pushed her cart forward once, then backward. "Lady, if my Roger has all those allergy medication samples, then I'm sure your Rob has at least one..."

But Mrs. Redding interrupted her. "I will ask him about it," she said.

I was so happy that I felt lightheaded. "That's really nice of you, Mrs. Redding. Thank you so much!"

"It's nothing," she said.

"It sure means a lot to me," I said. I wanted to hug her, but decided against it. "To me it means everything!"

She shrugged. "I have chocolate ice cream and popsicles inside my shopping cart. I need to finish my shopping before it all melts."

"Well, thank you again," I said. Then I added: "I'll see you tomorrow morning."

She shot a bewildered look in my direction. "Why would you?"

"Because, as I said earlier, Valerie said she was going to come to the party tonight and then spend the night at my house. I mean my *apartment*. Plus, tomorrow is Tuesday, and Tuesday morning is Valerie's, you know—" I looked at Joan, then back at Mrs. Redding.

Her face went hard as stone. "Oh, yes. I forgot."

"Okay," I said. "I'll see you tomorrow. And thank you again for asking Dr. Redding about the asthma inhaler."

I was all the way to the end of the aisle when she called back to me. "You forgot this," Mrs. Redding said as she handed me Nikki's birthday card. "And by the way, Marcy..." She narrowed her eyes at me. "You might want to think about choosing a different card. There's a tear right down the center of this one."


*A*s it turned out I didn't have enough money to buy the strawberries. And the baguette was five cents more than I had in my pocket. If I'd wanted to I could have picked out a different birthday card for Nikki but I decided to keep the one I had chosen, tear and all. Even with its imperfection it was still perfect for Nikki, I thought to myself, as I paid for the groceries.

The bagger used four plastic bags even though everything I bought could easily have fit inside one. Outside the sun was hot and blinding. I put my hand over my forehead and squinted. Walking toward me was a group of slender blurry bodies. The bodies got closer. Then, suddenly, one of them spoke to me. "What's up, Wonder?"

It was Robin Bell. My eyes adjusted just in time to see him, along with a group of his friends from the baseball team, or maybe it was the astronomy club, or maybe it was a mixture of both, walk past me into the supermarket.

*I* wish you would have left a note," Mom said as I walked into our apartment. Her voice came from the living room. "It's not like I didn't figure out where you went," she continued, "but still, I don't like it when I wake up and you aren't here. The house is so quiet. The only thing I can hear is my own breathing. It feels like—" But then she just stopped talking.

I placed the four plastic bags on top of the kitchen table and walked into the living room. Mom was in her bathrobe, sitting on the couch and holding a cup of coffee. Across the room the television was on. She looked at me, her face still puffy from sleep. "Sit and talk to me for a minute?"

"Okay," I said and sat down beside her. "Did you just wake up?" She nodded. "How was work last night?"

When Mom didn't say anything I thought about her stained uniforms and the double dose of Tide that I had dumped into the washing machine earlier that morning right before I had walked to CostMart. Any minute now the uniforms would be ready to go inside the dryer. Then Mom would take them out, iron them and hang them inside her closet. A couple of hours later she'd take them out, put on the BONANZA BURGER uniform, and place the Waffle Falafel uniform inside the backpack which, after her shift ended at BONANZA BURGER, she'd change into.

"It was nothing special," Mom said finally.

"Do you want some breakfast?" I offered. "I bought some eggs." She shook her head no. "I found a birthday card for Nikki. Do you want to see it?"

"Maybe in a minute..."

Mom looked so tired. She looked so tired... I got up from the couch and went back to the kitchen to put away the groceries. "No, Mercy, stay here with me a little longer," she said.

I sat down on the couch. "I found everything on the

list except the last three items you wrote."

A questioning look came over her face. Then she laughed. "I can't remember what I wrote on the list. Isn't that funny?"

I recited the list back to her, verbatim. "With the *l* crossed out," I told her.

"Oh, yes," she said. "That was for—" But she decided not to finish what she was going to say. Instead, she took a sip of coffee. She readjusted her bathrobe. "Ticket," Mom said. "I remember now. I wrote 'ticket' on the list so I could ask you to go to Nikki's house to use her computer to check her email for the information about your plane ticket to California."

"Can't it wait?" I said. "I have all week."

But she had already decided. "I talked to Nikki about it, and she said yes. She isn't home right now—she's at Clippers working a half-day—but she said she'd call home to Kurt and tell him to pick you up. He'll be here in just a few minutes. You can just stay at Nikki's house. Then tonight you can drive with them to BONANZA BURGER."

I sighed.

Mom said, "I could barely sleep at all this morning, I kept thinking about the plane ticket. What happens if it gets lost or something?"

"Mom, it doesn't work like that. It came through email. That means it is a digital ticket."

She looked lost.

"If it's not in Nikki's email—if the ticket was to get 'lost'," I tried to explain to Mom, "then I'm sure we can always ask them to resend it."

"Oh," she said and nodded her head. But I knew she had no idea what I was talking about. "All the same," Mom started, "I already talked to Nikki, and she said—"

"Okay, okay, okay," I said.

A pained look shone on her face, the one she gets when she feels both guilt and worry. "It's just that it means so much to me, Mercy," she explained. "I want to do everything by the letter on this one. I want to make sure I don't mess it up."

I nodded.

"So, when Kurt picks you up, please don't forget to take Nikki's birthday present with you."

"Okay, Mom," I said.

She took another sip of coffee. She squinted hard at the television, like she was thinking hard about something. "That's it," she said finally. "Now I remember why I wrote 'The End' on the list. Because yesterday I had to leave the theater to go to work before the end of the movie and I wanted to remember to ask you what happened at the end of the movie."

All I could think about was Fiona Wonder's big head on the giant screen.

"Mercy, what happened at the end?"

"Did you find your asthma inhaler at work like you thought you would?"

When she didn't say anything I became almost certain that I knew the answer to my question.

"I guess I better get ready to go to Nikki's," I said and got up from the couch.

She took my hand and squeezed it hard. "Promise me that later you'll tell me what happened at the end of the movie?"

"Okay, Mom," I said. "I promise."

Immediately, her hand dropped from mine.

"Are you sure you don't want breakfast?" I asked her. "I don't mind making it." She shook her head no. I looked at the clock. It read five minutes till one. "Maybe you should try to go back to sleep for a few hours?"

She looked across the room at the TV. "I'm not sleepy. And in any case, when I got up I checked the TV guide. In a few minutes they're going to play *Redemption Avenue* on the movie channel." She reached for the remote and started flipping through the channels. "Fiona Wonder is in it, but only in one scene. At least that's the way I remember it," she added. "It was made so long ago. She's just a girl in it. She's your age. She wasn't even a star yet."

I watched Mom stretch out on the couch. Watching the flashing images in front of her, she said, "I think I'll just lie here and watch it."

*H*i, Kurt," I said fifteen minutes later when Kurt arrived at our apartment to drive me to Nikki's house.

"Hi."

"Thanks for picking me up so that I can use Nikki's computer."

He shrugged.

"Hi, Kurt," Mom called from the living room. *Redemption Avenue* had already started. She did not make a move to get up from the couch.

Kurt waved back at her.

"Hold on a minute," I told him. "I have to get Nikki's birthday present."

He nodded, stuffed his hands inside his pockets and waited.

It's just like Kurt to not say much. He is forty years old and what both Mom and Nikki call ruggedly handsome. Kurt has wavy brown hair, a constant five o'clock shadow, and a small beer belly that Nikki says wasn't there when he was still working. The skin on his face and arms and legs looks like tanned leather from years of working outside. He has green eyes. They always look sad to me. As usual, Kurt had on jeans and sneakers and a gray Hanes T-shirt. Nobody knows this but one time I looked inside Kurt's closet at Nikki's house. Just as I'd suspected, it was full of Hanes T-shirts and sweatshirts, all gray. It must be his favorite color or something.

It had been a mistake to make that observation to Nikki. In response she had snorted and said that maybe it reminded him of all the cement he used to mix and pour before he got fired. If you ask me, there's a big difference between Kurt getting fired and Kurt getting laid off, because the company that he worked for went out of business.

Nikki is mad as hell that Kurt can't find work. I guess it's hard for her to understand when just a few years ago he did nothing but mix and pour cement. He mixed and poured the foundations of new strip malls and new office buildings, but mostly he mixed and poured it for the foundations of new houses.

At that time the construction business was so robust that Kurt decided to buy his own concrete mixer truck. That way, he had told Nikki who had told Mom and me, he could be the subcontractor and make more money. But mostly importantly, he'd said, he would be his own boss.

I remember the evening that Kurt bought his used mixer truck at an auction. It cost fourteen thousand dollars. It was a Thursday—Mom's night off. Inside our apartment Kurt drank a lot of beer, ate an entire pepperoni pizza, and told Mom that if she wanted to she could buy her own house. With his mouthful of cheese and pepperoni, he talked a lot about low interest rates and great deals on loans. He told Mom there was no better time than the present to buy a house, and that she could get herself a three bedroom house in this new housing development where he was pouring foundations. Kurt had popped the top of another can of beer, took a huge gulp, belched, and said that he'd buy one too—a house, he meant—for himself and Nikki, and that the four of us— and his kids Tucker and Brandi too, on weekends—could all live on the same block. On the weekends we could take turns having the other over for barbeques. It was the most I had ever heard Kurt talk. He was drunk.

It's funny how things turn out. It was only a month and half later that the big bank called Lehman Brothers failed. Then the stock market crashed. More banks failed. The media went crazy talking about it. A lot of people got scared. The developer that Kurt usually worked for ran out of money. Shortly after that it went out of business altogether. It was like somebody threw a pebble into a lake and one of the ripples submerged Kurt.

"If he doesn't find work soon," Nikki had said not long ago to Mom and me, "then I'm going to throw his ass out of my house. He can sleep in that goddamn truck he bought!" But I know she didn't really mean it.

"Is that the head?" Kurt said when I returned from my bedroom to the kitchen with Nikki's birthday present, the practice head named "Mandy" that was wrapped in shiny white paper. I nodded. He considered it a moment. "It looks like a basketball," he said.

"I think it looks like a big egg," I said. We both laughed.

"I think it looks like a little cloud," Mom called from the living room.

"She's never going to guess what it is. It's going to drive her crazy trying to figure it out," Kurt said. He smiled sadly, his hands still stuffed deep inside his pockets.

"Kurt," I said, "would you like to sign your name on the birthday card?"

He stopped smiling. He looked down at his feet. "Oh, well..." He shrugged.

I took a pen from the junk drawer and set it on top of the kitchen table. Then I opened the card, which both Mom and I had already signed, and placed it on the kitchen table so that he could sign it. *Happy Birthday, babe! Love you, Kurt*, Kurt wrote.

In the living room I bent down, gave Mom a hug and told her that I'd see her later at BONANZA BURGER. Mom said: "Bye, Mercy." And: "I love you". Then: "Honey, can you please move one foot to the left? You're blocking my view of the screen."

That's when I remembered Valerie. When I told Mom about Valerie wanting to come to the party, she said it was okay, that it was easy enough to fit a sixth chair around a table set for five, and that she would tell the hostess about it beforehand. "Okay, Mom," I said. "I hope you have a good rest of the day."

Mom went back to watching the movie.

$O$n the seat inside Kurt's truck I placed Nikki's birthday present. Taped on the paper and sealed in an envelope was the birthday card with our three signatures. Kurt turned out of the parking lot and onto Bird Road.

"Under Pressure" started to play on the radio. Kurt steered the truck onto the onramp leading to the freeway. A few seconds later, the truck veered from the slow lane to middle lane. Heritage Mall flew past. Then, at exactly fifty-seven miles per hour, we drove over the freeway underpass. CostMart appeared and disappeared from view. Three minutes later Kurt signaled, crossed from the middle lane to the slow lane, and turned onto the off ramp. We stopped at a red light. Kurt lit a cigarette. I rolled down the window. The light turned green. Kurt crossed the intersection, drove four blocks then turned left down Nikki's street.

"I like where Nikki lives," I said more to myself than to Kurt.

I looked out the window as we drove slowly down the residential street. Because it is an older neighborhood there are a lot of leafy trees and flowering bushes. I'm glad that Nikki never got the chance to move. Just like the neighborhood, Nikki's house is old, but not by any means worn out. Built in the 1940s, the house is made of yellow and red bricks. Inside are coved ceilings and hardwood floors, two small bedrooms, one bathroom, a living room, a kitchen, a front yard that is bigger than the house itself, an even bigger back yard, and a porch with a swing out front. Nikki not only grew up in the house, she's never lived anywhere else. Her parents bought it in 1970, a year before she was born. Then, when Nikki turned twenty-one years old and had graduated from cosmetology school, her mother, who had divorced her father a long time ago, gave Nikki the house and moved with her sister to a mobile home community in Jacksonville, Florida. The way I see it, Nikki's house is part of who she is.

I turned to Kurt. "Was Nikki still at work when you left to pick me up?"

"Yep..."

"Do you know what time she gets off?"

"Nope..."

He parked the truck on the street just outside Nikki's house. Looking up the driveway, I could see that the garage door was open. The Daihatsu was parked inside the garage.

"Nikki is home," I said. "They must have let her off an hour early because it's her birthday."

Kurt didn't say anything. Like me, he got out of the truck and went up the walkway to the front door. Just as we reached the top step the front door flew open. There stood Nikki, wearing nothing but a neon green bra, matching colored underwear, and an open silk robe, white with little red cherry blossoms on it. A half-smoked cigarette dangled from the corner of her mouth. Her short spiky hair was fire engine red.

"How come you're not wearing any clothes?" Kurt said.

Nikki looked at him like he was the stupidest man on earth. "Because it's hot and we can't afford to buy an air-conditioner?"

"What happened to your hair?"

"It was a slow day at Clippers. The hair Nazi wasn't there. It was the shampoo girl's idea—for my birthday. What do you think?"

"I think you look like an upside down strawberry."

Apparently this was the wrong thing to say. Nikki glowered at him.

"Nikki, come on. It was just a joke," Kurt said. When he went to kiss her, she turned her face away. "Have it your way," he said and pushed his way past her into the house.

Nikki took the cigarette out of her mouth and threw it past me onto the walkway. "By any chance are you going to mow the lawn today?" she called after him.

"Not now. I've got to pick up the kids from Alicia's mother's house."

Nikki left the door ajar as she followed Kurt through the living room and into the kitchen. "I thought what's-her-face was picking them up," I heard her say to him. She meant Alicia.

I didn't know what else to do but stand there in the middle of the living room.

"I thought *that woman* was going to pick them up from her mother's house, and that we were going to pick them up from her house right before the party," Nikki said to Kurt. "How come I didn't know about this change of plan? Is it because you talked to her on the phone this morning? Did you use *my* cell phone to call *that woman*?"

"No."

"Don't lie to me..."

"Jesus! You know we wouldn't even be fighting about this," Kurt said, "if you'd let them come over here during the day instead of going to their grandmother's house."

"So you did use my phone to call her..."

"What I said was that we wouldn't even be fighting about this if you'd let—"

But she stopped him. "Those kids are not coming over here every day of the week during the summer. They already spend every weekend with us. My house is not a goddamn day care center!"

"Calm down."

"If they start coming over here while I'm at work, and while *that woman* is at work, you're never going to find work, Kurt. That is, unless you want to start your own daycare center."

"Nikki..." he warned.

"It's not right, Kurt. You're a man. I can't wait till the day you find your balls and—"

But this time he stopped her. "You know what, Nikki?" Kurt said. From the living room I heard the refrigerator door open and slam shut. Then I heard the pop top of a beer can. "Just because it's your birthday doesn't give you a license to act like a bitch."

I could not hear it but I could easily imagine what came next: Kurt swigging in two swallows an entire can of beer. There was a long pause. Nikki, I imagined, was trying to figure out what to say next. At long last, she came up with it.

"Well, that's just swell," she said to Kurt. "I hope you're proud of yourself. It's not even two o'clock in the afternoon, and by my count, you're already on your fifth can of beer. If I don't miss my guess, you're going to be good and drunk just in time for my birthday party."

"That's the plan," Kurt said and belched.

"Congratulations," Nikki told him. "You're not only a pig, but a drunken pig."

"If you say so, darling," Kurt said, but it came out more like a song. At the very end of the lyric, I thought I heard a crack in his voice.

Before I knew it Kurt had stormed out of the kitchen, past me in the living room, and out the front door. From the picture window Nikki and I watched the truck rumble down the street and out of sight.

"Nikki, are you okay?" I asked.

"That's a dumb question," she snapped at me.

She looked out the window one more time, then turned, lit a cigarette, and walked to the other side of the room to the fish tank. Inside it a pair of angel fish glided from one end of the tank to the other. Both the fish tank and the angel fish had been a present from Kurt, before he was out of work. Their names were Fred and Wilma Flintstone. "Happy freaking birthday to me," Nikki said, smoking her cigarette and staring at the fish tank.

I winced. Suddenly I realized I had forgotten Nikki's present inside the cab of Kurt's truck.

Nikki looked at me. "What's the matter?" she demanded.

"Nothing," I said. Then I said, hopefully, for both our sakes, "I'm sure he's just gone to pick up Brandi and Tucker. I'm sure he'll be back soon."

"I know that!" Nikki said. She turned away from the fish tank, sat on the sofa and crossed her legs. Immediately her right foot began to twitch nervously. She stubbed out the cigarette in an ashtray on top the coffee table. Then she stood up again. "I hate my hair. I'm going to change it back," she announced. "Don't bug me while I'm in the bathroom. Go ahead and turn on my laptop so you can see about your plane ticket."

"Okay, Nikki," I said.

I walked from the living room to her spare bedroom where she keeps her laptop. I've often thought that even though Kurt's kids only spend weekends at her house, it would be nice for them to have their own space. If she wanted to Nikki could fix up her spare bedroom for Kurt's kids instead of making them sleep together on that old foldout sofa in the living room. As it stands, the only thing in Nikki's spare bedroom (which was her bedroom when she was a kid growing up in the house) is a collection of stuffed bears in one corner on the floor, a faded Vanilla Ice poster taped to the wall, an old desk and chair, Nikki's laptop computer on top of the desk, and, near the window, a huge chest with a padlock on it. The key to the padlock, I know, is inside a drawer in the vanity in Nikki's bedroom. I've never thought about taking the key, opening the padlock and looking inside the chest. I don't need to; I already know what's inside it.

I heard the bathroom door open then shut. Nikki's house suddenly became very quiet.

I switched on the laptop, waited for it to boot, then went online and typed "xtraemail" into the search engine.

Nikki's email is snipnik@xtraemail.com, and her password is "steelhead". I know because I set it up for her. There were five unread messages in Nikki's inbox. The first two messages were spam. The third message was a forwarded email showing pictures of half naked men. It was sent by one of Nikki's coworkers. The subject line read: HOT, HOT, HOT!!! The fourth message was from extraemail. It talked about the latest updates to the system. The subject line of the fifth message read: ATTN: FLIGHT CONFIRMATION AND TICKET CODE. I clicked it open. The message read:

*Dear Ms. Swimmer,*

*Attached to this email please find a copy of your confirmation and ticket code for your flight to Los Angeles on Western Airlines next Sunday at 6:15 am. Please print and take this document with you to the airport, as it will serve as your ticket. When you arrive in Los Angeles a representative from Almost There Magazine will be waiting for you outside the flight terminal. Look for a woman holding a sign that reads, WONDER/SWIMMER.*

*If you have any questions regarding your plane ticket next Sunday morning to Los Angeles, please do not hesitate to email or telephone my office at (401) 349-8923.*

*Warmly,*
*Mandy Simon*
*Assistant Marketing Director,* Almost There Magazine

It seemed a funny coincidence that the Assistant Marketing Director had the same first name as Nikki's present. I thought about the practice head, "Mandy", inside Kurt's truck. I imagined it rolling from one side of the cab to the other as he drove.

I looked at the computer screen in front of me, moved my mouse to the email attachment then clicked it open. Once it loaded, I reached to turn on the printer so that I could print the ticket. That's when Nikki's phone rang. I stopped what I was doing and craned my neck to look out the door. I saw Nikki open the bathroom door and run to the phone that was in the living room on top the coffee table.

"Hello?" Nikki said into the receiver. With her back to me she stood tall and tense. Her voice carried a heightened nervousness. I think she thought it was Kurt on the other end. Nikki listened. Then her shoulders sagged. "Wait a minute," she said, then turned and walked to where I was sitting at the desk in her spare bedroom. With the phone in her hand she stuck out her arm to me.

"For me?" I said. I think I was more surprised than she. I took the phone from her hand. "Who is it?" I asked her.

"That friend of yours. Mallory." Still at the doorway, she crossed her arms over her chest and started biting on her left thumbnail.

"Hi, Valerie," I said into the receiver.

Nikki took her thumb out of her mouth. "Don't stay on too long," she instructed.

"How did you know I was here?" I said to Valerie.

"I called your place," she told me. "Your mom gave me the number."

In the background I heard muffled voices and shoes squeaking on floors and the sound of an ambulance. "Is everything okay? Where are you?"

"At the hospital ER. My stupid brother broke his collarbone at football clinic."

"That's terrible," I said. "Is he okay?"

"He's purple and swollen and full of Valium. He's fine, the dumb ass. He's doing better than my mother. After she talked to Dad on the phone, and he told her that he was in a very important meeting with his accountant, and that he couldn't leave and that she'd have to deal with it herself, she started acting spastic."

"How?"

"Well, right now she's in the cafeteria eating a bowl of corn chowder. I know because I saw her."

"Maybe she was hungry."

"When Mom gets hungry she eats a carrot stick. Anything else has too many calories."

"Oh," I said.

"I just called Dad again," Valerie told me. "He said that I'd better stay here with her and my brother. Sorry, but I can't come to the party tonight...for your mom's friend Vikki."

From the doorway Nikki snapped her fingers at me—a warning to hurry up and get off the phone.

"I guess I'll see you tomorrow morning," Valerie said to me. "By the way, my mom told me that she saw you this morning at CostMart."

"Yeah," I said. "Guess who else I saw there?" As soon as it came out of my mouth I regretted saying it.

"Who?"

"Robin."

Her breathing quickened. "Oh, yeah?" she said. She was trying to sound nonchalant. "Inside the supermarket, or, like, somewhere else?"

"What's the difference? It really wasn't a big deal. I don't even know why I'm mentioning it."

"Did he say anything to you?"

"Nikki wants me to get off the phone now, so—"

"What did he say?"

"He just said 'what's up?'"

"He said 'what's up'? That's it?"

"He said, 'What's up, Wonder?'"

When Valerie didn't say anything, I said: "It wasn't a big deal, Val. Really."

"Quit saying it wasn't a big deal. I know it wasn't a big

deal."

"It was stupid of me to say anything about it."

"Yeah, it was. But why would he call you *Wonder*?"

"I don't know," I said. "He probably found out that I'm going to spend next week with Fiona Wonder."

"Oh," she said.

"So I'll see you tomorrow morning," I said.

It took her a few second to respond: "Yeah. Whatever..."

"I'm really sorry to hear about your brother. I hope your mother doesn't worry too much. I hope that Jeremy—"

But she had already hung up the phone.

"What did she want?" Nikki asked me.

I switched off the phone, placed it on my lap and looked up at her. "Valerie's brother Jeremy broke his collarbone. She's with him and her mother at the Emergency Room."

For a moment we were each quiet.

"I bet they have insurance," Nikki said finally. "He'll get five-star treatment."

I didn't say anything.

"I remember the last time that I was in the ER. You were there too. When was it again?"

I didn't even have to think about it. "Three months and five days ago."

Nikki crossed her arms over her chest again. Just like me, I'm sure she was remembering that ER visit.

What happened was that Mom had had an asthma attack. As usual, she'd taken a double dose of her rescue inhaler, except afterwards she still couldn't breathe. That's when I got scared. I ran to the phone to call 911, but then I remembered ambulances charge money to drive people to the hospital. So I called Nikki. Luckily, Kurt was with her. When he was still in high school he drove race cars, so he was experienced at driving fast and it took him only seven minutes to get to our house. Kurt, along with Nikki and I, drove Mom to the Emergency Room. The first thing the nurse behind the desk wanted from us was Mom's insurance card. I remember that Kurt had looked at Nikki. Nikki had looked at Mom. Mom, who was wheezing and panting and gulping for air, had looked at me. When I lied and said we had left the card at home the nurse pointed to the waiting room and told us to wait. Three and a half hours later we were still waiting. By then Mom could breathe again. We had left the hospital without Mom ever seeing a doctor.

"I hope she never has to go through that again," Nikki said to me.

I nodded. "But she might have to go back there if she doesn't get a new rescue inhaler. Do you know anything about that, Nikki?"

She opened her mouth then reconsidered and closed it. In response, she took the phone from my lap, turned and started to walk back to the bathroom. I went back to my ticket business. I turned on the printer to print my ticket. That's when we heard Kurt's truck pull up on the street outside the house.

This time I decided to get up, walk into the living room, and stand beside Nikki in front of the picture window. Outside, in the cab of the truck, sat Kurt and his kids, Brandi and Tucker. Kurt said something to them, and in response they both nodded. On their upper lips, I noticed, were purple half-circles: grape Kool-Aid, I imagined. Nikki stepped away from the window as Kurt swung open the heavy door of his truck. We watched silently as he marched up the walk to the house. In the crook of his arm was Nikki's present. I shut my eyes and prayed silently that they would be kind to one another.

I opened my eyes just in time to see Kurt open the front door. "Take this," Kurt said to Nikki. He held out the present to her but did not make a move to come inside the house.

Nikki acted angry at him even though it was pretty

obvious, at least to me, that she was relieved that he'd come back. "Tell your kids to get their behinds inside this house," she said. "I'll make them peanut butter sandwiches with the crusts cut off—just like Brandi likes them."

Kurt didn't move a muscle. "Are you going to take this from me or aren't you?" We all stared at the present. At that moment in time it looked precious and fragile and ultimately unreachable.

"Just give it to me, Kurt. And come inside," she said.

"I can't do that," he said. "I can't because I'm not coming back." He sounded sad and tired and exhausted, like an old dog about to be put down. "I'm just not enough for you anymore. Me leaving—just consider it my birthday present to you. It's what you really want. And anyway, I can't afford anything else." He dropped the head on the floor.

He pulled the door shut and walked back to his cement truck. He started the ignition then drove down the street.

Nikki stood frozen.

*I* have you down for a party of six," the hostess at BONANZA BURGER told us.

Her name is Courtney Liver, the hostess. Next year, just like Valerie and me, she will be a senior at our high school. Courtney plays the tuba in the school marching band and can look at people for extended periods of time without blinking or smiling. She has absolutely no sense of humor. Maybe it's because back in elementary school a lot of kids teased her about her last name. For example, instead of Courtney Liver they called her Chicken Livers.

"But your table is ready," Courtney protested, unblinking and unsmiling, after I tried to explain to her that our plans had changed and that it would be just the two of us—Nikki and me—that needed a table. "Your mom came in early to set it up. She decorated it and everything. Even though she could hardly breathe she blew up a whole bunch of balloons—six of them!"

"We Built This City" played overhead on the music system. BONANZA BURGER always plays upbeat songs like "We Built This City" and "Party in the U.S.A." and "Greased Lightning" and "You're the One That I Want" from the movie *Grease*. I have a hunch that the same songs play over and over again at every single BONANZA BURGER restaurant in the United States of America. I guess I think so because everything else from the big floppy menus to the posters on the walls is identical from one restaurant to the next.

"The person who eats at a BONANZA BURGER in Spokane, Washington, Houston, Texas, Jackson, Mississippi or here, the location in which you work, should have the exact same experience—a good honest burger made by a good honest cook brought to them by a good honest server" Mom was told recently at a BONANZA BURGER Employee Workshop.

The workshop lasted all day, no pay, mandatory to attend for all employees, and held inside a banquet room at a Best Western hotel near the airport. It was stressful for Mom because up until the last minute she didn't know how she was going to get there. The day of the workshop Nikki had to work and Kurt had what turned out to be an unsuccessful job interview for a position as a manager at a construction company (his effort as an independent had not turned up even one job). Mom started to cry when she found out the nearest bus stop with a bus going to the airport is twenty miles from our apartment. She was convinced that she was going to be fired.

Thankfully one of her coworkers, Gabriel, offered to drive her to the workshop. I've never met him in person so I don't know exactly what he looks like, but Mom has told me that he is over six feet tall with black curly hair and a tattoo on his right forearm. The tattoo reads, in capital letters, MARAVILLA. Mom hasn't asked him yet what it means in Spanish.

Gabriel has worked as the kitchen manager at BONANAZA BURGER for four years. On the drive to the workshop he explained to Mom that he used to cook at his family's restaurant which was called Tres Amigos, but then the Mexican chain restaurant called Trescientos Nachos opened across the street. It was a combination of the two-for-one margaritas on Mondays and plates of unlimited nachos on Fridays that did in Tres Amigos. Mom said she'd never eaten at Trescientos Nachos and didn't know anyone else (she meant Nikki, Kurt and me) who'd eaten there either.

I know someone who has eaten there: Valerie. The last time she went with her family she and her brother had a contest as to who could eat the most nachos. Jeremy ate four platefuls and Valerie ate five. The next day she didn't feel very well. We went to the mall anyway. At the food court she ate a corn-dog then, fifteen minutes later, a fudge brownie. To tell the truth, I wasn't surprised when she had to run as fast as she could to the nearest bathroom.

At Tres Amigos, Gabriel told Mom, he had made homemade tortillas, pico de gallo, green and red salsas, and mole. His favorite dish to make was posole—a hominy, meat and chili stew. "Posole is very old," Gabriel said to Mom. "It was once consumed only on very special occasions. That's because the ancient Aztecs believed humans were made out of cornmeal dough, so the combination of hominy, or whole corn kernels, and meat in a single dish was highly significant. Of course back then," Gabriel explained to Mom, "the dish was made with human meat instead of pork."

At the BONANZA BURGER Employee Workshop Mom, Gabriel, Chicken Livers and every other employee was given an official BONANAZA BURGER workshop packet. Inside it was a list of exercises to be performed throughout the day. All the exercises were aimed to help strengthen their senses of "Honor", "Loyalty" and "Trust", the three core principles required by Coreman National.

Also inside the packet was a coupon for half off the price of all the items offered to them that day during their fifteen-minute lunch break (Mom didn't get lunch that day because she didn't realize she had to pay for it), and a single sheet of white paper that read:

*Attention Employees:*

*Recently all Coreman National restaurants in California have been mandated by the attorney general to place a notice inside the lobby that reads:*

## WARNING
### Chemicals Known to the State of California To Cause Cancer, Birth Defects or Other Reproductive Harm May Be Present In Foods Or Beverages Sold Or Served Here.

*As you already know, because you are a vital part of our family, Coreman National strives to create and serve **affordable**, **delicious** and **safe** meals inside all our casual dining restaurants. The key phrase in the notice is "may be present". The notice is only mandated in California, not in our state or any other state in the United States of America. In the near future we feel confident our legal team will successfully fight to remove this overly-cautious notice from our locations in California. In the meantime, if a customer asks about the notice, then please refer them to our corporate web site where they can find information about how to contact our corporate office.*

*We thank you for your **honor**, **loyalty** and **trust** regarding this matter.*

Mom told me that Gabriel excused himself briefly from

the banquet room right after he looked at the back of the workshop packet. Arranged in a circle were five different restaurant logos. In the middle of the circle of logos was the Coreman National logo. Mom thinks that Gabriel didn't know until he saw the back of the packet and all those satellite logos together that Coreman National not only owned BONANZA BURGER but also Wong's New Chinese Experience, Little Vinny's Italian Eatery, Pat's Irish Pub and Grill and, last but not least, Trescientos Nachos.

Gabriel is serious and quiet and nice to everyone, Mom told me about him. She hasn't admitted it yet, but I'm pretty sure that she likes him. When I told Valerie that I'd like to see them go on a date, she just snorted then recommended to me that I recommend to my mom to find out first whether or not he has a Green Card.

*I* can seat you now, however it won't be at one of your mother's tables," Courtney informed me. She looked very official behind the hostess station. "You can wait for one of her tables to open up, but it could be as long as an hour."

Nikki looked like the last thing she wanted to do was wait for anything. She stood a few feet from me in the lobby next to a giant gumball machine and a five-foot-tall replica of the Statue of Liberty. Nikki had on her purple cowboy boots, a pair of stonewashed, super-tight jeans, a low cut silky black top and a colorful beaded glass necklace. Flung over her shoulder was her big black purse. Her hair was gelled back, slick-looking and, once again, jet black.

After Kurt had left she'd changed it back. First, though, she'd gulped down an entire can of diet soda, smoked three and a half cigarettes and paced half a dozen times from the kitchen to the living room. "Are you okay?" I asked her, but instead of answering me, she stubbed out the half-smoked cigarette, walked into the bathroom and slammed the door. I walked to the front door, picked up the slightly smashed present from the floor and carried it with me to her spare bedroom where I went back to printing my ticket confirmation to California.

Inside the mall on our way to BONANZA BURGER Nikki had, without warning, shoved her present at me before walking inside Mind, Body & Spirit, and I was still holding it. She hadn't invited me to go inside Mind, Body & Spirit with her, so I walked to the railing to wait for her. Across the atrium two more shops, Pets Plus and Coffee Way, had closed. Just like Mrs. Redding's favorite department store, Time & Luxingham, and Valerie's favorite shop, Mood's, the entrances to both Pets Plus and Coffee Way were gated shut. When Nikki emerged from Mind, Body & Spirit, and I pointed at the closed stores, she just shrugged and readjusted her purse over her shoulder. She was empty handed, of course.

"So do you want to wait or don't you?" Courtney asked, wanting a decision

"Let's just eat," said Nikki.

We were led to a two-seat booth, each handed a menu and told to enjoy our meal before Chicken Livers, her ponytail swinging behind her, turned and marched back to her hostess station. Halfway she stopped to talk to a busboy. She pointed at the long empty table with six balloons tied to six chairs, placemats with "It's Party Time" written on them, and, at the head of the table and placed on top of the placemat, a big pink button with writing on it that read, *It's My Birthday!*

If Kurt had not left with his kids in his cement truck, and if Valerie hadn't had to go to the Emergency Room with her brother and her mother, and if we had been a party of six, as planned, instead of two, then that's where Nikki would have sat.

Nikki flipped open her menu and held it just high enough in the air so that I couldn't see her face.

"What looks good to you?" I asked as I placed the birthday present at the middle of the table. Even though there are countless choices when it comes to ordering a meal at BONANZA BURGER, I already knew what I wanted—a cheeseburger without special sauce, or mustard, or mayonnaise, or ketchup, or any toppings except pickles, and a Sprite.

"Nikki, would you like to split a basketful of steak fries with me?"

She closed the menu then folded her hands neatly on top of the table. "Why do you always have to act like a baby?"

"I don't know what you're talking about," I said.

"Yes, you do. All the time you're saying stuff like *Is it okay, Nikki?* And, *Can I do this, Mom?* And, *I'm sorry to hear about your brother, Mallory.* Jesus Christ! You're sixteen years old and act like you're fucking six."

"I just asked if you wanted to share some fries with me..."

She repeated verbatim what I had just said except in a baby voice. "*I just asked if you wanted to share some fries with me...*" With her head tilted to one side, she said, "You sound retarded."

I watched her reach for her purse and slam it onto the top of the table. While Nikki looked for her cigarettes, I couldn't help but notice, between her wallet and her hair brush, the bottle of Green Apple Body Lotion from Mind, Body & Spirit.

"You know you can't smoke in here, Nikki. I know you're upset, but if you'd like to talk about what happened with Kurt then—"

She flung her purse back to the floor. Then she took one of my wrists and squeezed hard. "Just shut up! You don't know shit about anything, so just—shut—the—fuck—up!"

"Nikki, let go. That hurts."

"You don't know shit about how things work, which is

too bad for you, because you sure as shit aren't one of *them*."

I yanked my wrist away from her. "I don't know what you're talking about."

"You know who I mean. People like your friend Mallory."

"Here name is Valerie."

"I don't give a shit what her name is. I know all I need to know about her: she's a spoiled fat rich kid."

"Nikki—"

"Shut up and listen to me. You might actually learn something."

I waited; I had no choice.

"Five years from now, ten years tops, your so-called best friend isn't going to be your best friend anymore. You won't know her. She's not going to talk to you. You know why? Because you aren't going to be good enough for her anymore. She's going to college. You're not. She's going to marry some rich boy. You're not. She's going live in some big-ass house, pop out a couple of kids, take a couple of real nice vacations each year and not ever have to worry about anything. But you're not going to be living in a fancy house, or taking nice vacations. You're going to end up just like your mom—just another waitress living in some crappy apartment. You understand what I'm saying to you, M? Your friend is somebody because she's connected to things; and you're nobody because you're connected to nothing. Honestly, I don't even understand why she's your friend. The only thing I can come up with is that no one else will be seen with her. She's too fucking fat."

I said in a low whisper and after a very long pause: "Are you finished?"

"Are you finished?" she mimicked me. She laughed in my face. Then she stopped laughing suddenly. "You see, this is what I'm talking about. You are so naïve. You really need to grow the fuck up."

"Nikki," I said as quietly as possible, "Kurt loves you.

You love Kurt. It may be true you don't love or even like his kids, but you could try harder to get to know them. Who knows, if you just try, then you might not only like them but love them too. The problem is, Nikki, you think a job, or money, or a bottle of stolen Green Apple Body Lotion from Mind, Body & Spirit, which you're not even going to use but just stick in a chest with a lock on it, is more important than love. If anyone sitting at this table is retarded, naïve or just plain stupid, it's you."

She raised her hand at me. I squeezed my eyes shut and waited. I was sure she was going to smack me. Nothing happened. I opened my eyes again. Her hand had dropped back to the table. She had never done anything like that before. For a minute we just sat there, not saying anything. I think we were both in shock.

A waitress came to take our order.

"I want the grilled chicken sandwich with guacamole and fried jalepenos on it, and a diet soda," Nikki said. Her voice was shaking. She didn't even look at me, she just said "no" when the waitress asked if she wanted to order a basketful of steak fries.

The waitress locked in Nikki's order on her digital hand-set then looked at me. I ordered a cheeseburger and a Sprite.

"What kind of cheese, honey?"

"American, please."

*Beep* went the digital hand-set. "Toppers?"

"Just a pickle, please."

"Sauces?"

"No, thank you."

"Not even ketchup, darling?"

I shook my head.

The waitress finalized my order. She said Mom's name. "You're her kid, right?"

I told her I was.

The waitress said that she thought so, and that I looked just like Mom, except younger, and that Mom talked about me all the time, especially since I'd won a week with a movie star.

"Which movie star is it again?" she asked me.

"Fiona Wonder," I told her.

"That's right. I just love her, don't you?"

The waitress left our table just as Mom walked past. Balanced on her palm and supported by her shoulder was an oval tray loaded with drinks and plates with burgers and two red plastic baskets full of steak fries. When Mom saw us, she stopped walking. When the tray started to tip to one side she expertly rebalanced it on her shoulder. She looked at Nikki, then at me, then at the table in the middle of the room, then back at Nikki. Her mouth opened, questioningly. That's when a woman sitting at a table on the other side of the room called to her: "Waitress!"

Mom crossed to the other side of the room. Just as she set the tray on the edge of the table, I saw a bus boy make his way to the table that was meant to be ours. In his hands he held a large rubber tub, and it was amazing how fast he cleared Nikki's birthday table. First all the special placemats and the birthday button went inside the rubber tub. Then, with lightning speed, he untied each balloon from each chair. I thought maybe he'd take off his nametag and, with the pin on the back on the clasp, pop each balloon right there. Instead he held the balloon strings in one hand, the rubber tub in the other, and walked behind a wooden partition that led to the kitchen. That's when I noticed the silver foil stars in the middle of the table that Mom must have placed there when she was decorating it.

The bus boy reappeared from behind the partition. I couldn't believe it at first—it didn't seem possible. The bus boy was Randy—the pitcher on the baseball team, the boy who sat in front of me in economics class. In one hand he held a dishrag; in the other a bottle full of neon blue liquid. Just as he reached the table, Mom turned to face the center of the room, the empty tray tucked underneath her left arm and pressed against the side of her body.

"Wait!" Mom said just as Randy took aim at the mound of silver stars with his spray bottle. She ran to the table, grabbed the bottle from him, and tucked it into her armpit. With both hands now free, she collected as many of the little stars as she could from the center of the table.

"Hey!" he yelled at her. His face turned bright red with anger.

But Mom wasn't listening. She was too preoccupied, too determined to scoop up as many stars as she could. When she'd collected a handful of them she opened up her arm like a bird extending its wing and let the spray bottle hit the floor. Without saying anything to Randy, she ran to our booth.

I saw him turn his eyes toward me, then back at her. A chill ran through me.

"What *happened?*" Mom looked upset and concerned and confused. Cupped in her palms were all the little stars. "Where's Kurt?" she wanted to know. "Where's Brandi and Tucker, and Valerie, too, and—" She looked desperate. "Mercy, I don't understand, where *is* everybody?"

I guess Nikki couldn't stand any more questions, so she grabbed her present and ripped open the wrapping paper. For a moment she just sat there, staring down at "Mandy", the practice head.

"Do you like it?" Mom asked finally, her voice full of hope.

I saw Nikki's jawbone working. She looked up at me, fiercely. "I'll tell you one thing, Little Miss Mercy. You know why your mom can't wait for you to spend next week with Fiona Wonder? I know why. It's because she knows it's the first and last special thing that will ever happen to you."

When Nikki said that, Mom's face went white. It was like Nikki had just slapped her. Mom shook her head back and forth, back and forth.

"It's the truth and she knows it!"

The palms of Mom's hands dropped to her sides, dumping all the stars onto the table.

# TUESDAY

*I*t was more than obvious that Valerie was still mad at me the next morning when she and her mother picked me up to go to her therapy appointment. To start with she didn't say "Mercy Swimmer!" as she always does when we greet each other. She didn't even say hello or turn around when I got into the back seat of the Wagon. As Mrs. Redding turned off Bird Road onto the freeway and past Heritage Mall, Valerie stared straight ahead, chomping away on a wad of gum as she flipped through radio stations.

"Valerie, please!" Mrs. Redding turned to look at Valerie's pudgy fingers twisting the knobs on the radio.

She sighed, turned the knob again and settled on KYRX, a pop station. General Public sang about "Tenderness".

When I asked how Jeremy was doing it was Mrs. Redding who told me in detail about what had happened the day before at football clinic, about how he had been hit from behind and fallen hard on the synthetic field, about how he had yelped in pain and had lain on the field with his teammates surrounding him while the assistant coach, a man named Bud Lancaster, called an ambulance. Now Jeremy was at home, resting comfortably as a result of the Valium that the doctor had prescribed and watching ESPN with a bag of frozen peas and carrots wrapped in an old bath towel balanced on his shoulder. He had asked her to leave the front door unlocked just in case he got bored and wanted to call some of his friends to come over. Throughout the entire ordeal, Mrs. Redding told me, he had been incredibly brave.

Valerie snorted. "Give me a break. Last night I heard him cry when Dad helped him into the tub for his sponge bath. He's incredibly brave, all right: an incredibly brave baby!"

Mrs. Redding's foot tapped on the brake. She turned down the volume on the radio. "I see somebody woke up on the wrong side of the bed this morning."

Valerie turned the volume back up. "That expression is so stupid. It doesn't make any sense. It's like saying somebody peed on the wrong side of the toilet." She snorted again.

"Well, you know what I mean."

"Why don't you just *say* what you mean, Mother?"

"All right, I will. You seem like you're not happy about going to therapy this morning."

"Not happy about it? I hate Tuesdays. I hate therapy. I hate Dr. Zuwansky."

Once, at the end of Valerie's session, I saw her therapist. She appeared from behind the glass door and walked past the circular-shaped, steel-colored reception desk to the water cooler. In her hand was an oversized mug with a big chip on the rim and a rainbow painted on the side of it. She looked no more than five-feet-tall. Her hair was a mass of tight springy curls. When Dr. Zuwansky saw me sitting alone in the waiting room she smiled at me. She seemed nice enough.

"You don't hate Dr. Zuwansky," Mrs. Redding said.

"Yes, I do. She's a freak. She talks nonstop."

"I'm sure you're exaggerating."

"I'm not. Don't you remember the staff picnic last spring? She wouldn't shut up about her raw food diet and that stupid theory she's got about how there are cancer causing chemicals and metals and whatever else found in everyday products. For example, aluminum can give you Alzheimer's; therefore she refuses to wear deodorant." Mrs. Redding sighed. Valerie continued, "I can smell her armpits from across the room. Half the time I'm in her office I feel like gagging. Plus I'm so sick of looking at that gay rainbow mug that she's always carrying around with her. The bottom of it leaks. There are tea stains on the thighs of her pants and skirts. She's completely clueless. She doesn't even consider buying a freaking coaster, or better yet throwing the mug in the garbage where it belongs. So what if she's a lesbian? She doesn't have to announce it to all her patients."

"She is not gay, Valerie. I know the mug of which you are speaking. Her child made it for her."

She opened her arms wide in front of her. "So?"

"So, he died of leukemia when he was ten years old."

"Oh."

"He was the same age as your brother. Your father and I went to the funeral and you and Jeremy stayed at your grandmother Redding's house for the weekend. Don't you remember?"

"No."

"It was very sad."

Valerie looked out the window.

"She's divorced. It was her only child," Mrs. Redding continued. "I remember at the funeral—"

Then Valerie exploded. "Excuse me, but she is *my* therapist. She is supposed to deal with *my* issues. That's why Daddy is paying her one hundred and fifty dollars an hour. She's supposed to listen to *me*. Let her get her own therapist to listen to her talk about her dead kid. Okay?"

Valerie's statement had sucked all the oxygen out of the

car. Escaping the vacuum, I migrated to another time and place. Now floating in deep space, I hovered just a few feet away from a rainbow nebula that surrounded the supergiant red star Betelgeuse. I recognized my environment because Robin Bell had taped a photograph of the nebula on the blackboard in our science classroom, which doubled as the meeting place for the astronomy club. I remember that it was just five minutes before class ended, and Robin must have had a baseball game that day because he was wearing his baseball jersey, number 8, but not his hat. His sandy brown hair was long in back and ended in small curls. The ringlets looked like upside down question marks on the nape of his neck.

I admit that I spent a long time looking at the back of Robin's head. Most of the jocks wear their hair military style, including Randy. They march around school in packs with their square shaved heads and matching outfits— football or hockey or baseball jerseys, the associated sport's hat, blue jeans and sneakers, mostly Nike but sometimes Reebok—except for Robin. Sure, he wears his baseball shirt on game days and hangs out with the baseball team sometimes, but not all the time. He has other friends too, like the people in the astronomy club. A lot of times, actually, I see him on his own, walking down the corridors on his way to class with ear buds in his ears. He really likes music, I think. One time I stood in front of him and one of his astronomy club friends, a skinny boy with pimples and black glasses, in the lunch line. His friend asked him what he was listening to. "Pink Floyd," Robin had said. "Us and Them."

That day in science class, five minutes before the bell rang, Robin stood with three of our classmates looking at the photograph of the rainbow nebula around the star Betelgeuse that he'd taped to the blackboard. I remember how I had pitched my body forward in my seat so that I could listen to him explain that the star is six hundred times bigger than our sun, the eighth brightest star in the sky, and six hundred light years away from Earth in the constellation Orion. The rainbow nebula swirling around it is actually its own mass shedding itself. That's because Betelgeuse is destined to become a type II supernova. Someday within the next million years it will cave in upon itself and explode from the inside out.

After the bell rang I waited for everybody to leave the classroom. Then I walked to the blackboard to look at the photograph. It looked like a crown of flames and, within the flames, a liquid-like rainbow surrounding the star.

I didn't notice him until he was standing right beside me. Robin has pretty eyes. They are brown with some green in them too. Then something really funny happened: It was like there was a flash of light and I felt the heat from it radiate from my toes all the way to my head. Robin looked just as startled as me. Even though it was the first time that we had talked to one another, it didn't feel like it.

"What do you think about Betelgeuse?" he asked me.

"It's wonderful," I said to him.

"It's dying," he said to me.

A couple of months later he surprised me with an invitation to the Junior Prom. I'd thought about that star with the rainbow around it, and about Valerie too, when I made my excuse.


*M*rs. Redding pulled into the parking lot outside Dr. Redding's office. As she turned off the engine she said to Valerie, "I'll pick you up in exactly one hour. If you happen to see your father, please ask him what he would prefer for dinner—mushroom risotto or grilled eggplants." She pretended not to notice when Valerie made a face.

"Today in the newspaper I read that one of Georgia O'Keefe's paintings is on loan for the summer at the art museum. There was a picture of it in the paper. It's not one of her flower paintings but something called *Clouds* or *Sky* or *Clouds and Sky*. I'm not sure, I forgot. Anyway, I'd like to see it."

"Congratulations," Valerie said.

"If you would like to see it too," Mrs. Redding offered, "I'll take you both downtown with me."

Valerie rolled her eyes. I was not consulted.

Mrs. Redding started the engine. "Never mind then. Get out of the car now, please."

Valerie looked like she was reconsidering. "What about lunch?" she asked finally.

"I was planning on it after the museum."

"Can I pick the restaurant?"

"Yes. As long as the restaurant you choose is within walking distance of the museum. I don't want to spend the afternoon trying to find a parking place."

"Okay."

They both must have assumed that I wanted to go too since neither thought to ask me.

Valerie slammed the car door. She didn't wait for me to walk with her into the building. Dead center in the parking lot she stopped to adjust one of the straps of her sandals. Then, because she must have thought that no one was looking, she picked at the crack of her shorts.

"Mrs. Redding..." I started. I wanted to ask if she had decided whether or not to speak to Dr. Redding about a rescue inhaler for my mother.

"I don't have time to talk to you now, Marcy. Whatever it is can wait until later."

She sat facing forward, staring straight ahead with her hands placed firmly on the steering wheel. Her wedding ring glinted in the sun. In the rear view mirror I couldn't see her eyes behind her big black sunglasses.

Outside, Valerie swung open the door and disappeared inside the building.

Mrs. Redding sighed and shook her head. "Sometimes I can't believe that that's my daughter. Does she have any idea what she looks like?"

$F$or the next half hour I sat in the waiting room sucking on pieces of butterscotch candy that I got from a glass bowl on top the reception desk. I had forgotten to eat breakfast and I was famished. Flipping through a pile of old newspapers and magazines I found a three-month-old copy of *Better Homes and Gardens*. I read about how to make cheesy scrambled egg burritos. My stomach grumbled. I put the magazine down, picked up a two-day-old copy of *The Wall Street Journal* and stared at the head of a dot-matrix man until I got cross-eyed.

The next magazine I picked up had Fiona Wonder on the cover. She wore a midnight blue dress, matching shoes and dark red lipstick. She smiled in a teasing way, as if she had a wonderful secret that she might or might not tell. The index finger of her right hand touched her bottom lip. On her wrist she wore the Shooting Star Bracelet.

*Isn't She Luminous?* A question asked in the same color blue as her outfit. And then in smaller letters underneath it: *Inside: Read our exclusive interview with one of Hollywood's brightest stars.*

I opened the magazine and flipped through the pages until I saw her face again. There she was on page 88, wearing the same blue dress and shoes and red lipstick, except this time she lay on one side, on a blanket spread over ultra-green grass. Her head tilted toward the sky. She held the wrist—the one with the bracelet—to her forehead, almost as if she had a fever and was taking her temperature.

On the opposite page, in another photo, she stood at the center of the blanket, her wrist pressed against her chest and her hand holding onto a string connected to a big luminescent balloon. Her open mouth was shaped in a perfect "O". On her wrist the Shooting Star Bracelet sparkled. The opening of the article read:

*So what if her real name isn't Fiona Wonder? In this exclusive one-on-one with one of Hollywood's brightest stars, Fiona Wonder (born Clare Winkle) opens up about making movies, meeting men, and maintaining her madly divine figure while still indulging—at least once in a while—in her favorite all-time meal: a good old fashioned cheeseburger. Plus learn all about her new jewelry line as well as her inspiration for the widely popular Shooting Star Bracelet. Hint: she is not only a star but an avid star gazer.*

I closed the magazine and placed it on an empty chair next to me. I stood up, walked to the water cooler and took one of those triangular-shaped paper cups stacked high on the side of the cooler. Behind me I heard Jeannette, the receptionist, clear her throat. I drank the water, crumpled and threw the cup into the trash can next to the water cooler, turned and walked to the giant steel-colored reception desk. Sitting inside, like a soldier in a tank, Jeannette punched numbers into a calculator. She had a no-nonsense look on her face. Valerie was right: she smelled like mothballs.

I reached for another butterscotch candy.

"That's your fourth one..."

My hand froze, hovering over the glass bowl.

Jeannette took the bowl off the counter and placed it on the desk between the blinking phone and the calculator. "These are for paying clients. Sorry. There's a Columbo's Coffee across the street, for your information."

Suddenly my throat felt dry. I wanted another drink of water but didn't dare go near the water cooler. Instead I turned, walked across the room, sat down on the chair, placed the magazine, cover up, on my lap and stared down at Fiona Wonder's face.

When a man came through the front door and approached the reception desk, Jeannette placed the glass candy bowl back on top of the counter.

"Don't even sit down. I'm sure he's ready for you now. Wait a moment, please; let me check," Jeannette told the man. She picked up the phone, jabbed her finger down on one of the buttons, and said, "Dr. Redding, the accountant is here. Should I ask him to sit down to wait or—yes, sir. Thank you, Doctor."

A few seconds later the glass door opened and Dr. Redding appeared. I sat straight in my chair. All I could think about was Mom last Sunday morning at the bottom of the hill with her arms over her head, trying to breathe. I stood up, holding the magazine in my right hand, just as Dr. Redding placed his hand on the accountant's shoulder. He asked the man to follow him to his office.

"Dr. Redding..." I stammered. He turned to look at me.

That's when the shouting started. It wasn't just me but everyone else inside the waiting room that turned to look toward the door that led to the inner offices. Behind the frosted glass were two gray figures—one of which was a lot bigger than the other. Suddenly the door flung open. Out stormed the bigger of the two—Valerie. Her face was beet red and sweaty. And she was still screaming.

"Didn't you hear what I just said? I told you that I don't give a fuck! I'm glad you don't want to see me anymore. You don't listen to anything that I have to say anyway!"

Right behind her was Dr. Zuwansky, her springy curls bouncing on top of her head. The doctor's expression, I thought, looked calm and in control. In her hand she held the chipped rainbow mug.

"Valerie," she began, but first she took a moment to note everyone inside the waiting room. "Valerie," she repeated, "I don't think that now is the time or place to have this conversation. Please, let's go back inside my office so that we can finish—"

"Blah, blah, blah!"

"Valerie, please. I feel it is necessary that you understand how I feel about this. As I said to you before you stormed out of my office, I feel that we have reached an impasse. I feel that it would be best if we tell your father—" and with that she extended her arm to Dr. Redding, "that we agree that it would be best for you to find another therapist."

"Are you deaf? I already said I'm happy about it. You smell!"

Nervously, I looked to Dr. Redding. His jaw had noticeably tightened. He closed his eyes then opened them again. He stared up at the ceiling. Then, suddenly, he turned and looked at me. "You're her friend, right?"

It took me a couple of seconds to answer: "Who me?" I said. I was surprised. I nodded my head.

"Then do me a favor. Get her the hell out of here." He jerked his thumb in the direction of the door. "I don't have time for this." And with that he put his hand on the back of the accountant's shoulder and directed him past the reception desk. When he slammed the door behind him, I saw Valerie flinch.

"Val..." I started to say. I reached out my hand to her.

It was right there on the counter. If she really had to do what she did next, then she could have—she *should* have—chosen it: the glass candy dish rather than Dr. Zuwanksy's dead son's rainbow mug.

"Oh, no, please!" the doctor said right after Valerie grabbed the mug from her hand.

It went sailing across the room. Hot tea flew everywhere. I didn't see it but knew it must have happened because some of it landed on my arm. It burned. The mug hit the wall about a foot from my head. It smashed into pieces. "I'm glad your kid is dead!" I heard Valerie scream.

The magazine dropped from my hand to the floor. It was only then that I realized I had been holding the magazine with Fiona Wonder's face on the cover in front of *my* face—in an attempt, I guess, to protect myself from Valerie's explosion. As soon as I dropped the magazine I saw Dr. Zuwansky, her face in her hands, her entire body shaking, but I didn't see Valerie. She had disappeared.

*I* found her standing outside the building, unwrapping and jamming a piece of banana-flavored gum inside her mouth and waiting for Mrs. Redding to pick us up. She blew a huge yellow bubble that immediately collapsed all over her face. For a moment Valerie actually looked embarrassed. Then that passed and she went to work pushing the gum with her fingers and tongue back inside her mouth. It looked like she was about to swallow a surgical glove.

"So what!" she said finally, still struggling with the gum. "You're not talking to me now, Mercy?"

"That's the first thing you've said to me all day, Valerie. It's you who hasn't been talking to me."

All the gum was back inside her mouth now. She went back to chomping.

"Last night Nikki told me that this was going to happen," I said. "I was hoping that she was wrong about it, but now I don't know. Maybe she was right."

"I don't know what the hell you're talking about." I stared across the street at the Columbo's Coffee. "Whatever... Be a bitch. See if I care." I didn't move. "That's what I thought. Then fuck you too!" I turned and started to walk away. "Where are you going?" Valerie shouted at me.

"I'm walking home."

"No you're not! That's ten miles away. Maybe farther..."

"I can make it."

"Mercy, stop walking. I said stop!"

A few seconds later I heard feet slapping on pavement. I heard heavy breathing. Before I knew it Valerie had grabbed my arm, just as Nikki had grabbed my wrist the night before, and swung me around. I could feel her bitten-down nails digging into my skin. "Stop acting like you're all high and mighty!" she screamed at me.

"I'm not the one who is acting high and mighty."

"Yes, you are. You always do. I'm sick of it!"

"Then don't be my friend anymore."

She blinked. Her grip on my arm weakened but didn't let go. "You mean you don't want to be my friend anymore?"

"I didn't say that, Valerie."

"Well, that's the way you're acting."

"No, that's the way *you* are acting, Valerie."

"Yeah, but only because—" She stopped talking. She got all red in the face. She looked down at the ground. "You know..."

"Valerie, it's not my fault that I ran into Robin outside CostMart. It's not my fault that he talked to me. I know you like Robin, but—"

"Shut up. I do *not* like him!"

"Yes, you do. For some reason you just don't want to admit it. You think it's a better idea to slam your car into his truck. If you like him, then why don't you try to talk to him? So what if he talked to me outside CostMart? It's like you've forgotten that he talked to you first inside the Quick-E-Mart. For all you know, he—"

But she stopped me. "He *didn't* talk to me inside the Quick-E-Mart. Okay, Mercy? Are you happy now? Fuck!" she screamed at the top of her lungs. "That's why I smashed into his truck. Not because he said to me, 'What's up, Red?' It's because I said to him, 'What's up, Robin?' and he didn't say anything back to me. He just kept walking with his friends. He just completely—totally—" she swallowed her gum whole—"*ignored* me."

She let go of my arm. I looked down to watch her white hot handprint disappear from my skin. It reminded me of what Gabriel had told my mother about how the ancient Aztecs had believed that humans were made out of corn meal.

"I'm sorry I was like that earlier," she said. "Please don't walk home and leave me here alone." Her eyes filled with tears. "You're my only friend."

I didn't even have to think about it: I hugged her,

forgave her. "Val, maybe he just didn't hear you," I whispered in her ear. I was thinking about how Dr. Redding had slammed the door right before she had taken Dr. Zuwansky's rainbow mug and thrown it at the wall. "Maybe you need to try again."

A car horn sounded, startling us both. A few feet away, sitting inside the Wagon, Mrs. Redding stared at us. Without saying a word, Valerie and I got into the car—Valerie in front and me in back—and buckled our seat belts.

"I'm glad I drove home to check on Jeremy," Mrs. Redding said, oblivious to the trauma that had just happened both inside and outside Dr. Redding's private practice. "The bag of frozen vegetables had almost melted, plus he was hungry. I made him a tuna sandwich and French fries. I think he should be okay for a couple of hours while we look at the painting and go to lunch."

When neither of us said anything Mrs. Redding turned to Valerie. She frowned. She readjusted her sunglasses and started the engine. "How was your appointment?" Valerie was silent.

Mrs. Redding started to drive. "Did you ask your father what he wants for dinner?"

"No."

She sighed. "Because you didn't see him or because you forgot to ask him?"

"Because I—" The rest was a mumbled incoherent answer.

Mrs. Redding signaled, switched lanes, and steered the car onto the freeway onramp in the direction of downtown. "I thought as much. I'll just have to call him later and ask him myself."

Valerie hesitated. "He didn't call you?"

Mrs. Redding's head tilted. "You mean while you were at your appointment, and I was at home?"

"Yes."

"No. Why would he call me?"

For the rest of the drive downtown Valerie just stared out the window.

The art museum building looks like a gigantic piece of origami made out of gray concrete. Inside the lobby Mrs. Redding's heels clicked confidently on the hard shiny floor. She didn't seem to notice when Valerie and I veered away from her toward the drinking fountains. We stood together not saying anything as Mrs. Redding approached the front counter and took a pamphlet next to a sign that read, *Current Featured Exhibition.* She said something to a woman behind the counter. Then she handed the woman her membership card.

Mrs. Redding and Dr. Redding are patrons of the arts. That means that they donate money to the museum. They don't have to pay admission to enter. On a wall in the lobby their names are etched on a piece of black marble. Year round they attend fancy parties at the museum, including the annual Winter Ball held inside the museum's events room.

Before the Redding's had left for the ball last Christmas—I remember because that night I had stayed overnight at Valerie's house—Mrs. Redding had on a beaded white gown with a low-cut back. She looked quite beautiful, even luminous, I thought, when I saw her as I had walked from the living room into the kitchen to pour a refill of root beer for Valerie. Dr. Redding had on a tuxedo. He stood next to the garage door with the car keys in his hand while Mrs. Redding picked up the phone to order two extra large pizzas for Valerie and Jeremy and me. After she hung up the phone she slipped diamond earrings onto her earlobes as she walked to the middle of the kitchen where her white fur coat lay folded over the back of a chair. I was the first to notice Dr. Redding frowning at her.

"I just need to give Valerie the money for the pizzas,"

Mrs. Redding said, "and then we can be on our—Rob, what is it?"

"That dress," he said.

She froze; one arm in, the other arm out of the coat. "What about it? You don't like it?"

"No."

"Why not?"

"Frankly, Lady," he said, "I'm surprised that you even need to ask me that question. Perhaps it's because you're too preoccupied trying to call attention to yourself."

"I am not," she protested. "At least I don't think I am."

He just stood there, frowning.

With Valerie's root beer refill in hand I left the kitchen and went back into the living room. On the overstuffed leather couch Valerie sat stuffing jelly beans into her mouth as she flipped through channels on the flat screen TV. I sat down next to her just as Mrs. Redding walked out of the kitchen, through the living room and up the staircase that led to the bedrooms. Valerie took the root beer from my hand, her eyes not leaving the screen, and started slurping.

When Mrs. Redding came downstairs she was wearing a different dress—black with a zippered back. In the foyer, by the front door, she placed pizza money on the table where she always keeps a big vase full of fresh flowers. Staring into the mirror that reflects the living room, she told Valerie that when the delivery boy arrived not to tip him more than five dollars. "Are you listening to me, Valerie?" Mrs. Redding said. Her voice sounded strange and strangled, like an imaginary hand was choking her.

Valerie didn't even look up; she was too busy slurping the root beer and watching a tiger tear a terrified antelope to pieces on The Discovery Channel.

Mrs. Redding sighed. Still facing the mirror, her eyes moved from the reflection of Valerie and me sitting on the couch to what was immediately in front of her: her own reflection.

I blinked. I heard Mrs. Redding's heels clicking again inside the art museum's lobby. The clicking of her heels stopped. She stood between us, next to the drinking fountains. I watched her place her membership card back inside her wallet. She snapped the wallet shut and placed it inside her purse. Then she tried to hand the pamphlet that she had taken to Valerie.

Valerie folded her arms across her chest and announced that she had to go to the bathroom before we went upstairs to see the painting, *Sky in the Clouds* or the *Clouds in the Sky*. Whatever it was called, she didn't really care; she just had to pee.

"I wanted to wash my hands anyway," Mrs. Redding said as she threw the pamphlet into a trash can next to the drinking fountains. She followed Valerie into the women's bathroom.

From the corner of my eye I saw a man dressed in a dark gray custodian's uniform. Carrying a mop inside a bucket, he unlocked a set of double doors. He stepped through the doors then disappeared inside the room. Black letters above the doors read, *Events Room*.

The custodian had already started to mop the floor when I stepped through the double doors. It was a beautiful, circular space with a domed ceiling and green marble columns all around the rim of the room. He looked up from his mopping. "Can I help you?" He didn't smile or frown at me.

I cleared my throat. "I just wanted to look at the room."

He shrugged, didn't seem to care. "Just a room," he said.

I stood there, silently, trying to picture the Winter Ball, and trying also to picture the State Ballroom Dancing Competition. Instead, all I saw was Mom standing in the middle of the room, wearing her soiled red Waffle Falafel uniform with her misspelled nametag attached to it.

$B$ack inside the lobby it took me no time at all to find their names—Dr. and Mrs. Robert Redding—on the wall of plaques just outside the bathrooms. It was kind of amazing that I found their plaque considering every plaque looked exactly the same—black, shiny, envelope-sized, and, above each name, an inscription that read: *In honor, recognition and appreciation of your generous contributions to this establishment.* There must have been at least a hundred of them screwed onto the wall, arranged neatly in rows and columns that reached almost to the ceiling. A thin strip of sky-blue paint separated the top row of plaques from the ceiling. Dr. and Mrs. Redding's plaque was located in the fourth column from the right, the third row from the bottom. I'm not sure why, but it made me sad to look at it.

A toilet flushed. I heard Valerie's voice, her shoes squeaking on the floor tiles. She followed her mother out of the bathroom back into the lobby. I watched Mrs. Redding's eyes slide down then back up my body. Even though she didn't say anything I was pretty sure she had noticed the pamphlet that a few minutes ago she had thrown away and I had fished out of the trash, folded in half and placed inside my back pocket.

Valerie stood next to me, facing the wall. "Did you find ours?" But she didn't wait for me to answer. "There it is," she said, pointing.

"The painting is on the second floor," Mrs. Redding said. She had her back turned away from the wall of plaques. "That's where they keep the American Moderns. Should we take the stairs or the elevator?" Valerie's reply was automatic and not surprising.

Off the elevator, on the second floor in a small white room with a high ceiling, Valerie stared hard at the painting—*Sky Above Clouds IV*—before turning and walking away. She strolled into the next room to look at a display of multi-colored light installations.

"It's so..." Mrs. Redding frowned. We stood together in

front of the painting. "I don't know. I don't think I get it."

I took the pamphlet out of my back pocket, unfolded it, and read to Mrs. Redding about the eight-foot-tall by twenty-four-foot-wide mural. The inspiration for it happened when the artist, Georgia O'Keeffe, looked out the window at 30,000 feet on her first ride in an airplane. She was in her seventies, I read to Mrs. Redding. She was traveling toward the American West. The rows of clouds that took up ninety percent of the painting looked like misshapen white stones or eggs neatly lined against a background of blue sky. There was a playful, childlike quality to them. At the bottom of the mural the clouds were quite large, however they grew smaller and smaller until almost at the top of the painting they turned to haze and reached a peaceful blue and pink horizon. Many art scholars believe that in this massive abstract painting O'Keeffe's intention was to comment on the optimism of the American experience, especially in regard to those who journeyed west and therefore into the unknown. *Sky Above Clouds IV* had its permanent home at the Art Institute of Chicago. It was on loan until the end of the month. Then it would make its next stop on its traveling exhibition.

"Oh," said Mrs. Redding. I folded the pamphlet in half again and placed it back inside my pocket. She stood frowning at it. "I don't like it," she said finally. "There are too many clouds, or something. And all the clouds, especially the ones at the bottom of the painting, look like a child could have drawn them."

"I think she meant to do that," I said. I thought about Ms. Starburn and her green felt pen. "I think it's a metaphor," I said.

"A what?" Mrs. Redding said.

"A metaphor. The clouds at the bottom of the painting look like a child could have drawn them because, I think, the artist meant for the clouds to symbolize childhood. With each ascending row the clouds grow smaller until the very end, or almost the very end, of the picture. The clouds grow smaller until they reach the horizon, or the end of the journey. Until death. Maybe she's saying that as we get older our ideas and visions grow smaller. We grow up but shrink at the same time."

She just looked at me with her mouth clamped shut. That's when Valerie meandered back from the next room. She announced that she was starving and bored—in exactly that order.

$B$ecause it was the first sit-down restaurant that we came across outside of the art museum, Valerie chose to eat lunch at a Greek restaurant called Pleiades. Inside it smelled like grilled meat, lemons and olive oil. A white pillar divided the room in half. Heavy wine-colored curtains draped the windows. A huge painted mural on the back wall showed seven women standing in a semi-circle with their arms outstretched like dancers. They wore long, flowing, pastel-colored dresses. Their round, calm faces looked similar to each other—so much so that I just knew that they were meant to be sisters, including the one whose body was turned in such a way that her face was not visible. Above the seven braided heads shone a glistening bright blue star.

Mrs. Redding ordered a glass of white wine and a Greek salad. Valerie wanted a large pink lemonade with extra ice and something called gyros. I had never eaten Greek food, didn't really know what to order and ended up with a small bottle of water and something called tiropita. It turned out to be a pastry stuffed with feta cheese and honey with sesame seeds sprinkled over the top. It smelled good, tasted delicious and looked a lot better than Valerie's gyros, a mound of shredded pork on top of a soggy looking pita.

Mrs. Redding took a bite of salad. "I'm curious, Marcy, do you plan to go to college after senior year?"

"I—" I started to say.

"I already told you that she's not going," Valerie answered for me, her mouth full of meat.

Mrs. Redding closed her eyes as she spoke. "Please don't speak with your mouth full of food. It's unladylike and rude." She opened them again. "I know you already told me that she's not planning to continue her education after high school, however I wanted to know if she had changed her mind. You know, girls, the direction your lives take in the future depends on whether or not you invest in your education. Those who continue their schooling after high school will be rewarded; those who do not—"

Valerie set down her fork noisily on her plate. "I've already heard this speech a million times. You don't have to tell me again. I already promised Daddy that I would go to his what-do-you-call-it, his alma pater, just like Jeremy. So enough with the college speech, okay? It's tired."

"Alma mater, not alma pater. Perhaps, young lady, I was not making the tired 'college speech' for your benefit."

"Alma mater, alma pater: who cares? I know you weren't talking about it for my benefit because everyone knows that I'm already going. I still don't see the point of this conversation. I already told you that it's not that Mercy doesn't want to go to school; it's that her mother can't afford to send her. Her mom is just a waitress. Don't you remember last Sunday at the mall when we went to see that Fiona Wonder movie, *The Immortals*? Mercy's mom was with her friend, that woman who cuts hair at Clippers, Vikki."

I flashed to Ms. Starburn riding the escalator to the Home and Garden Center on the basement level of Coleanne's Department Store.

Mrs. Redding crossed her arms over her chest. "I remember. What about it?"

"Mercy's mom was wearing a waitress uniform. She works at BONANZA BURGER. Waffle Falafel too." Valerie rolled her eyes. "She's served us before."

Mrs. Redding looked startled. "What?"

Valerie sighed liked she was talking to a real idiot. "The last time we ate at BONANZA BURGER, Mercy's mother *served* us. It was on the same night that Jeremy came home from school. You got upset when Daddy called to tell you that he was working late—"

"Valerie—" she tried to cut her off.

"—so you dumped the salad and the lasagna down the garbage disposal and told us you were taking us to Heritage Mall. You bought a down-feathered blanket at Time & Luxingham and a new pair of Nikes for Jeremy at Sporty's, because he left his pair inside his dorm room. You said 'no' when I said I wanted to go to Moods. You said 'no' again when I said I wanted to eat at the food court. Does any of this ring a bell? You let *Jeremy* pick where we ate dinner. You always let him do whatever he wants. It's so unfair."

"I don't think that I—"

"During his junior and senior year of high school he had no curfew," Valerie interrupted her, "and yet my curfew is 10:30. He went wherever he felt like going, and yet you have a cow whenever I want to go to a party at a house in our own neighborhood."

Mrs. Redding looked confused. "Party? What party? You have never mentioned to me, ever, about wanting to go to parties. I just assumed it was because you were never—" but she decided not to finish that sentence. She picked up her wine glass, took a sip of wine, and set it back down on the table. She tried again: "Valerie," she said, "when Jeremy was in high school he got much better grades than you. Plus he was on the football team."

"What do you expect me to do, Mother? Become a linebacker?"

"Don't be ridiculous; of course not. But since you brought it up, I'll tell you that I still feel disappointed that you never showed interest in any kind of team sport."

"Like cheerleading?" Valerie said. She was being

sarcastic.

"Track, perhaps. Or soccer..."

"Both those things require running. I hate running."

Mrs. Redding sighed.

"So what you're saying is that Jeremy got to do whatever he wanted because he was on the football team. Or maybe the real reason is because he's a boy. Or maybe it's because you actually love him more than me. Or maybe it's because—"

"Valerie, stop it!" she snapped. "He had a girlfriend! He was popular! He was a good student and an excellent football player! He was even on the ballot for prom king! He didn't mope around with the same friend day in and day out. He never once settled for anything that was—" she looked at me quickly, like I was a reference in a book, then away, "below him. He never, *ever*, would have dreamed about crashing the front end of his brand new car into the back of somebody's pickup truck!"

Sitting across the table, Valerie had turned purple. When the waiter approached our table to ask if we needed any refills, Mrs. Redding shooed him away with her eyes.

"That day at the mall," Valerie said slowly, "you let Jeremy pick where we ate dinner. That's how we ended up at BONANZA BURGER."

"I don't remember."

"As soon she left our table to get our order, I *told* you it was Mercy's mom that was our waitress."

"I said that I don't remember."

"You ordered the Cobb Salad, except she brought you the Chef's Salad. You got really mad. When she left the table I remember you said that you hated it when you got a waitress that seemed dumb and—"

"Valerie, that's enough!"

Valerie's eyes widened. Because she didn't know what else to do, I think, she picked up her fork and shoveled meat into her mouth. Meanwhile, across the table, her mother picked up her wine glass and drained it.

"Higher education is not for everybody," Mrs. Redding said finally. Then she stood up and dropped her napkin onto the table. "Hurry up and finish your lunch. We need to get back home so that I can check on your brother. I'm going to pay the check."

Valerie swallowed and made a face in the direction of her mother's back. She pointed at my half eaten cheese pie. I told her to go ahead, that I wasn't hungry anymore.

She reached across the table, picked it up and stuffed it into her mouth. "She acts like she's such an authority on the subject," Valerie said. A whole bunch of cheese and pastry flew out of her mouth. "What a joke! She didn't even finish college. She got married to Daddy during her sophomore year. She's just a stupid drop-out. Don't even listen to her, Mercy."

I just stared at the mural on the back wall, looking at the seven sisters and counting and recounting the seven stars over each of their heads. I could have been wrong, of course, but the entire time that we were inside the restaurant I don't think that either Valerie or Mrs. Redding even noticed them.


The maid stopped vacuuming the carpet in what they call the great room when we walked through the front door of the Redding house. "Hello, Mrs. Redding. Hello, Ms. Valerie," she said. She did not wait for a response. Maybe she already knew that none would be given. She went back to work, steering the vacuum cleaner behind the big leather couch. Even though it was the middle of summer she wore gray sweatpants and a gray Mickey Mouse sweat shirt. The age spots on her hands looked as round as quarters. Her short, salt and pepper hair looked wilted.

"Hi," I said to her. She didn't look up from her vacuuming.

I wish I knew her name. I have no idea because no one has ever told me. She is simply referred to as "the maid".

She is from Mexico, Puerto Rico, or maybe Portugal, Valerie can't remember which. Mrs. Redding found her through friends at the country club. For the past seven years she has cleaned the Redding's house from one o'clock until four o'clock in the afternoon every Tuesday, Thursday and Saturday. She cleans everything including the garage, the downstairs rec room, and the long windows that reach all the way to the ceiling in the great room. She is not allowed to clean either Valerie or Jeremy's bedrooms. That's because Valerie and her brother flat out told their mother that it would be a total invasion of their privacy. Besides, Valerie had pointed out, and Jeremy had agreed, even though Dr. Redding pays her six dollars and fifty cents an hour, that the maid might not be able to help herself and steal something from their rooms; for example, one of Jeremy's old football trophies, or Valerie's gold charm bracelet that her dad had given her for her thirteenth birthday. Never mind that Valerie hasn't worn the bracelet since the eighth grade. That's when she gained too much weight and could no longer hook the clasp around her wrist.

Mrs. Redding's heels on the floor in the foyer made the exact same clicking sound as when we were inside the art museum. In a lot of ways the Redding house reminds me of a museum. It is really big with white walls and full of really nice, expensive looking things that I'm afraid to touch. The fresh flowers in the vase in the foyer are so perfect that they looked like they were made out of plastic. The great room is the size of our entire apartment.

Once inside the kitchen, Valerie immediately headed for the refrigerator. From it she collected a can of pop, three plastic-wrapped slices of American cheese, and a jar of pickles. She set the contents of her snack on top of the island in the middle of the room.

Mrs. Redding looked like she was deliberating whether or not to say something. Finally, she began to sort through the mail. Valerie uncapped the jar of pickles, stuck half of her hand inside it, fished out at least a half dozen slices then went to work stacking them together like a roll of coins. She was about to drop the stack into her mouth when Mrs. Redding picked up the cordless telephone. With her perfectly manicured index finger she started to punch in a number.

Valerie's hand froze just above her mouth. "Who are you calling?"

"Your father..." She punched in the last two digits. "...to ask about dinner." She held the phone to her ear and waited. "Hello, Jeannette. Yes, it's Lady. Yes, thank you, I'm fine. Is Rob—excuse me? How is Valerie?" She looked startled. "She's fine too. Thank you, I guess, for asking. I want to speak to Rob." She waited a moment then frowned. "I see. Well, will you please ask him to call me as soon as he's available?" Again, she waited. "Thank you," she said into the phone, crisply. "I will look forward to his call."

I thought that Valerie looked temporarily relieved. She dropped the pickles into her mouth and chewed.

Mrs. Redding went back to sorting through the mail. She dumped about half of it into the garbage can. Turning away from the island, she opened the refrigerator door and poured apple juice into a glass. Then she opened a cabinet to the right of the sink, took out a bottle of pills, uncapped it and shook out a small white pill into the palm of her hand. She held out the glass and the pill to Valerie. "Will you please take this downstairs to your brother?"

Valerie was busy unpeeling the plastic from the third and last slice of cheese . She folded the bright yellow square lengthwise, like a letter, dropped it whole into her mouth, chewed three times then swallowed. "Why can't you do it? You're his mother."

"And you're his sister." She looked at the digital clock on the stove. She turned back to Valerie and sighed. "I'd do it myself, Valerie, but it's almost four o'clock, and I want to speak to the maid before she leaves."

Valerie rolled her eyes. She opened the can of pop and took a huge slurp. "Let me guess: you want to talk to her about the missing cue ball from the pool table, right? Ever since it went missing last weekend, Jeremy hasn't shut up about it."

Mrs. Redding hands, one holding the glass of juice and the other—the one with the Valium in the palm of her hand—remained outstretched in front of her. "Your brother is upset about it. So is your father. It's impossible to play pool without the white ball."

"The cue ball," Valerie corrected her.

"Well, whatever it's called, it has gone missing. Perhaps the maid misplaced it last Saturday while she was cleaning the rec room."

"Maybe she stole it."

"Valerie, you know it's not nice to go around accusing—well." She stopped to think about it. She cleared her throat. "I don't know what she did with it. That's why I need to ask her about it." Then she frowned again. "On the telephone just now with your father's receptionist I did not like the way that she asked about you." Valerie swallowed hard and set down her pop on top of the counter. "Did something happen today in therapy?"

"No."

"Are you sure? Because the way that she—"

She snatched the glass and the Valium from Mrs. Redding. A bit of apple juice sloshed out of the glass onto the kitchen floor. "God, Mother, I said no!"

I didn't know what else to do but follow Valerie as she clomped down the stairs to the rec room. At the base of the stairs I turned right toward the media center. The rec room is one long room painted eggshell white with beige burlap carpet. There are no windows. The games area has a pinball machine, an old Packman machine and the pool table with, apparently, a missing cue ball. The media center gets a lot more use. On that side of the room is a flat screen TV, a surround sound music system, an actual working popcorn machine, and an over-sized, muted gray sofa set.

A sportscaster's overly cheerful loud voice announced the starting lineup of a baseball game between the Cubs and the Giants. In the center of the sofa Jeremy sat bare-chested with an ACE bandage on his right arm, a sling around his shoulder and the back of his strawberry blonde head fixed adamantly at the blaring flat screen in front of him.

He wasn't alone. On either side of him sat a girl—Ally, who had graduated with Jeremy last spring, and Gretchen, the cheerleader in the same grade as Valerie and me who lives three blocks from the Redding's house and whose party Valerie wanted us to go to on Friday night. Both girls wore high blonde ponytails, big gold hoop earrings and tight tank tops—green on Ally and red on Gretchen. It looked as if they had taken up the role of nursing Jeremy. On his left side Ally fed him tortilla chips from a big Tupperware bowl. Meanwhile, on his other side, Gretchen was busy rearranging a throw pillow on top of his lap. His bandaged right arm lay on top of the pillow.

The other person in the room—Randy, the baseball pitcher and busboy who worked with Mom at BONANZA BURGER—stood directly behind the sofa, facing the ball game on television and clutching a bright orange foam ball in his hand. He wore shiny silver knee-length shorts, a bright yellow sleeveless basketball jersey, really dirty tennis shoes, and a baseball cap.

"The Cubs suck," he announced. "Watching them is a waste of time because you already know who's going to win the game, and it's not them!" He took aim with the ball at Starlin Castro, the first batter for the Cubs. "If I were pitching this game I'd bean that nappy-haired Dominican in the head so that I'd get thrown out of the game and wouldn't have to play such a shitty team."

Valerie cleared her throat, and both Gretchen and Ally turned to look at her.

"Who is it?" Jeremy wanted to know, still facing forward and not moving a muscle. Apparently, because of his broken collarbone, he couldn't turn around to see who it was.

"It's your sister," Gretchen said.

"And her friend," Ally said.

Valerie cleared her throat again. She tried to look nonchalant, I thought, as she rounded the sofa to hand Jeremy the glass of apple juice and the Valium.

"Thanks," he told her. "Now move. You're blocking the screen."

Gretchen and Ally looked at each other knowingly.

Valerie didn't budge: "Hi, Gretchen... Hi, Ally," she said.

"Um, hi," Gretchen said.

"Yeah, hi," Ally said too.

"Did you see that I responded 'yes' to your invite, Gretchen?"

There was a pause. "Oh... No."

"Well I did, on Facebook. You invited me to your party and I responded 'yes'."

Gretchen repositioned herself on the couch. "Oh. Okay. Great."

"It's okay if my friend Mercy comes too, right?"

"Um... Yeah. Whatever."

"Is there anything else that we should bring besides beer? I don't mind bringing other things, like chips or—"

"Valerie, I'm serious," Jeremy yelled at her, "*move!*"

"*Okay*," she snapped at him. She circled the couch and stood next to Randy.

"Well, anyway, I can't wait," Valerie said.

Gretchen stared straight ahead at the ball game. Either she hadn't, or she was pretending that she hadn't, heard Valerie.

That's when Randy turned to look at me. "I know you," he said. He looked unimpressed. "You sat behind me in economics class last year. Your mom works with me at

BONANZA BURGER."

"You work with her mom?" Gretchen said.

"Uh-huh."

"That's weird."

"Tell me about it," he said. He just stood there, staring at me. "A couple of days ago you came into the restaurant with some older chick with short spiky hair and purple cowboy boots. Your mom stole my spray bottle." He looked at me expectantly, as if he might be waiting for an apology concerning the so-called theft. When I didn't say anything, he turned back toward the sofa and started bopping Gretchen on the top of her head with the bright orange foam ball.

"Cut it out!" she yelled at him. But she didn't sound like she really meant it.

He got bored quickly. Again he took aim with the Nerf ball at another batter on the television screen. Instead of throwing it, he turned around again to look at me. "She's waited on me before, you know," he said to me. "I mean your mother, at Waffle Falafel. On the night of Junior Prom."

I was thinking about the ballroom dancers, the prize money, the one hundred and fifty-dollar tip.

"Gretch was there too," Randy continued. "Remember, Gretch?"

"Not really," she said.

"It was after prom," he said. "Before we ended up at the restaurant we went to Ally's and drank tequila shots. By the time we got to Waffle Falafel we were drunk."

"How come I wasn't there?" Ally wanted to know.

"Because you were passed out on your bathroom floor," Randy said.

"I don't remember any of this," Gretchen said.

"Because you were drunk," Randy told her.

"What did we eat there?"

"Waffles, you dork! Then you and some other girl, Amanda I think it was, did cartwheels all around the perimeter of the restaurant. You still had on your prom dresses, so me and Andy and Steve and Josh got a real good show."

Her face turned red. "Shut up! I don't remember doing that."

"Because you were *drunk*," he said.

"Shut up, Randy!" She wasn't really that upset with him.

"We stayed for hours and hours. We had the place all to ourselves. We did some crazy shit in that restaurant that night. It was just us—" he looked at me, smiled, licked his lips—"and your mother, the waitress."

"That's not true," I said.

It wasn't just Randy but Gretchen and Ally, and Valerie too, who turned to look at me. The silence hung in the air, heavy and foul. "What did you just say to me?" Randy wanted to know.

"That's not true," I said again. "My mom told me about that night. She told me all about it from start to finish, and she didn't say anything about waiting on you."

"She *did*. Like I just said, she waited on us all night, practically. Then, in the morning, after her shift ended at six, she left the restaurant before we left, and I ended up giving her tip money to someone else—to another waitress. So she waited on me and got nothing. If I were you, I'd choose a different career than your mother. As for me, I'm going to be a doctor, a lawyer, or the owner of chain restaurants, whichever pays the most money. That is, of course, unless I don't make it into the majors."

And with that he turned toward the flat screen TV to take aim with the ball at the next batter.


The phone rang three times then stopped. Upstairs, Mrs. Redding must have picked it up.

Ally sighed heavily. "Can't we watch something else? Baseball is *bo-ring*."

"Shut up! No, it's not," Randy said. He bopped her

hard on top of the head with the ball.

"Ow!" she said. "That hurt."

"Then listen to me and I won't do it again. It's the Cubs that suck, I already told you. Baseball isn't boring, at least not when I'm on the mound."

Gretchen twisted her head and looked up at him. "Except you'd be a better pitcher, Randy, if you and Robin, the catcher, were friends instead of enemies."

I saw Valerie stiffen as soon as Gretchen said Robin's name.

"Half the time you don't make the pitches that he calls," Gretchen continued. "That's what I heard him say to the coach after the last game of the season."

Randy didn't even look at her. "Whatever... Half the time he just can't catch my pitches. They're too hard for him."

Gretchen rolled her eyes. "Just don't get into a fight with him at my party on Friday."

"Robin is going to be there?" Valerie chimed in. She sounded a little breathless.

That's when we heard grunting. Except Jeremy, everyone else turned around in the direction of the noise. "What's that? Who is it?" Jeremy wanted to know.

Nobody answered him. It was the maid. She was already on the other side of the room in the games area by the pool table. She grunted again, then bent down, her head below the table, her hands on the floor, searching. Her bottom stuck straight up in the air.

Randy leaned close to Ally and Jeremy and Gretchen's heads. "Oh, my, God," he said slowly, "look at that big fat momma ass. That is so *hot*," he whispered.

Gretchen and Ally burst out laughing.

"Who's he talking about?" Jeremy said. He still sat facing forward.

"The maid," Gretchen told him.

"Oh, God, I want to give it to her," Randy said. He stood up straight, rotating his hips and moving his arms up and down with clenched fists.

"Where is she? What's she doing?" Jeremy wanted to know.

"She's by the pool table. She's looking for something," Ally told him.

"She's got her ass sticking up for me, that's what she's doing," Randy said.

"You're a freak!" Gretchen said. Her face, screwed up from laughter, had turned the color of grape juice.

"I want to hump her doggy style."

"Ew!" Ally and Gretchen proclaimed in unison. They couldn't stop laughing.

Valerie looked at the maid, then at Randy, then at Gretchen, then back at the maid. She started laughing too, like she thought it was really funny.

"She's mine," Randy said, licking his lips and still thrusting his hips. He pumped his arms up and down. "Nobody else can have her but me." He took aim at her with the Nerf ball.

I didn't even have to think about it: I snatched the ball away from him, turned, crossed the room and marched up the stairs to the kitchen.

"Hey!" Randy yelled after me.

"Um, okay," I heard Gretchen say. "That was totally rude."

"Totally," Ally echoed.

"What happened?" Jeremy wanted to know.

I heard Valerie's big heavy feet clomping up the stairs behind me. I didn't turn around at first when she called my name. "Mercy!" she said again at the top of the stairs. When I turned around to look at her, I knew she was angry. "Why did you do that?" she said to me.

I looked down at the ball still in my hand: "Because I didn't want him to throw it at her."

"It's made out of foam. It wouldn't have hurt her."

"I know, but still—"

"It's not like he was about to throw a baseball at her.

No harm would have been done, that's all I'm saying. You shouldn't have interfered. Now he's pissed off. So is Gretchen. What happens if she *disinvites* us to her party?"

"Valerie, I don't really care what Randy thinks, or if Gretchen—"

That's when Mrs. Redding's heels clicked from the foyer into the kitchen. In her hand near her hip she held the cordless phone. When she saw us there together she opened her mouth to say something, but then she reconsidered and closed it. Softly, she placed the phone on top of the island.

"Who was that on the telephone just now?" Valerie wanted to know.

Mrs. Redding didn't say anything. Instead she turned, opened the refrigerator and just stood there staring at a gallon jug of milk and a couple of Chinese take-out boxes. She reached inside the fridge, picked up a bottle of ketchup, studied it for a moment, and then set it back in its place between the mustard and the mayonnaise.

"It was Dad, wasn't it?" Valerie said. "What did he say?"

"He won't be home until late."

While Valerie waited she shifted her weight from one foot to the other. "Did he say anything else?" she asked finally. "I mean other than about not being home until late?"

Mrs. Redding slowly closed the refrigerator door, turned and looked at Valerie. "Yes, he did. He said that you don't have to go to therapy anymore."

Valerie's face went completely white: "And?"

"That's it."

It was like her colorless face was a movie screen and each frame, one after the other, showed a clear emotion: relief then disappointment then, finally, anger.

"Oh," she said at last.

Mrs. Redding wiped her right hand against her left hand, like something dirty was there and she was trying to be rid of it. "You can forget what I said about dinner. If you're hungry, let me know and I'll order a pizza."

Valerie's voice sounded strained and weak. "Come on, Mercy," she said. "Let's go up to my room." I didn't move. She grabbed my arm and tugged. "I said, come on!" I didn't budge. She must not have believed me. She tugged on my arm again, hard. "Come on. I'm not *that* mad at you. I forgive you, okay?"

I felt incredibly tired from everything that had happened during the day. I stepped away from her. "No, Valerie," I said. "I think I want to go home."

Mrs. Redding just stood there, watching us. At last she reached for her car keys. She sighed. "I suppose you want me to give you a ride back to your—" she paused to clear her throat— "apartment building."

"No, thank you. I'll walk. I want to walk."

Valerie said, a little louder than necessary, "Fine. Don't stay. I really don't care. Just call me later. I'll see you on Friday."

"We'll see, Valerie," I said.

She looked angry and confused. Then, just as she'd done at her father's office, she grabbed the bright orange foam ball from my hand and threw it across the kitchen. It hit the picture window and landed in the sink. "You see?" she yelled. "He wouldn't have hurt her even if he'd hit her. Nothing bad would have happened!" She turned and ran out of the kitchen. A few seconds later I heard her feet clomp up the stairs, and then, another few seconds after that, the door of her bedroom slam shut.

"Marcy—" Mrs. Redding started, narrowing her eyes at me, but that's when the maid reached the top of the stairs. She was out of breath. In her hand she held the cue ball.

"Here it is, Mrs. Redding," she said, panting. "I found it on the other side of the games room underneath the pinball machine."

Mrs. Redding looked at the maid, blankly. After a few moments of intense silence, she threw out her arm, her palm up, in front of her. "Give it to me. How in the world did it end up underneath the pinball machine?"

The maid handed Mrs. Redding the cue ball. "That's what I was wondering too, Mrs. Redding," she said, still trying to catch her breath, "but then as soon as I found it and showed it to Jeremy he said that he remembered that the last time he played pool he hit it too hard and it went flying off the table and underneath the pinball machine and that he had just forgotten to tell you and—" she stopped to look at the digital clock on the stove. She took a big gulp of air. There was a pained look on her face. "Please, Mrs. Redding, you asked me to find the cue ball and that's what I did. Now it is ten after four and if I do not leave now I will miss my bus and—"

"All right. Go!"

Mrs. Redding and I stood looking at each other as the maid collected her purse, walked out of the kitchen into the foyer, then out the front door. She closed it softly behind her.

And then it was just the two of us alone together in the kitchen.

"Goodbye, Mrs. Redding," I said finally and turned to walk away.

"Wait a minute," she stopped me. I froze. "Look at me," she said. My heart started to race. I didn't really want to look at her but I did.

Her face looked as it always did—a mask of beautiful, forceful, cool indifference. If you peeled it back, you'd see the truth. "I thought about what you asked me," Mrs. Redding said to me, slowly, calculatingly. "I mean about asking Dr. Redding for an asthma inhaler for your mother." She paused to switch the cue ball from her right hand to her left. By the look on her face, and by the way that she was acting, I already knew what she was going to say before she said it. Still, I couldn't help but hope. I think that's why I held my breath. "The answer is no. I am not going to ask him about it. It is inappropriate and—well.

Perhaps your mother needs to find another means of employment, one which actually pays health benefits. I don't know what she needs to do to get the medication she needs. All I know is that it is not my problem, or my husband's problem, or my family's problem, so don't make it our problem. Do you understand me...Marcy?"

I didn't jump at all, but she did, when she accidently dropped the cue ball. It hit the floor, hard. Together we watched it roll across the kitchen into the foyer. It came to a stop in front of the table with the perfect flowers arranged in the vase where the recently cleaned mirror hung on the wall.

*I* stumbled outside into the summer evening. The air was hot and fresh and good. It felt like I hadn't breathed since word had come from *Almost There Magazine* that I'd won the contest. I walked down the street, reached the end, turned left, walked down another street, turned right, walked past Gretchen's house, kept walking up the hilly street with the big yellow speed hump, and found myself, finally, on a busy two-lane road that a quarter of a mile away connected with the freeway.

The maid was there, sitting at the bus stop, crying. "I missed my bus!" she sobbed. "She made me miss my bus!"

I didn't really know what else to do but start running. Without looking I crossed the busy two-lane road. A blue Subaru honked its horn, almost hit me. On the other side of the road I ran down a gully and up a steep hill. At the top of the hill I stopped to catch my breath. I turned around and looked behind me. The maid looked so small from there. I couldn't even see her face. Below me was the freeway and Heritage Shopping Mall.

*T*he door of Coleanne's had never seemed so easy to push

open. Right in front of me, as though in greeting, stood a mannequin on top of a circular pedestal wearing a white summer dress. A popular song was barely audible as it played over the loud speakers. I didn't recognize it right away because it had been re-recorded as an instrumental. I felt a little nervous but also certain that if I went downstairs she'd be there, and that she'd let me talk to her, just like she let me talk to her last year at school, and that she'd tell me that everything was going to be okay, and that she'd be more than a teacher, she'd be my friend. I felt full of hope as I stepped onto the escalator to take me to the Home and Garden Center.

There was a collection of La-Z-Boy chairs as I stepped off the escalator. Two little girls ran past them, then turned around, ran back and plopped down on two of them. They weren't sisters, I didn't think, but maybe cousins. One had blonde hair, the other brown. They were dressed in matching blue dresses with little watermelons on them and a little watermelon pin attached to the same place on the lapel of their dresses. A woman called them, and then another woman, and the two little girls jumped up and ran toward the women. They were standing near the photo center. I watched them go into the back to have their pictures taken.

I turned back to the empty chairs then made a half-turn toward the other side of the department store. There she was in the gardening section, standing next to a piece of bright green synthetic turf and a red lawnmower. Her hair looked different—way less frizzy, flat-looking, like she had taken an iron to it—and she wasn't wearing her square glasses. A brass colored nametag was pinned to her shirt in the exact same place where Mom pins her nametags on her uniforms.

When she saw me she just stood staring at me. When I waved, she looked away. I walked over to her. I waved again. That's when a man wearing a blue and white plaid shirt approached the display. He tapped the lawn mower with his foot. Then he asked her the price.

"$189.99," my teacher, Ms. Starburn, answered him.

Silently he nodded his head, as if the price was agreeable. "And what kind of fuel does it take?"

"Gas."

"How many horse power?"

Expressionless, she handed him an information sheet.

He circled the lawn mower once then put his hands on his hips. "Any assembly required?"

"No."

"What about a warranty?

"Two years."

"I'll take it."

Ms. Starburn stepped onto the turf, got behind the lawn mower and pushed it toward the nearest register. "I just hate mowing the lawn," he said, walking behind her. "Sometimes I think it'd be better if I stripped off all the sod and dumped rocks in the front and back yard. Then I'd have myself a big rock yard. I'd never have to think about mowing grass again." She went behind the register, rung up the lawnmower, took his money, handed back change and watched him wheel it away.

"Hi, Ms. Starburn," I said to her. I waited, but she didn't say hello to me. She wouldn't even look at me. Instead, she fiddled with the cash register, her face hard as a stone. "It's me," I said softly, trying to remind her, "Mercy Swimmer."

When she finally looked me in the eye I saw something that I wasn't expecting. "What are you doing here?" she wanted to know. I had never heard her use that tone of voice.

"I'm here to see you," I said. I felt weak again, just as I'd felt in Mrs. Redding's presence. "I saw you last Sunday, riding the escalator, so I thought that I'd come downstairs and—"

"I need to get back on the floor."

I didn't know what else to do but watch her walk away

from the register and back to the display of red lawnmowers on the fake grass. I stood there for a few minutes, my head reeling, trying to make sense of why she was acting so cold to me. I thought back to our time in the teacher's area during fifth period, grading papers, finding and circling metaphors in novels, feeling safe, with hope.

The only way out of the basement was to take the escalator. I'd have to walk right past her. So that's what I did. I was about to step onto the escalator, but then something stopped me. I guess I hoped she'd have a change of heart about me. I got up my courage, turned around and walked back over to her. "Ms. Starburn?"

Again she glared at me. In the same irritated voice, she said, "What do you want, Mercy?"

I took a step backward. "I just wanted to say hello, Ms. Starburn, and ask how your summer was going."

"It's not going very well at all."

I took another step backward. "I also wanted to ask you if you'd like for me to be your teacher's assistant again next year, because if you would, then I would really like—"

She stopped me. "There isn't going to be any next year. I've been made redundant along with twenty-five percent of the county's teachers because our state, like every other state, is broke."

She was talking too fast. I didn't understand what she meant. "I don't get it. What does redundant mean, Ms. Starburn?"

She laughed then, as if it were funny, as if it were a joke. "You're so naïve," she said to me. "You don't really know anything about anything. You have your head in the clouds. You're dreamy and naïve and, according to the local paper, you're on your way to Hollywood to spend a week with a movie star." She laughed and laughed; it was eerie.

"But Ms. Starburn—"

"Don't call me that," she snapped at me.

She grabbed her shirt and thrust out her nametag at

me. "I'm not your teacher anymore," she said, her voice cracking, "I'm *this*. So unless you need a lawnmower, or a chainsaw, or a tree trimmer, or a weed whacker, then I don't ever want to see you here—in my department— again. Do you understand me? Not *ever*..."

$A$t the center of the mall the water fountain had been turned off. Encircling the perimeter of it were orange cones connected with yellow tape with black letters that read: CAUTION—CONSTRUCTION ZONE— CAUTION—CONSTRUCTION ZONE—CAUTION. Inside the zone stood a man in a plaid shirt, faded jeans and a hard hat. He had a black mustache and eyes that looked like blue marbles. He was talking on a walkie-talkie and at the same time looking up at another man on a ladder who was slowly climbing toward the skylight. I stopped walking and looked up at him. I couldn't help it: I thought about Dad and the pole climbing contest.

"Hey!" the man with the mustache and blue eyes said, rushing over to me. I think that my face must have gone white. I fell flat on my butt and just sat there. "Are you okay, kid?" He smelled like spearmint gum and Old Spice. "You almost fainted, huh?"

I took another look at the man on the ladder. He had almost reached the skylight. I had to look away. "How come he's doing that?" I asked weakly.

"What? You mean him? That?" He pointed up.

I nodded. I felt like I was going to throw up.

"We're just doing some inspections. It's nothing to worry about. Do you think you can stand up? You can't sit here. You're too close to the construction zone. Something might fall on your head."

"She'll get up when she's ready," I heard another voice say.

I looked up and saw a tiny man with a wrinkled bald head, olive skin and big black glasses. He was smiling at me. I watched him walk away, around the fountain toward a shop front that, for some reason, I had never noticed before. It was called Stella and Apollo's Telescopes. The little man walked inside and disappeared. Then I saw him again, by the window. He was carrying a big silver telescope. He placed it at the center of the window then disappeared again. When he came back to the window, he had a sign that he taped to the window. It read: GOING OUT OF BUISNESS. EVERYTHING MUST GO.

# WEDNESDAY

*M*om's coughing woke me up. It was the deep, barking kind, the one that sounds like she's coughing up her lungs. I got up from bed, ran out of my room and down the hallway to the bathroom. She was there, sitting on the edge of the bathtub, barefoot, wearing her bathrobe, her hair in its usual before showering, after work ponytail. Her eyes were squeezed shut. Her face was red. In her right hand she clutched something—not her emergency inhaler but her daily asthma inhaler. At least that's what I thought.

I stood in front of her, trying not to panic. "Mom, are you okay?"

She waved her hand at me as an answer.

"Do you want me to call an ambulance?"

"No!" she just managed to choke out the word.

My heart felt like a little caged bird inside my chest. I pointed at her clutched hand. "Mom, take another dose of your daily inhaler. I know it's not your rescue inhaler, but maybe it will help."

Her mouth opened, searching for air. It was like she was a fish out of water.

"I'm calling an ambulance," I said and turned toward the door.

"Mercy—no!" she managed to gasp. "No—don't—ambulance—cost—too—much—"

I swung around to look at her. "I don't care how much it costs! You can't breathe!"

She looked at me, wild eyed. She wheezed and whistled and gasped for air. Her other hand, which had been clutching the edge of the bathtub, went flying and knocked a bottle of shampoo into the bathtub. The same arm spasmed again. Her hand went to her throat.

"Mom, please!" I said. "Don't stop breathing."

The palm of her other hand opened. It reminded me of one of those fast-forwarded flowers that you might see on TV—a delicate paper tissue thin flower that blooms and, just as quickly, closes and dies right in front of you. I had been wrong. It was not Mom's daily asthma inhaler that dropped out of her hand, bounced off her knee and fell to the bath mat on the floor; it was the Fiona Wonder Shooting Star Bracelet.

The wild eyed look left her eyes. She started to regain her normal complexion. She was getting air again. Suddenly, I could tell, the attack was going away. Mom eased herself from the edge of the bathtub to the floor, her back resting on the wall of the tub. She was careful, I noticed, not to sit on the bracelet.

"I think it's over," she said, still gasping for breath. She struggled but was able, finally, to take deep breaths. "I think it's going to be—" she inhaled, coughed, then exhaled, "better now."

As I stared at the Shooting Star Bracelet the muscles in my jaw showed my anger. How could I *not* feel angry when, for the second time in one week, I attempted to help her get through an asthma attack, except when I went to get her medications I found instead the Shooting Star Bracelet?

Mom tried to smile at me, still sitting on the floor and

almost, but not quite, breathing normally, as though everything was fine, as though the past five minutes had never happened. I watched her pick up the bracelet and place it carefully on her lap. "It's a good thing that one of us didn't step on it," she said, relieved.

My face felt hot all over, my heart pounded. I was furious. "You know, Mom," I said. "Fiona Wonder might be your favorite movie star, but she isn't going to help you breathe."

I'm not going to deny it; it felt good when she looked wounded.

"And another thing," I said, bending down to snatch the glittering star from her lap then clasping it around my wrist, "from now on I'm wearing this. It's supposed to be mine anyway, right?"

She looked hurt and confused. She reached out her hand to me. "Mercy—" she started to say, but I had already turned to walk out the bathroom door. I slammed it shut behind me as I left.

I went to my room, got dressed and brushed my hair. Then I just sat on my bed, trying to calm down. I sat there for at least ten minutes, maybe longer. When I finally felt better I looked out the window and saw a man in a yellow hard hat walking around on the roof of Heritage Mall. He circled the giant skylight then peered through it to see inside the mall. I felt uneasy all over again.

Mom wasn't in the bathroom when I finally came out of my room. The door to her bedroom was closed, too. She had probably gone back to bed, exhausted from the asthma attack. I went into the bathroom to brush my teeth. There was hair in the sink. The toilet needed a good scrub. Mom's nude-colored Waffle Falafel nylons lay in a pile, like a shed snakeskin, between the sink and the wastebasket. I don't know how long I stood at the center of the room staring at the bottle of shampoo that she had knocked into the bathtub. If it were only yesterday, and not today, then I would have cleaned the sink, scrubbed the toilet, picked up Mom's nylons to check for runs and put the shampoo bottle back on the edge of the bathtub. Instead, I walked out of the bathroom, leaving the light on behind me.

A clatter came from the kitchen. "Oh, shoot!" I heard her say. Walking down the hallway and turning the corner I saw her standing over the stove, holding a frying pan.

"Hi, honey," she said brightly.

She kept smiling, although less so, when I didn't smile back at her. I looked at the clock. It read just past nine in the morning. I frowned at her. "What are you doing? Why aren't you in bed?"

She set the frying pan on the stove. "I thought I would make you breakfast."

"You haven't made me breakfast in years. Anyway, I'm not hungry."

"Let me make it for you anyway."

I just shrugged, because the truth of the matter was that I really didn't care one way or another. I sat down at the kitchen table.

Mom looked relieved, like we had just done battle and she had won. Or at least managed a truce. She walked from the stove to the refrigerator. "What do you want? Eggs and toast? I think we might have bacon... No, I guess not. I could have sworn we had—"

"I know what's in the house, Mom. I bought the groceries on Monday."

She looked at me nervously then back into the open refrigerator. "Do you want scrambled eggs? What about French toast? Or you can have both if you—"

"I don't care."

"I'll make both," she said and got to work. She took milk and eggs and butter out of the fridge and set them on the countertop by the stove. She left the fridge door open. Her hands were shaking, I noticed. "I'm feeling much better now, Mercy."

She forgot about the fridge door and opened a cabinet

door instead. She took a glass bowl from the middle shelf and started to crack eggs inside it. "While you were getting dressed I took another dose of my daily inhaler. It really cleared me out. I'm breathing much easier now. I'm not wheezing at all." She looked at me quickly, then away. "I'm sorry that we didn't see each other at all yesterday. By the time I woke up you had already left with your friend, and by the time you came home I had already gone to work. Sometimes that's just the way the cookie crumbles. Did you have a nice day?"

I shrugged again and stared at the floor.

She opened the silverware drawer and took out a fork to beat the eggs in the bowl. "My day was just okay. There was a big party at BONANZA BURGER. There were thirteen children and five adults. It was really hectic and noisy and a lot of work, and the tip that they left me—well, never mind. Then at Waffle Falafel there were hardly any customers. Except, you know who came in at about one in the morning?" She waited for me to ask, but when I didn't she went on as if I had. "Gabriel," she informed. "He had coffee and pie. Apple... No, pecan... He sat there and talked to me for what seemed like hours." She blushed. "Oh... And before work I talked to Nikki on the telephone. All she talked about was Kurt and how she can't reach him on his cell phone. She's real upset about what happened with him on Monday."

I couldn't help it; I sort of scoffed.

She turned to look at me. "What is it?"

"Nothing," I said. "It's just funny to me what Nikki said to you, considering what happened with Kurt on Monday is her own stupid fault."

Mom tilted her head and looked at me questioningly.

"Never mind," I said. "Just forget it."

"She asked about you, you know? She said that she—"

"Do you realize," I said, cutting her off because I didn't want to listen to anything more about Nikki, "that there's some Cheerios underneath the table? They look like they've been there for a long time. It's pretty gross."

She wasn't expecting that. "Oh," she said. "Oh, well, no, I didn't realize. But yes, you're right. I'll give the kitchen a good sweeping right after breakfast. Why don't you tell me more about yesterday? Get me up to speed, as they say, on all the news. What did you do?"

It took me a minute to answer. "Mrs. Redding took us downtown to the art museum to look at a painting," I said at last. "Then we went to lunch."

"Oh, wow!" Mom said. She held the fork straight up in the air. It looked like a tiny pitchfork. A bit of egg yolk ran down the fork to her wrist. "Well, that sure sounds nice! Well, wow! What restaurant?"

"A Greek place; I don't remember the name."

"What did the painting look like?"

For some reason it surprised me when she asked that question. Suddenly, I felt like I might die of thirst. Without looking at her, I got up from the table and walked to the open refrigerator. There wasn't any juice or cold water. My choice was a bottle of diet soda or an open can of VeggieFit Juice. The VeggieFit wasn't even ours; it was Nikki's. I knew that because I remembered her putting it in the fridge about a week ago.

"It's so great," Mom said, "that you've got a friend whose family is so, you know, cultured and stuff. It sure is nice of Mrs. Redding to take you girls all the way downtown so that you can look at art and—"

I slammed the fridge door shut, got a glass from the cabinet and got some water from the tap. It tasted like metal. I spit it out in the sink. "Look," I said, sitting again at the kitchen table, "I really didn't have a very good time yesterday, so can we please just drop it?"

"Did you two girls get into a fight?"

Suddenly, it was like I was not in our kitchen at all, but rather back at the Redding's kitchen. I saw the cue ball drop from Mrs. Redding's hand and roll out of the room toward the foyer. "Look, I don't want to talk about it!"

Mom took in a big breath, coughed, let it out. She considered me for a moment then started to whisk the eggs as fast as possible with the fork. "That's okay. It's probably better if we don't talk about it. When I have a really bad day, I just try not to think about it. There's not anything that we can do about bad days, is there? So I suppose that it's best to think about the good days—I mean when they happen." Her face brightened. "Like next week! Like your week with Fiona Wonder! You're going to have such a great time, sweetheart. I just know it." Mom turned to the stove, put butter in the skillet and slid the eggs from the bowl into the pan. "Oh shoot!" she said. "I forgot all about the French toast. Is it okay if I don't make it?"

"I don't care," I said.

"I'll make it for you tomorrow," Mom decided. "It's my day off." She worked the eggs around the pan with a spatula. "And I'm so happy that tomorrow is Thursday. I can't wait to spend the entire day with my girl!" Again she waited for me to respond, to say, maybe, that I couldn't wait to spend the day with her too. "Your appointment at Clippers is at ten tomorrow," she said finally.

I shot her a look: "My what?"

She laughed nervously. "Don't you remember a couple of weeks ago Nikki said that she'd make your hair real pretty for your week with Fiona Wonder? Not that it's not pretty now, but if you just want a trim, then that's fine too." I stared blankly at her. "Of course it's up to you. Afterwards, I thought we could try to find you something nice to wear on the plane. Coleanne's is having a sale— 60% to 70% off. Can you believe it? I'm sure we can find you something nice to wear, something that goes with the bracelet. Then, when we come home, we can have a movie marathon. I mean a Fiona Wonder movie marathon. Doesn't that sound like fun?"

Again she waited, although not as long as last time. "When I talked to Nikki on the phone yesterday," she continued, "she said that after she gets off work tomorrow she'll come over and bring dinner with her—sandwiches and chips and drinks from the Sub Shop. Doesn't that sound like fun, Mercy?"

I swooped down, picked up the Cheerios on the floor, got up, threw them in the trash and then sat back down at the table. "It sounds like you've already made up your mind, so I don't even know why you're asking me."

She bit her lip. She turned away from the stove, walked to the refrigerator and opened it again. The light from inside the fridge shone on Mom's face like a spotlight. She looked like a hurt, scared animal. "I realize you're upset with me, Mercy," she said finally, "but do you think that maybe soon you can stop it? I mean stop being mad at me. I don't ever remember you acting like this before. It's making me feel—"

That was it: I couldn't take it anymore. "Screw how you feel, Mom!" I yelled at her.

"You don't mean that," she stammered. "That's not the Mercy that I know—"

"I have every right to be mad at you. And I'm going to keep being mad at you until you admit that you lost your rescue inhaler—"

"But I—" she tried to interrupt me.

"Don't interrupt me!" I yelled at her. "You lost your rescue inhaler, and either you don't have enough money to buy a new one, or you do have enough money but you don't want to spend it on that, or you're so preoccupied with my stupid useless week with Fiona Wonder that you're going around without one, which is really pretty dumb considering that you've got a condition called ASTHMA!"

She didn't say anything.

"Just admit that you lost it!"

"If I say that I lost it, will you stop yelling at me?"

I got up from the kitchen table. She looked alarmed. "Wait a minute. Where are you going? What about breakfast?"

"I already told you, I'm not hungry. I don't know where I'm going. All I know is that I feel like I can't breathe in here."

"Mercy, wait!" She pointed at my wrist. "Let me keep that for you, okay? I couldn't bear it if something happened to it. Just give me the bracelet, Mercy."

The skillet started to smoke on the stove. I left her in the kitchen with the smell of burning eggs.

*I* had nowhere else to go except Heritage Mall, and that's the truth; only when I went to open one of the doors of Pacy's, it was locked. I guess at first I couldn't really believe it, so I tried the door again, then the one next to it, then two others after that. When that didn't work I cupped my hands over my eyes and peered through the glass.

I turned away quickly, before what I saw had time to actually register in my head. I guess what I saw frightened me. Probably a lot of people had felt the same way and would continue to do so throughout the day. Probably it was exactly the way that Mrs. Redding had felt—although then again maybe not—when she had found her favorite store, Time & Luxingham, closed. The closure of Pacy's was just like that of Time & Luxingham—without prior notice, surprising, like an elaborate and unexpected disappearing act in a magic show.

Timidly, I cupped my hands again and looked inside Pacy's. It felt like I was standing on the edge of a black hole, peering into an abyss. The place was completely gutted. Even the carpets and the shelves had been ripped out. In my ears I could hear the faint hum of a vacuum cleaner. The aisle that led down the center of the store past the Women's Department on one side, the Children's Department on the other, now led nowhere.

My heart beat faster. I felt lightheaded and sick. I tried not to but couldn't help thinking about her—the teacher that was no longer my teacher, the woman whose name I was no longer supposed to say out loud—as I ran as fast as I could all the way to the other side of the mall to Coleanne's Department Store. At the entrance I took a deep breath and let it out before I got up the courage to try the doors.

Inside, everything looked exactly the same as yesterday. A mannequin wearing a breezy white dress stood on a circular platform in front of the Women's Department. An instrumental version of the song "Big Yellow Taxi" played overhead on the music system. In the center of a sea of clothes racks stood a sales lady with salt and pepper hair, gold hoop earrings and a brass nametag. She looked bored as she fiddled with a shirt on a hanger. She looked like she had been there for twenty years and was fully expecting to be there for twenty more.

Across the aisle from the escalators a man wearing a yellow hard hat stepped onto the stairs. I watched him disappear by degrees down to the lower level. Wedged inside his right armpit was a long plastic tube. Written on the side of it were the words, HARDMAN'S DEM. CO.

"May I help you?" said the sales lady with the gold hoop earrings. While I was watching the man in the hard hat she had made her way through the clothes racks and walked over to me. A look of determination, and something else too (Was it resignation?), shone on her face. The determination came from her wanting to do a good job, and the resignation, I guess, came from spending years doing just that. What came next was anyone's guess. "May I help you?" she repeated.

I felt like I might burst into tears. Instead I began to walk as fast as possible away from her. I walked along the aisle that led down the center of the store and then, because it felt like I wasn't moving fast enough, I began to run. I ran past the escalators and the Women's Department and the makeup counter and the perfume ladies, then through the aisles between the racks of clothing. I kept running until I saw the other end of the store and the wide opening that led into the mall. I let out a relieved breath as I exited the store. It felt like I had come out of a black hole. I started walking, refusing to look back. Too many memories there: red lawnmowers; green pens marking metaphors in books; and a teacher that was no longer my teacher *or* my friend... No one knows what goes on inside a black hole unless you're actually in one, and if you're in one then you're already gone.

*I* walked the entire length of the mall then turned around and walked back again. On my third stretch I veered off into the wings, meandering down those long passageways only to stop at the five-door exit, turn and walk back again. Those wings were the loneliest parts of the mall. More shops here were closed than open. The few still in business actually looked out of place.

"TiK ToK" played loudly inside Spinner's Gifts and Accessories. This is where Valerie had gotten her ears pierced in the fifth grade and had been dragging me to ever since so that she could spend some of her weekly allowance on whatever suited her—a purple lava lamp that ended up cracked and broken and in the garbage just two days later; a Madonna bobble head that she immediately drew a mustache on and then later tried to flush, unsuccessfully, down the toilet; a tiara; an oversized margarita glass that read, THIRSTY BITCH; a key chain that read, simply, FUCK YOU!, and that, no doubt, had swung violently back and forth as she had repeatedly crashed her car into the back of Robin's pickup. Out of all of her purchases throughout the years at Spinner's, my least favorite was a full length mirror with warped glass and a plastic frame that made us look strange and ugly and distorted no matter at what angle we looked at ourselves. The shop's owner, a skinny man with pockmarked cheeks and a shaved head, sat behind the counter, waited for customers, and stared emptily across the aisle where The Candlewick used to be located.

Nobody had even bothered to turn on the lights in this particular wing, probably because other than Spinner's the only two businesses still open, the movie theater and BONANAZA BURGER, weren't actually open yet. The same Fiona Wonder movie that had been playing since last Sunday began again at two, four, six and eight. I didn't even look at her face on the poster outside the ticket office. I didn't bother looking across the aisle at BONANZA BURGER either. At six o'clock Mom would be there to begin her shift. I should have just kept walking right out the exit into the parking lot, but instead, like a sleep walker, I stepped onto the escalator that led to the second level.

The big clock at the center of the food court read ten past noon. It smelled like pizza and corn dogs. HaiSheng was gone. So was Yogurt and Sprinkles. Dead center in the mostly empty food court three men wearing hard hats stood up from a table. They must have just eaten lunch. Marching in a straight line, like boys in a school cafeteria on their way outside to recess, they carried their food trays loaded with empty hamburger boxes and French fry containers to a trash can. They stacked the trays on top of one another then jig-sawed between the empty chairs and tables. The man walking in the middle of the threesome said to the other two: "Ben said he wanted one of us to go up to the roof again."

"For Christ's sake," said the man on the left. "We've already been up there three times since yesterday. What's he so worried about?"

"I hear that," the man on the right said.

"Remember the job last month two states over?" the man on the left said.

"Yup..."

"This one's almost a mirror image of that one."

"Yup..."

"I'll tell you one thing: there's no way that this is going to happen by Sunday; not unless everybody really hustles."

"Oh, it'll happen," the man in the center told the others. "I mean, it's got to. Don't forget; we're lined up for another one right after this one, starting on Monday."

The other two nodded in agreement.

They walked at a leisurely pace about ten steps in front of me, past Dickie's Formal Wear and Tuxedo Rental, American Experience Jeans, Hollywood Accessories, Pawable Pets and Hard Line Electronics. Except for Hard Line, the other stores were closed, metal bars over the entrances. At the center of the mall the men stopped walking to wave down at more men who were standing at the center of the switched-off water fountain. The number of bright orange cones had increased, I noticed, since yesterday.

"Hey guys, sorry we took so long with the project manager," the man in the middle called down to the men below. "We went ahead and had our lunch. You guys can go eat now if you want." The men gave the thumps up signal.

$That$'s when I saw Valerie and Mrs. Redding. Even at the other side of the mall they were unmistakable. As usual, Val looked liked she'd just woken up and thrown on the first thing that she'd found on the floor by her bed. Both her hands were jammed inside the back pockets of her jeans. Her stomach thrust out from underneath a tight tank top the color of mildew. I had never before noticed, but Valerie walked with both feet pointing out, like an overweight duck wearing dirty pink Sketchers.

Walking next to her, Mrs. Redding looked like she had just walked out of a high fashion magazine. She wore a white button-down shirt with a high, upturned collar and oversized cuffs tucked into a pair of low-rise black pants. She must have been wearing big heels because her legs looked like they went on forever. Her lipstick matched the color of her hair, which she'd put in a low, tight ponytail held in back with a black barrette. On her right arm was an expensive looking purse.

They made their way along the railed walkway in the direction of the escalator, not looking at each other but straight ahead, and they were, as usual, arguing.

My mind flashed to yesterday when Mrs. Redding had told me that she wasn't going to help me get an asthma inhaler for my mom. All over again I saw her drop the cue ball from her hand and watched it roll away from us into the foyer, stop at the table with the flowers and the mirror. I panicked. I couldn't see them now. Not after yesterday. I didn't know what else to do but turn away from the railing, and without looking, march straight into the first shop that I encountered.

It turned out to be Limit-Ex, a fancy women's fashion clothing boutique that I knew Mrs. Redding shopped at because the one and only time before this that I had been inside the store it was with her and Valerie. Waiting for her, Val and I had sat on an upholstered bench in the middle of the store while she tried on that beautiful, low-backed, white sequined dress that she had wanted to wear to the Christmas Ball—the one that Dr. Redding had told her to take off.

Inside Limit-Ex I didn't know what else to do but walk around, knowing full well that I looked out of place. For effect I picked up a sequined tank top from the rack and held it up. Two sales ladies standing behind the register gave me the once over, then went back to talking. The price tag on the shirt read ninety-nine dollars and ninety-nine cents. I put the shirt back in its place on the rack and was about to move across the room to the accessories wall, but first I decided to chance a look toward the exit.

They seemed oblivious to everything and everybody around them, walking in the direction of the food court, continuing to argue. If I waited a few more minutes, I figured, then I could walk out of the store, turn in the opposite direction of the food court, keep going along the railed walkway, winding my way through the center of the mall...

I heard Valerie's voice, angry and shouting and unmistakable, and then, after that, the hard-as-nails clicking sound of Mrs. Redding's high heels on the floor. Suddenly they were back again.

"Why do we always have to do everything *your* way?" Valerie said.

"You act as if it will take five years instead of five minutes to return a pair of pants," Mrs. Redding told her. "Just go to the food court without me if you're going to make such a fuss. I'll meet you there after I'm done."

"I don't have any money. Give me some money and I will be happy to go to the food court without you. Did you hear what I said? I said, *give me money!*"

"For God's sake," Mrs. Redding said.

To my horror, I watched as she veered into Limit-Ex with Valerie trailing behind her. My heart started to pound. I didn't know what else to do but take the sequined tank top off the hanger, run into the first fitting room that I saw, and lock the door behind me. There was a metal chair in the corner of the room, a full length mirror on the back wall, and three big hooks on the door. I sat on the chair, the back of my head touching the mirror, the shirt still on its hanger in my lap. I was pretty sure that they hadn't seen me.

Outside the fitting room I heard one of the sales ladies ask Mrs. Redding if she could help her. "Yes," I heard her voice reply crisply, "I want to return a pair of pants. They don't go with anything in my closet."

"Okay, ma'am, that shouldn't be a problem, as long as you brought your receipt with you."

"Of course I brought it."

"If you would please come with me to the front counter..."

I heard Valerie groan. It was the extended version I knew so well, the I-want-to-eat-now version.

"Five minutes, Valerie," Mrs. Redding's voice snapped at her. "Go sit down on that bench and wait for me." She actually snapped her fingers. "*Go!*"

But she didn't go. Instead I heard Valerie muttering to herself as she fussed over clothing on the racks. Then, suddenly, those dirty Sketchers were right on the other side of the door to the fitting room in which I was hiding. I held my breath and waited. Her foot kicked at an imaginary stone. She started muttering again: "...never listens to me, always so goddamn bitchy... How would she like it if she hadn't had anything to eat since breakfast? ...makes me want to puke; I'd like to—"

Something must have caught her eye then because suddenly the muttering stopped. The feet shuffled away. I heard her pick up a hanger. More silence. And then the sound of Mrs. Redding's heels again.

"All done. And just look: during the amount of time it took me to return a pair of pants, you didn't waste away. It's a miracle!"

"Ha-ha."

"We can go to the food court now."

"I don't want to go to the food court. I want this dress."

Mrs. Redding must have been just as surprised as I was to hear that Valerie was suddenly more interested in shopping than eating. Even though I couldn't see her, I sensed her taking the dress from Valerie and giving it a look. "It's pretty," she said at last, "but I doubt that it will fit you."

"I love it. I want it."

"Try it on then."

"I was planning to do just that, Mother."

"Well no one 'is stopping you, Valerie. But wait a minute. Let me find a bigger size."

"No, I want this dress."

"But—"

"I said I want *this* dress."

The door of the fitting room next to me swung open and then closed. The lock turned. I saw those Sketchers again. Not that I thought she'd take the time to notice, but just to be sure I picked up my own feet and hugged my legs to my chest.

What happened next was typical Valerie behavior: she started to bang around in there like an angry zoo animal in a cage. First she kicked off her shoes and then, for some reason, both her socks. Sitting there on the other side of the wooden partition that divided the two fitting rooms, I could smell her feet. Her jeans dropped to the floor, then the green tank top. I heard her start to pant, saw for a moment the bottom of a party dress. It was an iridescent orange color with threads of smoky gray woven through it. She slipped it up her legs, around her middle, through her arms. "Umph," she said. I heard the sound of a zipper making its way up the fabric of the dress.

"Valerie, how's it going in there?" Mrs. Redding wanted to know.

She didn't say anything for a minute. Then: "The zipper is stuck."

"Let me get you a bigger size."

"No. I can get it. Just wait."

"Well at least let me in so that I can see it."

"I said wait!"

Silence followed by more panting and then a deep breath. She was sucking in her stomach, I imagined, trying to get the zipper unstuck so that she could move it up the dress.

Mrs. Redding sounded really annoyed now: "Valerie, you're going to tear that dress, I just know it. Now let me in. I mean it."

I heard her breath collapse. She must have decided to give up. The lock unbolted. The door swung open then closed. Inside the adjacent fitting room were now two pairs of feet—Valerie's chubby, smelly ones with an old cracked coat of purple nail polish on both her big toes, and Mrs. Redding's beautiful and chic black pants and matching black heels.

"What's that?" Valerie immediately wanted to know.

"Just relax and stop looking at me in the mirror. Put a nice smile on your face and be happy that you have a sensible mother who brought the same dress one size up. You can try it on as soon as I get you out of this one."

"But I don't need a bigger size."

"Don't be ridiculous. Of course you do. Now turn around, face the mirror, and hold still so that I can unzip you."

"No, Mother, I don't want you to unzip me, I want you to zip me *up*."

"Valerie, stop it! Now suck in. Come on. I said *suck in*, Valerie."

It sounded like she was about to dive underwater.

"You know what?" Mrs. Redding said. "This dress is actually really cute. I'm surprised that you like it."

"Thanks a lot."

"If we can manage to get you out of this one so that you can try on the bigger size, I think it will probably fit you. It might actually look good on you. Do you have any idea where you'd like to wear it?"

She exhaled, and then said in annoyed tone, "I thought you didn't want me to talk."

Mrs. Redding let out a small grunt. It sounded so strange, that noise, coming from her. She must have been tugging at the zipper and lost herself completely to allow such an animalistic noise to come out of her.

"If you suck in just a little more, then maybe... Wait a minute. Let me rest my fingers." She let out a big sigh. I heard her backside squash into the foamy material of the dressing room chair. "You're not thinking about wearing it on Saturday to the office barbeque, are you?" she said quite sternly to Valerie. "Because it's too nice for something like that. Everybody wears shorts and shirts, not party dresses."

Valerie groaned. "Crap! I forgot all about the stupid barbeque on Saturday. Do I really have to go?"

"Yes."

"Ugh. Is it going to be at the same park as last time?"

"No. It's at Chatfield. It has better basketball courts, apparently."

"Nobody plays games anyway."

"That's not true. At the spring barbeque some of the kids threw around a baseball. There was touch football too. Jeremy scored a touchdown, don't you remember?"

"No."

"You simply chose not to participate. As I recall, you just sat there like a lump at one of the picnic tables."

"Mom, don't start."

"I'm not starting anything. I'm just telling you."

Her feet suddenly hit the floor as she repositioned herself behind Valerie. I guess she was going to try to unzip her again.

"Chatfield is forty minutes from the house, so on Saturday morning we'll be on the road at ten-thirty sharp."

"Ow! That's my skin! Don't zip my skin!"

"Calm down and keep your voice down. It's your own fault. How many times do I have to tell you to suck in, not push out?" Mrs. Redding let out an exasperated sigh. "This isn't working. The zipper is really stuck." She sounded extremely put out—like she didn't deserve to have to deal with this situation, like Valerie being stuck inside a dress was the biggest inconvenience she'd had all week. "Before I forget to ask," she said to Valerie, "is your friend Marcy still planning to spend the night at our house on Friday night?" I felt my face blanch. Mrs. Redding continued: "Because it's fine if she is, but the next morning she'll have to leave early. She is not invited to the barbeque on Saturday."

"I know that."

"Good. Now turn around. Let me try again."

Without objection, Valerie followed her mother's command. After a pause, she said, "It'd be embarrassing to have her there anyway. I mean at the barbeque. She's just not—you know."

"Stuck," Mrs. Redding said. "Just won't budge. Not even an inch."

"I guess what I mean is that she's not like me. Not at all."

"If I have to rip this dress, Valerie, then we'll just try on the other size and, if it fits, we'll buy it and leave this one here and not say anything to anyone. No one will ever know the difference."

"Okay." She paused, and then said, "It's really not her fault."

"Not whose fault?"

"Mercy's. It's not her fault that she's not like me. It's not her fault that she's poor. That could have been me instead of her, and she could have been me instead of me. You know what I mean?"

"No."

It made me flinch the way that she said it: so certain, so definite. Her words were like a needle piercing my eardrum.

"You are you, and Marcy is Marcy—"

"You mean Mercy," Valerie corrected her.

"There is a huge difference between you and her and there always will be. Next year, when you go away to school, you'll meet more interesting people. People like you. People up to your level. You'll see. You'll forget all about what's-her-face."

"Mercy," Valerie said again. And then: "I guess you're right. You know what I think?"

"What?"

"I think that if she came to the barbeque on Saturday she'd be a real pain. I think she'd just spend all her time bugging Daddy about mooching a free asthma inhaler for her stupid pathetic mother. The waitress."

They both laughed, agreeing. As she ripped the fabric, my eyes blurred with tears.

"Hurry up, take it off," I heard Mrs. Redding whisper.

The dress dropped to the floor. Valerie's legs stepped out of the hole in the middle of the material.

What happened next really shocked me. It wasn't so much what she did but the way that she did it: one of Mrs. Redding's black heeled shoes kicked the ripped dress underneath the partition that divided the two dressing rooms. Without apology.

"Now hurry up and try on the bigger size," she said to Valerie.

I just sat there with my legs hugged to my chest, staring down at the torn dress. I felt a searing pain in my heart, and then everything just seemed to blur. Everything felt numb, including my face. It was like I wasn't awake but in a dream.

The bigger size dress fit okay—a little small but wearable, especially if she took off just a couple of pounds, and then it would fit—that's what I heard Mrs. Redding say to her; so Valerie took off the dress and put on her normal clothes. The door to the fitting room swung open, and together they walked toward the cash register. A few minutes after that there was the clicking sound of Mrs. Redding's heels, and Valerie saying something about a corn dog, and Mrs. Redding saying something to her about how she might like to try a garden salad instead, and then Valerie saying no, and Mrs. Redding not saying anything more after that, and then the sound of Valerie's voice and the clicking of Mrs. Redding's heels getting softer and softer until I didn't hear them anymore.

On the floor in front of me the glowing orange material looked soft and delicate. I picked up the dress. The smoky-gray threads encircled the waist. The rip that Mrs. Redding had made down the back of the dress looked like an open wound. The price tag read four hundred dollars. I turned the material over and held the dress up to my body. I saw myself in the full length mirror—the shooting star bracelet on my right wrist, twinkling white hot against the neon material. I took a step closer to the mirror and stared straight at my face.

Sometimes when I am alone in the bathroom in the apartment I do the same thing—I look at myself in the mirror and wait until the other faces appear, and they always do. If I stare at my face long enough what always happens is that my face starts to twist and distort and change shape, the contours and the lines shifting into something that definitely is yet definitely is not still me. Another second goes by and then my face isn't mine anymore but the face of a laughing man with short hair, a beard and glasses. My father. I have only seen him in pictures, and when he is there on my face he looks a bit blurry as he stares back at me, but still I recognize him. Usually he is only there for a second. Then his face collapses into mine and a new face emerges—Mom. Unlike my dad, Mom usually looks like she is crying. Another second goes by. Just like Dad, Mom changes into a fat-faced baby who changes again into an expressionless wrinkled old person.

It's not just Mom and Dad and the baby and the old person that I see, but other faces too. A day after Valerie slammed her car into the back of Robin's pickup truck I saw him—I mean Robin—in the mirror, very briefly, like a flashbulb. But probably it wasn't him after all. Maybe it was another boy with similar facial features. Another time I thought I saw Mrs. Redding. When that happened, she quickly turned into Valerie, who quickly turned into Nikki, who quickly turned into Ms. Starburn.

But now, inside the dressing room of Limit-Ex, it wasn't working—the ever-changing faces were not appearing. I saw only myself. I felt like crying. I kept trying. And then, instead of another face appearing, as I was hoping one might, something else happened. It was that thing that had happened to the main character in a novel that I had read last year in Ms. Starburn's class—it had just happened to me too, I was sure of it! There was a word for it, this thing that happened, except I couldn't remember it now, and I wasn't about to go downstairs to the lower level of Coleanne's to ask my former teacher about it. Because she'd said that she didn't want me down there... And she wasn't my teacher anymore... Because when she'd looked at me she hadn't seen me at all but her own reflection—or at least a reflection of who she used to be. It was that way over and over again, not just with Ms. Starburn but with Nikki and Valerie and Mrs. Redding and Mom, too. They looked at me and saw themselves, or an image of themselves from the past, or what they might like to be in the future... So why should I care so much for them when they didn't bother to care about me? Why should I keep looking at them, trying to see them, I mean truly see them, and especially the very best in them, when they didn't try to see me—the good, the bad, the *anything*?

Suddenly a new face started to take shape in the mirror. It was *her*, of course. But instead of fleeing from her, as I had all week long, I interrupted the connection by throwing Valerie's torn dress right at Fiona Wonder's laughing face. If I did not exist to her, then she did not exist to me.

There was a loud rapping sound on the other side of the door. A woman's voice asked if I needed any help. I looked down at the dress on the floor, and then unbolted the lock. On the other side of the door a sales lady frowned at me. "What's this?" she said as she picked up the torn garment.

I did not answer her: I just walked out of the store heading in the direction of the escalators.


Like an idiot, I made the mistake of looking inside Clippers as I walked past it. Nikki was there, not at her station but near the back of the salon talking to another stylist with choppy blonde hair and big hips. The stylist was listening to Nikki, nodding her head emphatically and mixing hair dye inside a plastic cup with a tongue depressor. When Nikki saw me she stopped talking. She stood there looking at me for a time then began to walk toward me. I started walking as fast as possible in the direction of the escalators.

"M!" I heard Nikki call to me.

I ignored her and kept walking. I was about five steps from achieving my getaway—those collapsible gray mechanical stairs leading to the ground floor—when I heard her voice again. "Hey, M," she yelled again. And then: "Mercy, wait a minute!"

It was like yesterday all over again, outside Dr. Redding's private practice with Valerie. Nikki reached for my arm but I turned away.

"What's the matter with you?" she said. "Didn't you hear me?"

I looked down at my feet and shrugged.

"What are you doing?" she asked.

"Nothing," I said. "Just walking around."

"Oh yeah?" she said. "You look sort of out of it, sort of weird. Not yourself. Like—"

I shot her a look that told her to shut up.

She continued to study me. Finally she said, "I don't have any appointments. I doubt there's going to be any walk-ins. Andrea and I were just talking about how dead the mall is again today. I know you have an appointment to get your hair cut tomorrow, but you're standing right here, aren't you? And I promised your mother I'd do it, so we might as well get it over with now. Don't you think? Unless, of course, wandering around aimlessly is more important." I did not answer right away, so Nikki continued to bait me. "Hello? Paging planet M? Anybody out there?"

I followed her as she walked back inside Clippers.

"Well," she said to me, "don't just stand there. Sit down."

I sat down at her station. In the mirror I watched her drape a solid black smock over me. She gathered all my hair in her hands, lifted it outside of the smock, divided it on either side of my head, and then spread it in front of me on my shoulders. She put her hand on her hip and stared at me in the mirror. "So, what do you think we should do with this? Any ideas?"

I didn't answer. Instead I listened to "Go Your Own Way" by Fleetwood Mac playing on the stereo. I avoided looking at myself in the mirror. Instead I looked at the glittery dolphin stickers stuck to her mirror that I had seen her steal from the thrift store on Madison Street, then at all the spray bottles lined up on the shelf, then down at a big potted plant between Nikki's station and the next one. The plant wasn't real. The plastic leaves needed to be dusted.

"No ideas at all, huh?" She tapped her foot and sighed impatiently. "All right then. Get up."

I got up.

"Follow me," she said.

I followed her to the shampoo station.

"Sit down," she said and pointed at the chair.

I sat.

She turned on the spray hose and tested the temperature of the water with the tip of her right elbow. Then she got my hair all wet with warm water. She squirted a large dollop of shampoo out of the bottle into the palm of her hand and in a no-nonsense way began to massage my head. I have to admit that Nikki's fingertips rubbing the fragrant floral shampoo into my scalp actually felt okay—almost relaxing. She didn't tug or pull at all, as I thought she might. She doused my head again with the hose. Water got into my right ear. When I went to tilt my head to try to get it out she pushed me back down in the chair. "Don't move," she said and began to rub conditioner in my hair.

I opened my eyes and looked up at her. The first thing that struck me was how she had tried but failed to hide those puffy, deep circles underneath her eyes with make-up. Since the last time I'd seen her, on Monday, Nikki's face had changed. It was hard to explain; it was like she had lost something and tried to replace it with an all-too-obvious mask.

If it had been yesterday, then I probably would have asked her about Kurt, and more specifically if she had talked to him since Monday. I would have asked if she thought they might find a way to work things out. I knew that Nikki loved Kurt and Kurt loved Nikki, no matter what the obstacles, kids or money or anything else.

Instead, all I seemed to see was a replay of last Monday. I saw Nikki inside her house, yelling at Kurt and telling him that he was no good. I saw the two of us sitting across from one other at BONANAZA BURGER, she holding onto my wrist and telling me that she and Mom and I counted for little to nothing. Then I saw her alone inside CostMart, shoplifting something that she would never use but lock away in her trunk along with everything else she had stolen throughout the years. I saw the ugliness and stupidity and greediness in her, plain and simple and undeniable.

Nikki stared down at me, startled. It was she, not I, who blinked and looked away. She doused my head again, the palm of her hand flat against my head, pushing down. Suddenly the water shut off. "I'm done. Sit up," she said and wrapped a towel around my head. She led the way back to her station, waited for me to sit, then began to comb out my long hair.

"So, M," Nikki said, "since you don't know what you want, I'm going to suggest that we first layer it a bit. Also, I think you'd look good with bangs. As far as color goes—"

"I want a trim; that's it," I told her.

She put her hand on her hip. "Don't be so boring. If you're worried about what it's going to cost, then don't think about it. It's my treat, all right? Now, like I was saying—"

"I said I just want a trim. I don't want you to try to do anything special with it."

She kept her hand on her hip. "That's silly. There's plenty that I can do with this mass of hair if you'll simply let me—"

"Look, it's not like we're in a big fancy salon or something," I cut her off. "This is just Clippers, after all. Home of the nine ninety-nine hair cut, uneven bangs and razor burn."

In the mirror I saw her mouth tighten. "Well, that's a crummy thing to say to me."

I shrugged. "I don't mean to hurt your feelings. I'm just trying to be honest. What I'm saying is that I don't want you to attempt anything that is beyond your abilities. I mean, everybody knows that the—" I raised my hands in front of me. From my curled fingertips I squeezed out quotation marks "quote, unquote stylists who work here do so because no other salon will hire them."

"Excuse me?" she said in her most accusatory voice.

"Remember when my friend Valerie and her mother came in here to get their hair cut, but then Mrs. Redding changed her mind and they left?" I didn't wait for her to answer. "That's because Mrs. Redding suddenly remembered that Jeremy—that's Valerie's brother—showed her a picture of a razor burned head that he had found on the Clippers page on Facebook. Apparently there are loads of pictures like that from people who got bad haircuts from this quote, unquote establishment."

Stunned, she just stared at me in the mirror. "I don't believe you about the pictures on the Internet," she said at last. "You're making that up, M."

"No I'm not, *Nik*. If you don't believe me, then go on Facebook and look for yourself. I should have told you about it a long time ago; I should have said something about it right after Valerie told me about it. I didn't because I was trying to be nice, but really, now that I think about it, it's nicer to tell the truth, no matter how pathetic the truth is, and it is actually pretty pathetic. Don't you think, Nik?" Again, I didn't wait for her to answer. "So just trim the edges and try to cut my hair in a straight line, okay?"

The look on her face was priceless.

"As I said, I'm just trying to be honest—like you always try to be honest. Like the last time we saw each other. Like on Monday..."

She looked confused, hurt, shocked—a range of emotions that I don't think I'd ever seen from her before. "So that's what this is about?" she asked slowly, in a thick voice. "You're upset about what happened Monday? That's why you're saying these things? That's why you're acting like this?"

"I'm not upset about Monday. In fact, I don't care."

"You don't care?" she repeated. "You don't care about *what*, exactly?"

"Any of it," I said matter-of-factly. I meant it. "I don't care about what happened on Monday, or how you treated Kurt or Mom or me or yourself, for that matter. I don't care. I did before, but now I don't."

What came next didn't surprise me at all: Just as Valerie had done, Nikki exploded. "What the hell is the matter with you?" she yelled at me, loud enough for the other stylist, Andrea with the choppy blonde hair and big hips, to be startled and drop a cupful of dye to the floor.

I got up and struggled to get the smock off my neck.

"Where you are going?" she wanted to know. "What about your haircut?"

"Just forget it!" I threw the smock on the floor between us. "Why don't you go steal something?"

I left her standing there, open-mouthed and holding a pair of scissors.

*I* don't remember running out of Clippers, along the aisle and down the escalators to the turned-off water fountain. If there were other people near me, then I didn't notice them. I guess you could say that I wasn't aware of anyone but myself.

I couldn't help it; I laughed out loud. My entire body tingled. Everything felt new and strange and thrilling. It felt as if I had just drunk a radioactive cocktail—volcanic red, atomic orange, mushroom cloud yellow—and now the mixture coursed through my veins and entered my brain, shining a light on the obvious, that up until now I had been blind to see.

"Hey you!" I heard a man say.

I found myself standing in front of the turned-off fountain, my legs touching the yellow tape that read: CAUTION—CONSTRUCTION ZONE— CAUTION—CONSTRUCTION ZONE—CAUTION. The tape made a circle around the fountain. At the center, where clear water had once flowed freely, a ladder now reached all the way to the skylight.

The same man that I'd encountered yesterday looked at me and frowned. "For some reason you really seem to like this spot, don't you?" he said to me. "But you're going to have to move, just like yesterday. Sorry, but this is a construction zone and—whoa," he said and put his hand to his head. "Holy shit, I just got that—what do they call it?"

"Déjà vu," I said.

"Yeah," he said. "That's it; déjà vu." He shook his head about, trying to rearrange his perception. "But listen, kid. You're going to have to move along."

Turning to leave the construction zone, I saw it—the astronomy store—Estella and Apollo's. Again, it struck me as strange that I'd never really noticed it before. Maybe that was because it was tucked into a corner, or maybe it was because...

My feet seemed to sink into the dark blue carpet as I

stepped inside the shop. All the telescopes, as well as the binoculars, had big red stickers attached to them. The stickers read: HALF OFF and BUY NOW and LIQUIDATION PRICE.

The funny little man with the bald head, olive skin and big black glasses didn't seem to be around. I was about to look into the eyepiece of one of the bigger telescopes when I thought I heard a voice coming from the back of the store. "Hello?" I said, but I did not receive an answer.

I walked across the store to the back counter. I put both hands on top of it. "Hello?" I said again. Again, I heard no answer. I waited a few seconds then decided to cross a boundary. I walked behind the counter to a doorway that was covered with a dark blue curtain with little yellow stars on it. "Anybody back here?" I called as I pulled back the curtain.

Still receiving no answer I began to back away from the curtain, but as I did I felt a presence very near me. I turned toward the front of the shop and the funny little man was now behind the counter, not more than a foot away from me. There was a hoagie sandwich on the counter, an orange soda, and an open magazine with a picture of a huge red planet that took up the two-page spread.

"I didn't mean to startle you," he said. His voice sounded reedy. "Or stop you from going back there," he added. He pointed at the curtain. "By all means, be my guest. Have a look. You'll probably like it."

"No, that's okay," I said. I backed away from the curtain.

"Suit yourself. Are you interested in buying a telescope?" he asked me.

"Not really," I said. "I mean, yes, I am. But I can't because I don't have any money."

He took a big bite of the hoagie. A bit of mayonnaise remained at the corner of his mouth. He shook his head. "They gave me pickles again, and I asked for cucumbers." He took another bite of the sandwich. Pointing at my wrist, he asked, "What about that?"

I looked down at the Fiona Wonder Shooting Star Bracelet.

"I'll trade you that bracelet for that telescope over there," he said, pointing at the exact telescope I had just been looking at—the fat gray one with the huge lens.

"How did you know that I like that one?" I said.

"Just a guess... It's a reflector, not a refractor."

He reached for the orange soda, put the straw in his mouth and slurped. "With that telescope you'll be able to see every nook and cranny on the moon, plus a lot more," he told me. "You'll see the moons of Jupiter—at least five of them—and the rings of Saturn, too."

"What about the rainbow nebula around Betelgeuse?" I asked him.

"No," he said. "Too far."

I thought about Mom and how she'd feel if I traded the Shooting Star Bracelet for a telescope. "I don't know," I said at last. "I'll have to think about it."

"Better make up your mind by Sunday; that's my last day here and then—*whoosh*—I'm gone, and your telescope too. That is, if you decide to make the trade."

"What do you mean you'll be gone?" I said.

"The store is closing on Sunday."

"It sure does seem like a lot of stores in the mall are closing."

"Eventually, all the stores will close here," he told me. He picked up his sandwich and started eating again.

"Actually," I said finally, looking in the direction of the dark blue curtain with the stars on it, "do you think that I—I mean, you said that it didn't bother you if I—"

He set the sandwich on the table, walked to the curtain and opened it. "Be my guest," he told me. "Stay as long as you like."

*I* wasn't at all expecting what happened next. When the

funny little man let go of the curtain I found myself in absolute darkness. Something inside me wanted to scream, but instead I extended my arms on either side of my body. I felt like I was falling, just like sometimes when I'm about to fall asleep it feels suddenly like I've fallen off a cliff. When that happens, I always jerk myself awake, except I couldn't do that now because I *was* awake. The funny little man had shown me a secret doorway, one that led to outer space, and now I was falling, falling, falling...

I looked above me and saw stars, brilliant stars so close that I could almost touch them. Once I saw the stars I didn't feel scared anymore. I reached out my arms, as if I were blind, and started to walk forward. I felt a chair, then another. Slowly, I was able to navigate my way between two rows of chairs. The seat on which I sat was deep and plush and comfortable but also a bit stiff and small, like an old movie theater chair. I put my head back and looked up. The stars circled above me in multi-colored clusters, white hot, blinking and twinkling, some shooting away, others swelling and then exploding into glorious nothingness.

I put my hand on my wrist and touched the Fiona Wonder Shooting Star Bracelet, my finger tracing all eight points. Then I laid the palm of my hand over the star. It must have been my imagination, but it felt as if heat were emanating from it. I must have sat there staring into the universe, all the while my hand on my wrist, for at least an hour—maybe longer. The longer I remained there the calmer I felt. Suddenly what had seemed unthinkable— trading the bracelet for a telescope—now became a real consideration. A particularly bright star caught my eye. It twinkled at me. I winked back at it. If I traded in the bracelet for a telescope, Mom would just have to get over it.

Suddenly, I felt a presence other than my own. I turned my head in the direction of the curtained doorway. I waited, breathing evenly. Slowly, the curtain drew open. I saw the silhouette of a body—long and tall and masculine—with the recognizable brim of a baseball cap on his head. Then the curtain closed and the room was again engulfed in darkness. I heard rustling, felt a body trying to navigate through the darkness. There was no way that I could actually see who it was, yet the newcomer somehow felt familiar to me as he sat down on the chair next to mine. The moment his arm touched mine I felt heat, like electricity running through me.

The arm tensed. "Sorry," said a voice. "I thought I was alone. Who's there?"

"It's me," I said, "Mercy Swimmer."

Immediately the arm relaxed. "Imagine that! What's up, Wonder?"

"Robin?" I said. "Is that you?"

But I already knew it was him. To tell the truth, I think I knew it was him as soon as he lifted the curtain to make his way into the darkness. Even now I couldn't see him but I pictured Robin—his half-boy, half-man face, his soft and serious, inquisitive dark eyes, the upside down question mark that his hair made on the nape of his neck. I couldn't be sure, but I thought I sensed him touching the brim of his baseball cap. His other arm, now touching my arm once again on the armrest, felt warm and nice. Then he said: "Yeah, it's me. I didn't know you knew about this place."

The way he said it made me think he didn't like me being there, that in his mind this was his special place where he came to be alone. If he did feel that way, then it wouldn't surprise me, because most people have places or things that they consider personal and worth protecting, like Nikki with her chest full of stolen crap. It felt like I was back in the fitting room, listening to Valerie and her mother's secret conversation about me. Or watching Mom watching a Fiona Wonder film, her eyes glued to the screen. She could sit there all day, oblivious to everything and everyone else around her. "If you want me to go, I will," I said. Before he had time to answer I stood up.

"Wait a minute," he said. "Where are you going? Sit down. It's fine with me that you're here. I mean, I'm glad you're here." His hand touched my hand in the dark. "Come on, Wonder," he said. "Stay!"

I sat down again. After a couple of minutes I slowly put my arm back on the arm rest next to his. "I didn't know about this place until today," I said. I let out a big breath then continued: "I really like it here. It's like one of those places—I can't remember the name of it right now... We went to one on a field trip in the sixth grade. Remember?"

"A planetarium," he said.

"Yeah, a planetarium; except this place is even better. It's more realistic. It feels like we're actually floating in space together." My entire face went hot when I said that word, "together".

"Yeah," he whispered his reply, "it does."

For a while after that we didn't say anything. We simply gazed into the funny little man's private cosmos.

"I remember the field trip to the planetarium," he said finally. "We went to the moon and to some really cool, far away constellations." He paused for a moment then said: "And you sat right in front of me."

"I don't remember."

"I do."

I settled back in my chair and looked up as a star whizzed past us, burning white hot into the dark abyss of the universe. "I remember the moon but not the constellations," I said. "And I remember sitting next to Valerie." I heard him shift on his seat. Then his arm disappeared. I sat up straight in my chair. "Robin?" I said. "Are you still here?"

"I'm here," he said.

"Sorry that I mentioned Valerie," I said. "You probably hate her guts. Because of what she did to your truck," I clarified. I closed my eyes for a moment and thought about yesterday. And about today... "I wouldn't blame you at all. I mean about hating her and everything."

"I don't hate her."

"You don't?"

"No."

"Oh."

She would have killed me right then and there if she had known what I'd asked him next.

"Do you have any idea how she feels about you?"

"I know," he said. I sensed him hesitate; he wanted to say something else.

"What is it?" I said, finally.

It took him a few seconds to actually speak. Then, when he did, it was in a soft, shy voice. "Is Valerie the reason why you said no to me when I asked you to—" he didn't finish. He didn't have to.

"Yes," I told him.

He let out a big breath. "That's what I thought. If she wasn't your best friend, then would you have—"

"Yes," I said, quietly. His arm touched mine again. "Robin," I asked him, "how come you like space so much?"

He didn't say anything for a minute; he must have been thinking about it. I could feel the heat from his body radiating off him and onto me. It made me feel strange inside—good and a little giddy. I sensed him touch the brim of his baseball cap again. Felt him slouch down further in his seat and look above us.

"It's not that I like it or don't like it," he said at last. "It's that it's there and we are a part of it, so how can I not be interested in it? You know what I mean..." It was not a question but a statement.

"So, are you going to be an astrologer?" I asked.

"You mean an astronomer?"

I felt my face flush with embarrassment. "That's what I meant."

"I don't know what I'm going to be," he said. "I guess that I'll be whatever I end up being."

"That's easy to say when you can be whatever you want

to be," I said.

"Sorry?" he said.

"Nothing," I said. I was quiet for a while but I knew that he was waiting for me to clarify my statement. "What I mean is that it's easy to be so nonchalant about the future when you already know that you have one."

It's a funny thing, really. Even though I couldn't see his face, I could actually feel his confusion. "We all have a future," he said at last. "Not just me, but you too. All of us."

"I guess I mean one worth having," I said. "Like I'm sure that you're going to college..."

"What has going to college got to do with having a future, or a future worth having?"

"You're joking, right?"

"No."

We didn't say anything for a minute after that.

"I haven't decided yet if I'm going to college," he told me finally. "I know for sure that I'm not going right out of high school. I want to wait at least a year. I want to travel."

It really surprised me when he said that.

"You know where I'd like to go?" he said.

"Where?" I whispered.

"Cerra Paranal. It's in Chile. That's where the VLT, Very Large Telescope, is," he told me. "Europeans built it. They have special quarters for the astronomers because it's so high up; it's hard to breathe. You are literally above the clouds."

Georgia O'Keefe's painting, *Sky Above Clouds IV*, flashed suddenly in my mind.

Robin explained: "The VLT is actually four telescopes that act as one. When put together the four telescopes act as the biggest mirror on Earth. That's pretty awesome, right?"

"What do you mean, the biggest mirror on Earth? I thought we were talking about telescopes?"

"That's what a telescope is; it's a mirror that collects

light."

I frowned as I stared straight ahead. "What about the other stuff besides planets and stars and constellations?"

"You mean the dark matter..." Again, it wasn't a question.

"Yeah. What about that? Does the mirror collect that too?"

"Of course it does. It's just that we can't see it."

"Well, just because we can't see it doesn't mean that it's not there, Robin."

I don't know why, but I thought I sensed him smile in the darkness. "No kidding, Wonder." Then he said: "Hey! Look up!"

The stars were moving, changing shape. They were falling and circling overhead.

"He must have changed the program," Robin said. "It looks like number 8, but I can't tell for sure. Listen! If you don't like it, then I won't call you that anymore. I mean 'Wonder'."

We didn't say anything for a while after that. Then he asked me if I planned to buy a telescope. I moved my arm away from his and placed my hand back on top of my wrist, covering the star. "I don't know yet," I said. "Maybe."

"In case you're thinking about joining the astronomy club next year, then just so you know, you don't have to have your own telescope. You can borrow one of mine, if you want."

"You have more than one telescope?"

"I have two, a refractor and a reflector."

"Aren't they kind of expensive?" I sensed him shrug. "Of course it doesn't matter to you," I said. "You're rich."

"Huh?" he said. I heard it in his voice again—surprise and confusion.

"Because your parents are members of the country club," I tried to explain. "I know because Valerie's parents are members too. What does your dad do, anyway? Is he a doctor or a lawyer or something?"

"He's a scientist."

"Oh," I said. "Is he one of those guys who figures out how to make a can of aerosol spray smell like lavender? Or a package of chips taste like they've been barbequed? Or did he help figure out how to put chemicals inside cigarettes so that people got even more addicted to them?"

"What kind of attitude is that?" he said. "Truth is that he's part of a team that is trying to find a cure for ALS. Otherwise known as Lou Gehrig's Disease."

"Oh."

"During the weekends he's in a rock band called The Other Side of the Sun. It's a Pink Floyd knock-off, I guess you could call it, but sometimes Dad and the other band members come up with some cool new stuff. Anyway, he tries, and that's the important thing."

"I bet you have a real nice house."

"It *is* nice, but not because it's huge or anything. It's really old and kind of small. It's in Crestwood."

Again, I felt surprised. Crestwood was Nikki's neighborhood.

"Does your mom work?"

"Yes, of course. She's an artist. She paints."

"Oh yeah?" I said. "Like what?"

"Portraits."

"You mean faces?"

"Yes."

"Oh," I said. I tried but couldn't quite manage to hide the disappointment in my voice.

"What?" he asked.

"Nothing. It's just that I think that if I were a painter, then I'd like to paint something other than people. Like maybe I'd paint the sky or something."

"Mom loves people's faces. She thinks the human face is the most interesting, and the most beautiful, and maybe the most important image in the entire world."

I looked above and tried to picture an interesting,

beautiful, important face. I could, actually, but I didn't tell him so.

"And they canceled their membership to the country club over a year ago," he told me. "They only joined because my mom wanted to try to get all the members to agree to host some art events there for kids, but after she set up this big long complicated board, well, she just got fed up with it because she realized that she was the only one who really wanted it. Who really cared, I mean. So she and Dad quit."

"Your grandpa went to Dr. Redding," I said.

"Yes, he did. He had emphysema. He went because he was dying."

"He could afford to go?"

"Yes."

"Some people can't. I mean can't afford to see him. Even if they're really sick and need help."

"I know," he said quietly. "And I think it's wrong. Worse than that, I think it's pointless. Scratch that. I think it's murderous."

We were quiet for a long time after that. Finally, to break the silence and also because I wanted to know, I asked him what was the difference between a reflector telescope and a refractor telescope.

"Reflectors have two mirrors, unlike refractors," he told me. "The mirrors are bigger, so you can see a lot more detail and further into space. The downside is that the image you see is upside down, so you can't look at long distance views. I mean on Earth. With a refractor you can look at things happening here on Earth. With a reflector, you can only look into space."

"If that's the big difference, then I definitely want a reflector," I said. "I don't need a refractor to look at things here. If I don't ever have to look at things here on Earth again, then that'd be fine by me."

He didn't have anything to say about that.

"The man who owns this shop told me that I could

trade my Fiona Wonder Shooting Star Bracelet for one of the telescopes."

"Oh yeah?" he said. "But I thought you really liked the bracelet. I mean, it won you a week with Fiona Wonder. And even if it hadn't won you a week with a movie star, you must have liked it enough to buy it."

"But that's the thing," I said. "I didn't buy it. My mother did. It's really my mom who loves the bracelet. It's really my mom who can't wait for me to spend a week with Fiona Wonder."

And then I told him the story my mother had told me about how she had gotten the money to buy the bracelet.

Sitting next to me in the pitch black room full of stars, I thought I sensed Robin thinking really hard about something. "What is it?" I said at last. "What's the matter?"

"When did you say that this happened?"

"On the night of the Junior Prom."

"You're sure about that?"

"Yes."

"And the dance competition—are you sure that she said that it happened in the events room at the art museum?"

"Yes."

Sitting there next to me in the dark, he suddenly went very quiet.

"What is it?" I said finally.

"Nothing."

"I don't believe you. It's something. Tell me. Please," I added, softly.

"Are you sure you want to know?" he said.

"Yes."

"Sometimes it's better not to know. Sometimes it's better to be left in the..."

"Robin, tell me."

He took a deep breath. "It didn't happen that way," he said at last.

I sat there for a moment, whirling with the stars.

"What?" I said finally.

"I mean there was no ballroom dancing competition on the night of Junior Prom at the art museum. I know because that room was being used for something else. It was being used to showcase local artists. I know because my mom had a couple of pieces in the show. Two portraits—one of a woman, the other of a man. I know because I was there that night. I decided to go after you told me—"

But I cut him off before he could finish what he was about to say. "So, what you're saying is that she—"

And then, suddenly, the lights came on. I don't mean figuratively, either. I mean literally. The lights came on in the room. It was blinding and shocking. The stars disappeared. We were just in a tiny, dusty room with a domed ceiling, sitting next to each other in a row of actual old-time movie house chairs.

I don't know why but I found it really hard to look at him. He was too close. In the dark it felt okay—even safe—but now it was like we were starting all over again.

"Sometimes that happens," Robin said to me. "The lights—they just go on suddenly. You want me to turn them back off? I know how to do it."

"No," I said. I stood up. I felt embarrassed, flustered. "I really should be going. What time is it, do you know?"

He looked at his watch. "Almost six o'clock," he said.

I looked around, and what I saw really depressed me. I wasn't in space anymore. I was back inside Heritage Mall.

"She lied about the entire thing, didn't she?" I said. "There were no ballroom dancers that came into Waffle Falafel that night. There was no dance competition. There was no prize money, and no one hundred and fifty-dollar tip. She got the money from somewhere else. She got the money from—" But the truth I perceived was too harsh for me to say out loud. The truth still felt unreal, like an unexpected punch in the stomach. Like falling from a very high place. Like falling from a vertical wooden pole and

175

hitting the ground with a smack!

He stood up next to me. "Mercy, are you okay?"

"I have to go."

"Mercy—"

Excusing myself, I made my way quickly toward the exit. Reaching the doorway, I drew open the curtain. The shop was empty. The little man was nowhere to be seen. I ran past the telescopes and out of the shop, past the water fountain, the lit-up stores and the empty stores too, up the escalator, past Clippers (Nikki called out my name but I was running so fast that she didn't even try to stop me this time), all the way to the food court. I didn't wait for the escalator to transport me; I ran down the stairs two at a time and almost fell flat on my face. These days it seemed as if I were constantly running away from unpleasant confrontations, with Valerie, with Nikki, with my mom, and with Ms. Starburn. I'm not a runner, I told myself.

I guess it was serendipity, running into Mom at that excruciating moment. Except she wasn't alone. A man with black curly hair and dark circles underneath his eyes pulled open the door for her.

"Mercy!" Mom said when she saw me. She had on her BONANZA BURGER uniform and the backpack with her other uniform inside it flung over her shoulder. "Sweetheart, where have you been all day? I've been worried sick. I thought maybe... Honey, what's the matter?"

It took a lot of restraint not to hit her. "You lied to me!" I yelled at her. "You didn't get the money to buy the bracelet from a big tip left by ballroom dancers. You got it from somewhere else."

I watched her face fall.

"You used the money from your medical fund, didn't you? You didn't lose your rescue inhaler; you don't *have* a rescue inhaler anymore. I bet you don't have a daily inhaler either, do you?"

The look on her face answered my question.

"You don't have a rescue inhaler or a daily inhaler because you used the money in your medical fund to buy me that stupid bracelet!"

She put her hand to her chest. "Oh," she said. "Oh..."

"You did!" I screamed. "I can't believe you did that!"

"Oh," she just kept saying. "Oh..."

"Just calm down," the man with the curly black hair and dark circles underneath his eyes said to me. He went to reach for my arm.

"Don't touch me!" I screamed at him.

He put both his arms in front of him. That's when I saw the tattoo on his right forearm that read MARAVILLA. This was Gabriel, the kitchen manager at BONANZA BURGER. "Be nice to your mother," he said to me.

"Screw you!" I yelled at him.

"Now look—" he started to say.

But I cut him off. "You made a choice, Mom," I said, turning to her, "and now I'm going to make one too. I'm not going next week. You can just forget about it. I'm not going to spend a week with Fiona Wonder, because I don't want to, I never wanted to, I was only going to do it for you, but now I don't care anymore, just like you didn't care about taking care of yourself, about buying your medication instead of this stupid bracelet," I said and held out my wrist at her.

"Oh, no, Mercy. Please—"

But I was already on my way toward the door.

# THURSDAY

*T*he ringing phone at three o'clock in the morning woke me up. I had to get out of bed and hurry to the kitchen, barefoot and in my pajamas, to answer it. Mom wasn't home yet. She still had three hours to go before her shift ended at Waffle Falafel.

It was Nikki. She didn't even say hello, or apologize for calling so early in the morning. "Call Kurt," was all she said. She sounded all hyped up, like she was high on something. "His number is 555-236-9056. Did you get that? And if he doesn't pick up his cell, like he hasn't for a number of days now, then find out where he is."

"What?" I said.

"I said, call Kurt's cell phone: 555-236-9056. And if he doesn't pick up, then find out where he is. I don't know where he is and I need his help, and I'm only allowed one phone call."

"Nikki, where are you?"

She didn't answer me. "Did you write down the number?" she said finally. "It's 555—"

"Nikki," I said, "I have it. It's in our address book."

178

"Okay, good. If he doesn't pick up, then you have to find him. I think he might be staying at his friend's house. Call the operator if you have to and ask for Bob Neaman. N-E-A-M-A-N," she spelled it out for me. "He lives in Maple View. If he's not there, then try this other guy, Stan Hatching. He lives in Coal Valley. Do you need me to spell his last name for you?"

"No."

"If he doesn't pick up his cell, and if he's not at Bob's or Stan's, then you've got to call—" she stopped for a minute to clear her throat—"*that woman.* You know who I mean. I know you have her number in your phone book because I remember that I wrote it down. It was right after I'd met him and he didn't have a cell then, and they'd separated, but he was still living at the house and—"

"Are you talking about Alicia?" Of course I already knew exactly who she was talking about. Just for the hell of it, I added, "The mother of his children."

"The number is under 'L' in the phone book. It's under Kurt's last name, Lovell."

"How come you need me to call him, Nikki?"

"L-O-V-E—"

"I know how to spell it," I interrupted her. "You got arrested for shoplifting, didn't you? And now you're at the police station. You're only allowed one phone call, just like in the movies. You need someone to bail you out. Well," I said, not waiting for her to answer, "I'm surprised that this didn't happen sooner."

"Look," she said, her voice meek and muffled and strained, "can you please just find him? And tell him to come and get me at the police station on Third Avenue and Quincy Street? And if he is at that woman's house, and if you talk to her, then don't tell her what this is about. I mean it, M." Then she actually started crying. "I didn't know who else to call... Please help me."

"What'd you steal, anyway?"

She hung up on me.

I put the phone back in its cradle and just stood there in the dark kitchen. I don't think that I realized that I had been looking out the window at the string of street lights from the freeway until one of the lights blew out.

*Call Kurt*, I heard Nikki's voice say to me.

I turned, walked back down the hallway to my bedroom, got into bed and pulled the covers over my head. I lay there like that for about half an hour, maybe longer. First I tried to picture Nikki calling me from inside a police station. I saw her standing there with her ear pressed against the receiver. Behind her an unsmiling policeman penciled something into a big brown book. Down a long white corridor came the sudden, jarring sound of bars slamming nosily against the latch of a lock.

I couldn't help it; I cracked a smile underneath the covers. Let her stay there for a while. Maybe it would teach her a lesson. I'd find Kurt when I was good and ready to find him. In the meantime my mind decided to make a detour; it ended up back inside the astronomy store and the roomful of stars. At first I was alone, sitting on one of the chairs and looking up at the constellations, but then Robin returned. Just like in real life he sat down beside me and we just sat there for a long time, looking up and feeling like we were floating together in space. In my half-awake, half-dream state he reached over and put his hand on top of mine. I looked down at my wrist and saw the bracelet.

Another fifteen minutes passed. Half an hour, tops.

When I got out of bed I knew exactly where to find our address book—in the junk drawer underneath the silverware drawer next to the sink in the kitchen. I knew exactly where to find it because I had just been through that drawer as well as almost every other drawer in the apartment last night after I had returned from Heritage Mall.

To be honest, as soon as I had gotten back from the mall I had torn through the entire place in the hope of finding Mom's daily asthma inhaler. I looked everywhere, not just inside every drawer in the kitchen, but also in the bathroom and in both of our bedrooms. I looked underneath the beds, between the cushions of the couch in the living room, and in all the pockets of our jackets even though it was the middle of summer.

The more I looked and didn't find the inhaler, the more I allowed the truth to be just that—the truth. And the more I allowed that to happen, the angrier I felt. I wasn't just angry at her but at myself. Angry for believing so easily Mom's whopper of a lie about where she'd gotten the money to buy the Fiona Wonder Shooting Star Bracelet. I was finally beginning to understand that the truth is usually not very complicated and almost always devoid of any wonder. Instead of her fantastic, magical story, the truth was simply that Mom had stopped buying her asthma medications. Because she was so hung up about a person who she'd never met, she'd decided that it was more important to use her medical fund to buy a stupid, useless hunk of cheap metal and clear glass beads instead of the medicine vital to her breathing. The fact that the bracelet she'd chosen had the winning sixteen-digit code didn't mean anything. There wasn't any magic to it. It was just dumb luck. Nothing more...

I didn't even try to find Kurt's cell phone number. I knew exactly where he was. Just like Nikki had said, I found the number in the phone book under "L".

The phone rang five times before she picked up. She sounded confused and groggy. In the background I was pretty sure I heard a man's voice.

"Hello, Alicia," I said into the receiver. "Sounds like I woke you up. Sorry about that. You don't know me but my name is—well, I guess it doesn't matter what my name is. I'm calling about Nikki. She got arrested for shoplifting. She didn't know who else to call for help because other than my mother she doesn't have any friends. Nikki needs Kurt to pick her up at the police station, the one on Third

Avenue and Quincy Street. If you ask me, I'm not surprised that she's in this predicament—I mean that she got caught shoplifting. If Kurt hasn't told you already, Nikki is a kleptomaniac. Anyway, Kurt's there, isn't he? That's all right, you don't need to answer. I can hear him talking in the background. Hey, listen, you should probably tell him to bring some money with him before he sets off for the jailhouse. I don't know how these things work exactly, but he'll probably have to pay something to get her out of the slammer. Since Kurt doesn't have a job at the moment, he'll probably have to ask you for a loan. Don't worry, though, I'm sure he'll pay you back for bailing out his girlfriend, or ex-girlfriend, or whatever she is to him, just as soon as he finds a job. Oh, and before I forget, go ahead and say hi to Brandi and Tucker for me. You know I've never actually met them, not even when they stayed weekends at Nikki's house. It's because she hates their guts, you know. She hates yours too, but you probably already know that."

*A* couple of hours later I heard Kurt's truck pull into the parking lot outside our building. From the landing I looked down and saw Mom and Nikki sitting next to him in the cab. Obviously, Kurt had decided to pick up Mom from Waffle Falafel after he'd picked up Nikki from the police station. Without saying a word, they got out and slammed the doors. In single file they marched up the stairs, their heads hung low, Mom in her bright yellow Waffle Falafel get-up, Kurt in a pair of dirty jeans and a wrinkled Hanes T-shirt and Nikki still wearing her maroon colored CLIPPERS T-shirt. Her hair, for the record, looked horrible.

Watching them walk up the stairs to our apartment, I had a thought: each of them had always been this way—a misfit, a dropout, a loser. On the other end of the totem pole of humanity was someone like Lady Redding. At that moment in time I could not imagine her being something other than what she was—rich, beautiful, privileged. Not like Mom or Nikki or Kurt. The more I thought about what she had told Valerie in the dressing room yesterday, the more I thought she must be right: Valerie would always be Valerie and I would always be me. We might be carved into the same log, but Valerie was already near the top, and I was all the way down at the bottom. If I tried to climb up to her, then I'd probably end up like Dad. I'd make it to the top of the pole only to fall off and kill myself. That's the way those things almost always work.

Mom came in first, followed by Kurt then by Nikki. Behind them the sun poked through the trees and shone on the concrete surface of the freeway. Of course by then all of the street lights that lined the highway had been turned off for at least an hour, perhaps longer.

In the kitchen Mom looked at me, searchingly. Her eyes went from my eyes down to my wrist, and the bracelet still attached to it, then back up to my eyes again. She tried to hide it, I think, but I saw the look of relief on her face. "I'll brew some coffee," she said.

Nikki sat down heavily on one of the chairs at the table. She smelled like cigarettes and body odor. She looked like she hadn't slept all night. She probably hadn't. *Serves her right*, I thought to myself.

"No coffee for me. Thanks anyway, I better get going," Kurt said and started to make his way to the door.

"No, Kurt. Stay..." Nikki reached for his hand. He let her hold it.

I rolled my eyes and smirked.

Nikki shot me a look. "Do you have something to say to me?"

"Not really. Do you have something to say to *me*?" I shot back at her.

"Like what?"

"Well, for starters, how about an apology for waking me up in the middle of the night? Or how about a thank you for finding Kurt?"

"Apology?" Nikki said. "Thank you?" She stood up, not letting go of Kurt's hand. She looked like she wanted to hit me. *Let her just try it*, I thought to myself. "It took you two and a half hours from the time I called you to call Kurt. What the hell were you doing?" she yelled at me. "Didn't you care where I was or what was happening to me? Didn't you grasp the urgency of the goddamn situation? And then, when you finally *did* decide to call him, you told *that woman* all about—"

"That you can't stop stealing stuff? So what? I'm sure she already knew all about it. It's not like your little recreational hobby is any big secret."

"Hey, now, come on—" Kurt started.

"What'd you steal this time, Nikki?"

"Guys, come on," Kurt said, trying to stop us. He hadn't let go of Nikki's hand.

"What'd you steal, Nikki? What'd you steal?"

She looked like she wanted to murder me.

"What'd you steal?"

"Hey, Mercy, come on," Kurt said. "She's had a hard night. Give her a break."

"Give her a break? Give *me* a break," I said. "So what if she's had a hard night. She did it to herself. It's not like anyone made her steal whatever it was that she stole."

"Mercy—"

"She's a thief!"

"She has a problem," Kurt said. "She has a problem that she needs to get some help with and—"

"She's a thief!" I screamed at him. Then I looked at her again. "What'd you steal, Nikki? What'd you steal?"

"I think you'd better shut your mouth, Mercy, before you get my boot upside your backside!" she warned me.

We stood glaring at one another, defiantly.

"It was a bar of soap and a package of hair bands from a twenty-four hour Walgreen's. Okay? The pharmacist who caught me was going to let me go but then the manager found out. He remembered me from the other time that I—" But she stopped before she came out with the truth. "The manager just had to act all high and mighty and call the cops. Okay? And now I'm completely humiliated. All right? Are you satisfied?"

Instead of continuing my verbal assault on Nikki, I looked at Mom. She had forgotten about making coffee. She stood next to the refrigerator with her hands pressed over her ears, her eyes squeezed shut, and her lips pressed together.

"Okay," Kurt said, trying to calm us both down. "That's enough."

But I couldn't calm down. I didn't want to calm down. I spun around and pointed a finger at Nikki. "A bar of soap? A package of hair bands? A twenty-four hour pharmacy? Ugh, I can't believe you!" I screamed at her. "You're so stupid! Who steals soap? It's soap! And your hair isn't even long enough for hair bands. If you were at a pharmacy, then you could at least have stolen something useful!"

"Oh yeah?" she screamed back at me. "Like what?"

I marched over to Mom, took both her hands and yanked them away from her ears. Her eyes flew open. "Like a rescue asthma inhaler!" I screamed at the top of my lungs. Mom looked at me with panic written all over her face. "Like a goddamn rescue asthma inhaler, you morons!"

Mom put her hand to her chest and started to cry. Kurt and Nikki stood there looking at me like they didn't know who I was anymore.

"Mercy—" Mom said, holding out her arms to me.

"Just leave me alone!" I yelled at her—at all of them. I turned and ran as fast as I could down the hallway to my bedroom. I slammed the door behind me, got into bed and threw the covers over my head. I was shaking really hard. My teeth chattered. I had never felt this way before. I felt capable of real violence. It felt good, but also scary. Even though my eyes were already shut, I squeezed them until it hurt. It was crazy that my teeth wouldn't stop chattering considering it was the middle of the summer, and that it was hot inside the apartment, and that I was all the way underneath the covers.

In the kitchen I heard Kurt trying to calm down Mom.

"Just try to breathe," he said to her.

"It's not like her," Mom sobbed.

I must have slept. I don't remember falling asleep, but I must have, because suddenly I was back at the Greek restaurant where Valerie and Mrs. Redding and I had eaten lunch on Tuesday. I was looking at the mural of the seven women with the seven bright stars over their heads. They were no longer just a painting, but actually real people inside the painting. They were us.

In the next sequence I was near Nikki and Kurt. They were still holding hands. It was like I was looking at them, but I also *was* them, I mean both of them, and there were no words because there was no need for words. I felt pure, deep love between them. And then, the next time I looked, it wasn't Nikki and Kurt anymore, but Robin and me, and the same pure love was still there, like the love was its very own thing that had been with Nikki and Kurt and was now with Robin and me.

Then I was alone in space. I was orbiting the earth when a very powerful but invisible force sucked me backwards. Earth just got smaller and smaller until it was gone altogether. This is what it must feel like to be inside a black hole, I thought to myself quite calmly.

I woke up gasping for air. My heart was pounding. My forehead was drenched in sweat. I threw back the covers. Sunlight poured into my room through the window. I sat there, waiting for my heart to slow down as I wiped away the sweat from my forehead. When I looked at the clock I could barely believe what time it read: twenty-five minutes past three in the afternoon.

I got out of bed, kicked off my pajamas and got

dressed. I opened the door and walked down the hallway. Turning toward the kitchen I saw Nikki outside the door on the landing, looking over the railing and smoking a cigarette. In the living room Mom lay on the couch still wearing her waitress uniform and staring at the television. On top of the TV the DVD player made its familiar humming noise.

"You know that person wasn't me, Henry," she said onscreen. "It was the other one. The one that just shows up sometimes. There's nothing I can do about her. But I'm still me, Henry, even when it seems like she's taken my place. I'm still here when that happens. That's what you've got to remember. I'll always be me. You've got to promise to never forget me."

I don't even know why I looked to see what movie was playing, because she had already seen it a hundred times, just like all the others that you-know-who starred in. On top of the DVD player was an opened sleeve. On the cover her face tilted downward, her expression was inquisitive yet serene. Just above her head read the title of the movie: *Never Forget Me*, and right underneath it, in smaller red letters: starring Fiona Wonder.

If memory serves me right the movie is about an untreated schizophrenic who falls in love with an investment banker named Henry. Just like Nikki's boss Cliff, he drives around in a Porsche, although unlike Cliff's car, it's not yellow but red. The untreated schizophrenic and the investment banker spend most of the movie trying to figure out who she really is, until the very end when she decides she can't take it anymore and throws herself off a building while, down below at street level, Henry holds out his arms to save her. The screen goes blank before you see what happens, but I'll bet anything he doesn't catch her.

Loud enough for Mom to hear, I said, "Some day off."

She turned her head and looked up at me. Her eyes looked puffy, like she had been crying on and off for hours. It looked like she hadn't slept at all. She wheezed a little. She looked at me quietly, hopefully. "Did you have a nice long sleep? Do you feel a little better now, Mercy?"

"I see that you haven't even bothered to change."

She looked down at her soiled waitress uniform. "Oh, well, I—" she started to say.

"I thought you said that you couldn't wait for today, your day off. I thought we were supposed to do all these fun things together, like go to the mall and buy me a new outfit and get my hair cut."

She sat up straight on the couch. When she wheezed again, which turned into a coughing fit, she had the sense to at least turn her face away from me. "We can still do all those things, honey." She stopped to cough again. "I'd like to go to the mall with you. Let me just take a quick shower and get myself ready and—"

"No, just forget it."

"Are you sure?"

"Just watch your movie. I know that's what you really want to do anyway."

She looked like I'd just hit her in the face—again. Her eyes watered up. She didn't know what else to do, I think, but turn back to the screen and watch Fiona Wonder implore the investment banker named Henry to promise to never forget about her.

"I know somebody around here—namely me—who'd sure like to forget about her," I said loud enough for Mom to hear. I didn't turn around to see her reaction. I entered the kitchen at the same moment that Nikki threw her cigarette butt over the landing, then turned and walked through the door.

At least she had taken a shower and changed into different clothes—a pair of ripped jean shorts that were hers and that she'd left here, and one of Mom's many old T-shirts. The shirt was pink with a big blue shooting star on the front of it. (I remember that once it had had silver glitter on the tail of the star, but didn't anymore.) The shirt was so old and holey and gross that it wouldn't even have served well as a kitchen rag.

"Well, look who finally decided to grace us with her presence," Nikki provoked.

I walked right past her and got myself a glass of water. The water tasted horrible, as usual, like it was full of bad stuff that would eventually kill me, but I was so thirsty that I didn't care. Anyway, there was nothing that I could do about the water. I thought about Mrs. Redding's friend, and her shopping cart loaded with Evian. Of course, we didn't have enough money to buy the bottled kind. And whose fault was that?

"You feeling better now?" she asked me at last. Her voice had a hard, no nonsense edge to it.

I drank the last of the water and slammed the glass down hard on the counter. I answered in the exact same tone of voice that she had just used with me. "I feel fine. What are you still doing here, anyway? How come you're not at work?"

Instead of answering me she walked to the refrigerator. I watched her open the door, take out the VeggieFit Juice she'd left, open the cap and sniff it. She put the bottle back in the fridge and shut the door. "Your mother didn't tell you?"

"Tell me what?"

Again, instead of answering me, she went instead to her bag and started to rummage through it. "I'm out of cigarettes. Shit." She walked out the door onto the landing and looked down at the parking lot. "I hope Kurt gets back soon, like he promised, so that he can drive me over to CostMart."

"Didn't Mom tell me *what*, Nikki?"

She just kept looking down at the parking lot. She said, finally, not turning around to look at me, "Clippers closed yesterday."

Immediately I knew what she meant. I don't know why I even bothered to ask for clarification. "You mean permanently?"

She nodded her head. And then, for whatever reason, she just started talking, telling me *everything*.

"Cliff showed up at the very end of the day. I knew as soon as he walked through the doorway that something was up. He asked us to gather round him in the center of the salon, like we were a bunch of Indians about to listen to the Big Chief. He didn't even care that there was a lady sitting underneath a dryer. He didn't even prepare us, he just blurted it out. 'I'm closing down the salon. Today's your last day.' It was so crazy and out of the blue and— well, I think we were all in shock. 'Don't look so shocked,' he said. 'In case you girls haven't noticed, the mall is dead. There just isn't enough foot traffic to sustain us anymore. First Time & Luxingham, and now Pacy's is gone. And it's only a matter of time before the entire operation shuts down. Usually, when a mall dies it happens slowly; it's like a slow cancer with the patient hanging on for dear life, in a coma and on life support, but still alive. That's the condition that Heritage Mall is in right now,' he told us. 'In a coma, on life support. But not too long from now, the cancer's going to have its way, and the only thing left to do is pull the plug. After that—curtains.'"

Her hands clutched onto the wooden railing of the landing. She kept leaning over the side, looking down at the parking lot.

"Then he started talking about all those guys in yellow hard hats walking around the mall and measuring things. He said he stopped to ask one of them what they were doing. 'Just making plans for improvements,' he was told. 'Improvements, my ass,' Cliff said. He'd seen the name of the company on the long plastic tubes that those workmen were carrying around with them. Something Dem. Co. *Dem* as in demolition.' He said he wasn't going to wait around for someone from mall management to tell him the truth. He wasn't going to waste one more day paying rent on a piece of property that wasn't producing now and wasn't going to produce ever again. Especially since, not long from now, the place would be nothing but a pile of rubble."

She scratched furiously at the back of her neck, as if something had just stung her. She stood first on tip-toe then flat-footed. She kept doing it, tip-toe then flat-footed, again and again, like her life depended on it. She must be aching for a cigarette, I thought to myself.

That's when I remembered a half-pack of cigarettes in the junk drawer next to the kitchen sink. I knew they were there because I'd seen them last night and then again this morning. Nikki must have left them there by accident, and instead of throwing them away, Mom must have kept them for her.

Nikki kept scratching. I didn't say a word.

"So that's it. End of story. All the girls at the Heritage Mall Clippers are up shit creek. No severance, no benefits, no nothing. And Cliff is not even going to try to help us find a job at any of the other locations. He said that all positions were full at his salons off Cripple Creek Road and Sandy Boulevard and at Patriot—" She cleared her throat. Then, like she had suddenly developed a nervous tic, she frantically scratched at the back of her neck again. Her nails left a long red imprint on her skin. "He talked for about half an hour. No, longer. He just wouldn't shut up and let us all deal with it. By that time I wasn't paying any attention to him. I'd listened to all I needed to hear."

I thought about Kurt, all those months ago having had the same thing happen to him at the construction company, and then not being able to find any work on his own. I thought about how Nikki had treated him ever since, like it was his fault that he'd lost his job, like he was less of a person because he couldn't find another one.

When she turned from the landing to look at me I saw fear in her eyes. And also the slightest glimmer of hope that I'd say something nice.

I walked outside onto the landing, stood next to her, and peered down at Mom's designated, empty parking space. Out of nowhere I flashed to the dream that I had just had about Nikki and Kurt, but as soon as I flashed to it, it erased itself completely from my memory. That's the way it is with dreams sometimes. It's like your real life doesn't want your dream life to remember some of the dreams, because even though the dream is pure and true, it just won't fit into real life.

"I bet you're just dying for a smoke," I said.

She let out a sigh. Without looking at me she walked through the front door and started going through her bag again, looking for the cigarettes she already knew weren't there.

I followed her back inside the kitchen.

"Kurt will be back any minute now," she said, rummaging frantically. "I'm sure of it."

"Where's Kurt now?" I asked. She didn't answer me. "Is he at Alicia's?"

"No."

"Are you sure about that?"

"Yes, I'm sure."

"Then where is he?"

"Doing errands."

"How do you know that?"

"Because I just do."

"I bet he's at Alicia's."

She slammed her purse on top of the table. "I just told you that he wasn't, so knock it off. Quit trying to piss me off."

"I bet he's at Alicia's," I said again, circling the kitchen table. I stopped walking and looked right at her as she stood opposite me. "I bet he's there right now trying to explain to her just what happened last night and why he felt so compelled to bail you out of jail."

"Listen, kid, I'm warning you."

"It's not because he loves you, he's telling her, but because he feels sorry for you. He's promising her that he's never going to leave her again. Probably Brandi and

Tucker are there too, telling them how happy they are that their mommy and daddy have decided to stay together. They're all one big happy family now that *that woman* is out of the picture."

"Goddamn it, Mercy!" she screamed and hurled her purse at me. It hit me right on the chest.

I picked it up and hurled it right back at her. It hit her in the gut, hard. "Don't ever do that again!" I screamed at her.

She wasn't expecting that. She put both hands up like she was a criminal caught in a police man's flashlight, like she had been caught and was ready to surrender. "Okay," she said. Her face looked green, like she was about to puke. "Okay, okay..."

"I wish you'd just go home!"

"Mercy, calm down."

"Why don't you just go!"

"Because," she said, softly, "I don't want to be alone."

I looked at her and saw that she was serious. I couldn't help it; I cracked up. I put my hands on my hips and doubled over. I laughed and laughed. "I'm sorry, it's just funny to me to hear you say something like that, that you don't want to be alone—" I pointed my finger right at her. "Just last Monday your behavior toward Kurt made it perfectly clear that all you want is to be left alone!"

The look on her face—it was like I had just hit her again in the gut with the purse. This time I loaded the bag full of rocks, took aim, and hurled it at her again.

"Instead of being in a relationship with him, you'd much rather be in a relationship with yourself. Yourself and your locked-up trunk full of stolen loot, of course..."

She opened her mouth but no words came out.

"It's funny to me how things change so quickly for you, Nikki, now that you know what it feels like 'to be let go'. It's funny to me that after everything is said and done that out of the three of you, the one left with a job is *that woman*."

The bruises that covered her body from the beating were invisible yet apparent.

"It's pretty damn funny to me that she's the one who's going to end up with him, because you were too selfish and too stupid to let him go."

That did it. Her face went into contortions. Her hands were two tight fists in front of her. Then, suddenly, she was a tree branch that had snapped in a fierce wind. Broken, she collapsed into a heap on the linoleum. She grabbed her knees and started rocking back and forth, back and forth. Then she started to cry.

"I'm sorry!" she cried out between sobs. She kept rocking. "I had no idea that it would feel so... so..."

"Awful and scary and out of control and lonely," I answered for her.

"I'm sorry!"

I didn't say anything. I just stood there, looking down at her. Still rocking, she grabbed my right foot and looked up at me. "Please, stop acting like this. Just be yourself again. You were good when you were yourself, not like this..."

"Like what, Nikki?" But I already knew what she meant. Finally, I opened the junk drawer, rummaged through it, took out the package of cigarettes and tossed them on her lap. My voice was barely a whisper. "Try to calm down."

She snatched the cigarettes, jumped up from the floor, ran outside and slammed the door behind her.


The last thing I wanted was for the phone to ring, but that's exactly what happened. I decided not to pick it up, but after the tenth ring I couldn't stand it anymore.

"Halfway House," I said into the receiver.

"Mercy, is that you?" Valerie said on the other end of the line.

I thought about yesterday at the mall. I thought about

what she and her mother had said to one another while unaware that I was inside the adjacent dressing room. Then I thought about the day before and the way that Ms. Starburn had treated me at Coleanne's.

"Look," I said into the receiver. "This isn't the best time. What do you want?"

It took her a moment to answer. She must have been surprised by the tone of my voice. "I was just bored," she said finally. "And I was wondering if you wanted to come over. Nobody is here right now. My mom took Jeremy to a doctor's appointment for his collarbone. After that she's taking him to the football clinic so that he can watch his teammates from the sidelines. My mom's got a million errands to run, so she won't be back for hours, and my dad's at work, as usual. He won't be home until late. So we'll have the place to ourselves. We could just hang out. We could drink a few beers. I'm sure that my dad won't even notice, and look through the yearbook, and talk about Gretchen's party tomorrow night and—"

"No," I said. "I don't want to."

An extended silence followed. Finally she said, "Are you okay?"

"This isn't the best time," I told her again. I waited for her to register what I had said.

"So I guess I'll just see you tomorrow," she said uncertainly.

"I doubt it."

"Really... And why is that?"

"You know, I saw you and your mom yesterday, at the mall."

I could hear her munching away on some sort of junk food. "God, you're acting weird. So you saw us at the mall. So what? How come you didn't say hello? Where'd you see us, anyway? At the food court?"

"No, inside Limit-Ex." I waited.

She decided to pretend to neither understand nor care about what I had just said. For all I knew she really didn't understand. Or maybe she did understand but just didn't care.

"So, are you coming over tomorrow night or what?" she wanted to know. "Because it would really suck to have to go to Gretchen's party all by myself. I mean, if you don't come and make me go by myself, then, I don't know, I probably couldn't forgive you for doing something like that to me."

"I already told you that I doubted it."

Suddenly, she sounded desperate. She was thinking about Robin, of course, and how much she wanted to see him tomorrow night. "But you have to come! I mean, you know how much I've been looking forward to it."

She was so transparent, it was embarrassing.

"Valerie, do you know for sure that Robin's going to be there?"

She hadn't expected me to say that. "Oh, well," she stalled. "Oh, well, yeah. He is. The only reason why I know for sure is because this morning on Facebook I visited Gretchen's party invite page. I just happened to see his profile picture and that he'd ticked off that he was attending. How come you want to know if he's going to be there?" she asked me.

"No reason," I said to her.

"So are you coming tomorrow to spend the night, or aren't you?"

"Yeah, I will."

She sounded relieved. "Good. Come early, like two or three in the afternoon, and then we'll just hang out. For dinner Mom said that we can order whatever we want. Then, after my parents go to sleep, we'll sneak out and go to Gretchen's." She sounded nervous and excited and flustered by the plan.

I couldn't help it: I just couldn't stand listening to her anymore like that. I wanted to kind of mess her up. "Are you planning to wear your new dress that you bought yesterday to the party, Valerie?" I thought I heard her catch her breath.

"Of course I haven't seen it on you yet. I mean the dress. I only saw the one that your mom ripped off your body and kicked underneath the wall in the fitting rooms. It's a real nice dress, Val. When he sees you in it, I'm sure that Robin's going to fall instantly in love with you. Just like in the movies. That's what you're hoping for, isn't that right, Valerie? Oh, and by the way, he asked me to Junior Prom. I really wanted to go with him, but I told him no because of you. I wish now that I had said yes. Maybe he'll ask me again next year for Senior Prom. It's really Senior Prom that's important anyway. Isn't that right, Valerie?"

She didn't dare respond. She just hung up.


*I* left the kitchen and crossed the hallway into the living room. Mom was still there, sitting on the couch and staring at the television. A mournful symphony accompanied the end credits for the movie, *Never Forget Me*.

It's not like our apartment is huge. She must have heard everything that Nikki and I had said to one another in the kitchen. Ditto regarding my conversation with Valerie. She sure looked like she'd heard everything. Her face was as white as a ghost. When I sat down next to her, she jumped. That's when I saw what she was playing with in her hands. It was her Waffle Falafel nametag. She kept hooking and unhooking the pin onto the clasp.

Suddenly, I wanted her to talk to me. I wanted to see things from her perspective. I wanted her to explain to me why it had made sense to her to spend the money in her medical fund on a bracelet that was marketed by a movie star. I wanted her to tell me why I shouldn't be mad at her. Instead she said, "I'm going to play another movie." She kept hooking and unhooking the clasp on the back of her nametag. "Will you stay here with me and watch it?" she asked me. "Do you want to choose which one to watch? We can just sit here together and be real quiet. We can just sit here and watch a movie. What do you think?" She looked at me hopefully.

It felt like she'd just ripped out my heart. "No, thanks," I said.

Her shoulders sagged. She placed the unclasped nametag on top of the coffee table, got up from the couch, walked across the room and got down on her hands and knees in front of the TV. I watched her open the cabinet door below the set and start to pull out DVD cases. Wordlessly, she spread out a collection of at least twenty DVDs in front of her.

I looked down at Mom as she knelt on the floor in front of all the DVDs. The back of her head looked small and unremarkable. And the way that she looked at Fiona Wonder's many faces, all staring back at her, seemed almost as if she were having a religious experience.

I snatched Mom's nametag from the coffee table. Turning it to the front, I read her misspelled name. I struggled to clasp the pin. "How come you never told the manager to change your name?" I wanted to know.

"What?" She looked up at me, surprised.

"On your nametag..." I held it up to her. "Your name is misspelled. It's been that way since you started working there. How come you never told the manager to make you a new one with your name spelled correctly?"

She looked at me, then at the nametag, then back at me. "Oh, gosh, I never even noticed. And what does it matter if my name isn't spelled right? I mean, in all the years that I've been waitressing, not one person has ever called me by my name."

I felt my face harden. I placed the nametag, still unclasped, back on top the coffee table.

"Mercy," Mom began, "I think that you two—I mean you and her—"

"You mean Fiona Wonder?" I said.

"Yes. I think that you and Fiona Wonder are going to—"

"You know that's not her real name," I cut her off.

She looked at me, confused.

"It's not. It's just her stage name. I read it in a magazine."

She looked as if I had just told her that Nikki's name wasn't really Nikki. Or that my name wasn't really Mercy.

"What is her real name then?" Mom wanted to know. She had placed her palm on top one of the DVDs, right on Fiona Wonder's face.

*Clare Winkle*, I thought to myself. I shrugged and looked away from her. "I don't remember now," I said.

"It doesn't matter," she said. "But I really think, Mercy, that you two are going to hit it off." She looked down at the collection of movies, the palm of her hand still on top of Fiona's face. "Maybe after the week is over she'll invite you back to stay with her sometime. I could see that happening. In fact, it would surprise me if it didn't happen."

"I meant what I said yesterday about not going next week."

She wouldn't look at me. "You don't really mean that."

"Yes, I do. Unlike you, Mom, I tell the truth. And the truth is I've decided that I'm not going next week. I'm going to trade in the bracelet for a telescope."

She just sat there, shaking her head back and forth.

"What made you think that you could just stop taking your asthma inhalers?" She opened her mouth then closed it. "What went on in your head when you decided to use your medicine money to buy *this*." I held out my wrist with the bracelet attached to it.

Her voice was barely a whisper. "I did it for you."

My chest was heaving, not violently but in exasperation. "No, you didn't. You did it for *her*!" I pointed at the screen. Then I pointed at her. "You did it for *you*!"

Her face fell again. More tears, quiet tears, streamed down her face. She looked so pathetic, still on her knees.

"You care more about her than you do me!"

"That's not true!" she wheezed.

"Yes, it is! You care more about her than you care about yourself!"

She put her face in her hands. Her palm print, I noticed, had made a mark on Fiona Wonder's face. And that's when I saw it—the two ballroom dancers on the cover of the DVD from which she'd just removed her hand. Just as Mom had described the ballroom dancer who had come into Waffle Falafel with her partner and left her a one hundred and fifty-dollar tip, Fiona Wonder wore a sky blue ballroom dress, her partner dressed in a tuxedo, his hair wet and slicked back.

Now I felt like I couldn't breathe. So that's where she'd gotten her story—her big lie—about where she'd gotten the money to buy the bracelet. She'd lifted it out of one of her movies. She hadn't even used her own imagination to come up with the story. Somehow it made the lie all the worse.

I thought about the morning after Junior Prom, her wheezing and crying alone in the bathroom. And I saw the ketchup stained uniform. I thought about what Randy had told me in the media center at Valerie's house—how he'd been there that night, how she'd waited on him and his friends, how she'd left the restaurant before they did, that she'd left without even collecting her tip money. It was Randy who was telling the truth, and my mother who had told the lie. My head started to spin. I felt sick.

"I did it for you," she sobbed. She was still sobbing when I got up from the couch, walked down the hallway and slammed the door to my room.


From my bedroom window I watched a group of men wearing yellow hard hats climb out of the skylight onto the roof of Heritage Mall. From this distance they looked like a swarm of yellow jackets climbing out of a beehive. I just sat there on my bed, feeling numb and staring out the window.

The next time I was aware of anything in the present was when I heard the front door open and slam shut. I was still sitting on my bed, staring out the window. I turned to look at the clock. It read six-thirty. I heard Nikki's muffled voice telling Mom about how she had walked all the way to CostMart. "Did Kurt come back?" I heard her ask Mom. "Or did he call?"

I didn't get up from my bed or turn away from the window when Nikki rapped hard on the door. "M, are you in there?"I didn't say anything. "I know you're in there, M, because your mom told me." She waited about ten seconds. Then she informed me, "She also told me that you haven't eaten anything all day." This time she only waited about five seconds after I hadn't answered her. "It's a good thing that I got some stuff from the supermarket. It's nothing special—just some ham and Swiss cheese, a nice loaf of French bread, some pickles, a couple of packets of potato chips and some orange soda. I thought I'd make some sandwiches, but if you're not up for that then I can look through the cabinets to see what's there. I know I've never cooked for you before, but I'm actually pretty good at it. What do you think?" When I didn't answer I heard her sigh. "Well, I'll let you know when dinner is ready."

I heard her walk down the hallway, say something that I couldn't quite make out to Mom, then start to bang away in the kitchen. Outside my window, on the roof of the mall, the group of men stood near the open skylight, talking and gesturing with their hands. It looked like they might be arguing, then suddenly I changed my mind and thought instead that they looked like they were agreeing about something.

This time Nikki didn't even bother to walk down the hallway and knock on my bedroom door. "Food's ready. Come out of your bedroom—now!"

One of the men stepped onto the ladder and started to

make his way through the skylight back down inside the mall. Another followed, then another, then another one after that, until there was only one man left. Instead of following the rest, he just stood there. He seemed to be looking back at me.

"Mercy!" I heard Nikki shout, "Get out here!"

$T$ogether we ate our dinner sitting on the couch in silence, while in front of us on the television screen Fiona Wonder walked peacefully through a beautiful, dense forest. She wasn't alone. She held someone's hand, although the way the camera angle depicted the scene it was as if the viewer was holding her hand. She looked back at us, smiling, as she made her way slowly through the trees. When she said something, we couldn't hear it because I had put the sound on mute just before picking up my sandwich.

Mom had showered and changed clothes. Her hair was down and still a little wet. She wore a knee-length jean skirt, a lilac sleeveless knit top, tan sandals and a matching belt. Out of the corner of my eye I saw her giving me nervous glances but she was smart enough not to talk to me.

Nikki was the first to jump when the doorbell rang. She must have thought it was Kurt. As she started to make her way to the door she knocked her plate from the coffee table onto the floor. Potato chips went flying. Her half-eaten sandwich landed on the carpet about six inches from the plate. The pickle disappeared completely; it must have rolled underneath the coffee table. Together Mom and I watched as she ran to open the door.

It was Gabriel. His enormous figure was unmistakable. Immediately I looked at the green tattoo on his right forearm. Even in the fading light I could see it— MARAVILLA.

"What are you doing here?" I said to him. I didn't get up from my place next to Mom on the couch.

He didn't step over the threshold. He took off his baseball cap and held it in his right hand, close to his chest. He was wearing tennis shoes, blue jeans and a tucked-in short sleeve shirt. His hair was a mass of matted, sweaty black curls. The circles underneath his eyes looked even darker today, almost black.

"I'm sorry to disturb you," he said, "but I'd like to speak with your mother." He looked past me to Mom. "That is, if I'm not intruding... If it's okay...."

She didn't sound at all breathless when she answered him: "C'mon in, Gabe."

He walked through the door, past Nikki and into the living room. He didn't pretend that the mess that Nikki had made wasn't there or step over it like I thought he would. Before he sat down on the couch in the place that I had just vacated, he picked up the overturned plate and Nikki's half-eaten ham and cheese sandwich from the floor. Then he started picking up potato chips and placing them, one at a time, onto the plate. He found the pickle underneath the cofee table and put it on the plate too.

"I'm sorry to bother you like this on your day off," he said to Mom.

"That's okay." She actually blushed. "We were just having something to eat. Are you hungry? Would you like me to fix you a plate?" He shook his head no and thanked her.

Mom looked nervous. It was then that I realized that other than Kurt, or the manager of the apartment building, or the occasional visit from a plumber, a salesman or a census taker, this was the first time that a man had come to visit her at our apartment.

"Do you want something to drink?" she asked him.

Again he shook his head. And again he thanked her. "The reason I'm here is because I have something to tell you about BONANZA BURGER."

Immediately she looked disappointed, and worried too. "Did something happen?"

"Yes. I don't really know how to say this except to start from the beginning. I'm sorry in advance if I ramble."

"No," Mom said. "That's okay."

"So what happened was that the owner came in this morning during kitchen prep. Have you ever met him before?" Mom shook her head no. "It was only the second time that I'd met him. The only other time that I'd talked to him was a couple of years ago, after the big fire in the kitchen. Do you remember the fire?"

"Sure..."

"Right after the fire, he came to the restaurant because he wanted to see how much damage had been done. I remember that he kept asking me: *Who started the fire? Who started fire? I have to know for legal reasons. I have to inform my lawyer... So who started the fire?* But of course I didn't tell him. I knew who'd done it, but it wasn't really the kid's fault, and nobody had gotten hurt, it was only a little damage, plus, if I had told him, and if they'd done some research on this kid, then they would have found out that, you know, the kid wasn't actually, I mean legally, allowed to work in the kitchen. And then God knows what would have happened to him. So, like I said, early this morning during kitchen prep the owner just appeared. He said that what he was about to tell me was only to be shared with the cooks, not any of the wait staff, and I wasn't even supposed to say anything to the cooks until tomorrow after closing. The only reason he told me first is because I'm the kitchen manager. But when he told me, well, I thought of you. I wanted you to know ahead of time, and in a quiet place, not in front of a whole bunch of people, because you have problems, you know, problems with your lungs and with breathing, and I didn't want the news to upset you, so that's why I'm here."

"I see," she said.

Gabriel took Mom's hand and held it. "The restaurant is closing a week from Sunday," he told her.

She looked down at her hand in his. But she said

nothing.

"At least we still have another week of work." He was trying to sound encouraging. "And after that, you still have your job at Waffle Falafel. I was thinking maybe that I could get a job there too. That is, if they're hiring."

Mom looked up from her lap to the television screen. Fiona Wonder wasn't in the forest anymore but bathing in a calm, moonlit pond. She looked back at Mom, her skin and hair wet and glistening, and winked.

"If you need another job, then I'll help you look. Maybe we can find something better—I mean together. Maybe we could—"

That's when Nikk started shouting. "Kurt!" She ran out the door onto the landing. "I knew you'd come back. I just knew it!"


*H*e had come back, after all. No one was more surprised than I. The three of us—Mom and Gabriel and I—went outside to the landing to watch Nikki run down the stairs to meet him at his truck. They hugged and kissed for a long time, followed by "I love you" and "I'm sorry" and "Never again". It was sweet and corny and kind of like watching a scene in a movie. I don't think that I'd ever seen Nikki happier. She was crying again—the second time in one day. Kurt said something to her then placed the palm of his hand on the small of her back and kissed the side of her neck.

"Come downstairs!" she yelled up at us. "He says he wants to take us somewhere but we've got to hurry. Come on!"

I looked at Mom, then at Gabriel. He put on his baseball cap and said that he'd be on his way. But he stood waiting on the landing while Mom went back inside to get her purse and keys. She took time to brush her hair, I noticed, but not to turn off the television. In her mind Fiona would stay behind, waiting for her to return.

"What are you doing up there?" Nikki shouted below. "Hurry up and come down here!"

Downstairs all three of them—Nikki and Kurt and especially Mom—were in agreement that Gabriel should come with us to wherever it was we were going.

"Okay," Gabriel said, laughing. "Thanks. Okay." He turned to Kurt. "It looks like there's not enough room in the cab of your truck, so I'll just follow behind you in my car. Where are you going?"

"We don't know yet," Nikki told him. "It's a surprise." Her face beamed. She looked like a kid.

Kurt unlatched and lowered the tailgate. "Just hop in the back." Gabriel looked a little skeptical.

"It's okay," Mom told him. "I'll ride in back with you."


$M$om and Gabriel rode in the back of the truck lying flat on their backs. From my place in the cab of the truck I could see that they lay facing each other, as if on a bed together. In the yellow glow of the street lamps I saw Mom's face looking back at Gabriel, and Gabriel's face looking back at Mom, and they were both smiling.

Kurt steered the truck onto the highway, switched to the middle lane immediately, then another second later to the fast lane. I looked at Nikki, who sat in the middle, then at Kurt. He had his arm around her shoulder and she rested her head on his shoulder. Both windows were down and the breeze whipped my hair. The sky was clear and starry. Nikki looked at me and smiled. "What a beautiful night!" she said.

"Hey Kurt," I said, leaning over Nikki so that he could hear me, "why don't you just tell us where we're going?"

"Because it's a surprise," Nikki answered for him.

I placed my arms across my chest and stared straight out the windshield. "I don't like surprises."

Nikki pinched my arm, softly. "Yes, you do. At least you always did before. So stop being so grumpy and just enjoy yourself."

I turned toward the passenger window. I started to rearrange my feet. They kicked at something—an old, wrinkled Pacy's shopping bag. On top of the bag was a pile of blankets.

Kurt signaled and then slipped over two empty lanes to the slow lane. Then he drove the truck onto the same off ramp that Mrs. Redding always takes when she drives to Dr. Redding's office. I was really hoping that he'd turn left instead of right at the stoplight. But Kurt turned the truck due west. I knew this road well. A couple of blocks later and we'd be back at the same place where I had been on Tuesday with Mrs. Redding and Valerie.

The light turned red just in time, of course, so that Kurt had to stop the truck. Across the street Columbo's Coffee was open but empty. At night Dr. Redding's office looked completely different. From the truck I could see the parking lot and the big plate glass windows that looked inside the reception area, which was dark. There was light behind the frosted glass door, however. I saw silhouettes of people.

We all sat there waiting for the light to change from red to green. I couldn't stop looking at the building. Suddenly the light behind the frosted glass door switched off, and then people started coming out of the building. I saw a several people I didn't recognize; then I saw Dr. Zuwansky, Jeannette the receptionist, and finally Dr. Redding himself. He walked straight to his car. He looked very upset. He opened the door of his car, got in, and then slammed the door in anger. Then he just sat there behind the wheel, staring straight ahead, his hands clutching onto the steering wheel. It was like he was one of those crash dummies that they use to test the impact of collisions. That's when the light turned green and Kurt started driving.

The truck turned onto a smaller road, and then onto an even smaller road that wasn't paved. There were no other cars behind or ahead of us. Above there were no street lights. The truck followed the winding road, the headlights beating down on the red dirt. Kurt kept driving until we reached a locked chain-link gate. *Private Property. No Trespassing*, a sign read on the gate. He put the truck in park but didn't turn off the ignition. "Just a second," he told us.

He got out of the truck. From the light of the headlights Nikki and I watched as he walked to the gate. He reached for something in his back pocket. It was a pair of wire cutters. "What is he doing?" I said to Nikki.

"It looks like he's cutting through the lock on the gate," she said.

"He's breaking the law," I said.

Nikki didn't say anything.

"That sign says private property. No trespassing. What is it with you people? First you're stealing stuff, and now you're breaking and entering..."

But then I shut up. I remembered how on Sunday morning I had lain on the grass looking up at the sky, taking Mom's nametag and puncturing a hole in the blue with it, then taking Nikki's scissors and making the hole bigger, cutting it open so that I could look past the blue into the infinite. And then Mrs. Redding's manicured hand zipping it back up.

"You okay?" Nikki wanted to know.

I watched Kurt push open the gate. He got back into the truck, not saying a word, and drove through the now open gate. The truck worked its way up a steep hill. There were several big old trees—old oaks and one big willow. The stars were in sharp focus, like we were looking up at them through a high powered telescope. Finally, the truck crested the top of the hill. On the other side of it was Kurt's surprise.

"Oh wow!" Nikki said when she saw it. By the lights of the dashboard I could make out Kurt's face. He was smiling.

Nikki turned and rapped hard on the glass of the back

window to get Mom and Gabriel's attention. Meanwhile, Kurt steered the truck in a circle so that the front faced the other side of the hill and the road that he'd just driven up. We all looked down at the trees, at the dirt road, and into the big sky full of twinkling stars.

I got out of the truck first. Nikki took the blankets. When the three of us circled round the truck we saw that in the bed of the pickup Mom and Gabriel had already sat up, their faces bathed not in moonlight, because there was no moon, but in the glow of cinema light.

There she was again, on celluloid, beaming—a close-up shot, behind her nothing but space. It was the same movie—*The Immortals*—that Mom, Nikki, Mrs. Redding, Valerie and I had watched last Sunday at the movie theater inside Heritage Mall.

This was Kurt's big surprise. He'd cut through the lock and opened the gate, he had driven us to this place because at the bottom of the hill we could clearly see an outdoor movie theater screen. The distance between Kurt's truck and the screen looked close yet faraway all at the same time. On screen Fiona's mouth moved, yet her voice was silent to us because we weren't actually on the grounds of the drive-in theater. We hadn't paid the admission price to enter.

Of course no one seemed to care. Everybody seemed quite thrilled—especially Mom. When Nikki asked Kurt how he knew about this place—this quiet grassy hill that looked down on the outdoor movie screen—he said that he had known about it since he was a teenager.

"Oh," Nikki said. "Does that mean..."

Kurt looked sad all over again.

She thought about it for a moment, and then reached for his hand. "It doesn't matter," she said. "I don't care."

There was a happy, carefree discussion about where everyone should sit. When Mom asked Gabriel where he'd like to sit, he told her that wherever she wanted to sit was fine with him: it was her choice. That made my mom blush, which made Gabriel blush too.

On the movie screen below Fiona Wonder blew us all a kiss.

"Mercy," Mom said, and held out her hand to me, "won't you sit down with us?"

Everyone was quiet. So was I. It was so stupid, being here like this. We couldn't even hear the soundtrack. What was the point? I walked over to the willow tree and sat facing away from the screen. Then I looked up through the branches at the stars. I put my hand on my wrist, touched the bracelet, and thought about my decision to trade it for a telescope.

Thirty minutes passed—maybe longer. I heard them talking and laughing. I looked over in their direction to see that Kurt and Nikki had settled in the back of the truck, while Mom and Gabriel lay on a blanket spread out on the grass, their bodies close but not quite touching. I turned my back to them and looked at the stars.

Absorbed in my star gazing and in my thoughts, I was surprised to see Gabriel's huge body standing over me. He asked me if I would mind him sitting there with me. I shrugged and kept looking up at the stars. "I don't care."

He crouched down on his knees, about a foot away from me. "You don't want to watch the movie?"

I didn't look at him: "No."

"Why not?"

"I've already seen it. Anyway, I can't stand the actress who plays in it."

"You mean Fiona Wonder?"

"Yes."

"Oh."

But I could tell he wanted to say a lot more than just that.

"What?" I said at last.

"Maybe you'll decide you like her—I mean Fiona Wonder—after you spend next week with her."

So he knew about it too. Everybody did, apparently.

"Well, there's been a change of plans," I told him. "I'm not going next week." I felt his eyes on me. Looking down at my wrist, I kept talking: "I'm going to trade the bracelet for a telescope—reflector, not a refractor."

He didn't say anything for the longest time. And then, finally, "Mercy..."

I felt exasperated, fed up; I wished that he wasn't here. "What?"

"I want to know why you're so angry."

I shot him a look. "You don't even know me, so how do you know whether or not I'm angry."

"Excuse me, Miss," he said, "but you're raging mad. Anybody could see it."

"How can I *not* be angry at her?"

"You mean your mother?"

"Not just her. All of them!" I said and pointed at Mom, Nikki and Kurt watching the film. "They've got no jobs, no prospects, no nothing, and yet they can sit there like nothing's wrong, like everything's going to be fine. Especially her! Look at her! Her entire world is caving in around her, and she just sits there, oblivious. And it really pisses me off! It pisses me off that she's hung up on people who aren't even real and situations that don't even exist. It's like she cares more about Fiona Wonder, a movie star, than her real life."

He didn't say anything for a long time. His silence started to make me feel nervous. And then he just started talking. "Maybe that's just the place where she finds hope, you know? Maybe it's there that she finds a little wonder in her life. Everybody's got to have some of that, don't they? Does it really matter where it comes from? Is looking at stars in a telescope any better or worse than watching a movie star on a screen? Isn't it the same thing? Isn't it really more about looking at yourself, and allowing yourself to dream and wonder and, most importantly, to feel a sense of connection to something bigger than yourself? To feel a sense of love or admiration for something or someone outside yourself?"

I was starting to allow his words sink in—to actually think about what it was he was saying to me. But then something stopped me. I remembered how I felt in the dressing room of Limit-Ex. If I let my guard down again, then I'd probably just be trampled. I'd just be used to facilitate other people's reflections of themselves. When I spoke again it felt like I was a snake with venom coming out of my mouth. "Not at the expense of her real life," I told him. "And that's exactly what she's done. She's gotten so wrapped up in a make-believe world that she cares more about it than her own life."

"She lives in the real world every day," he said.

"I know she does, but she could do a better job of it."

"How is that?"

"It's obvious! She could toughen up. Not let people walk all over her. She could fight more. She could try to find a better job with better benefits and...she could just try harder!"

"Try harder to do what?"

"To make more money, to buy nicer clothes, to get a nice haircut from a decent salon, to hang out with better friends, to just—" I had been searching for the right expression. And then I remembered another face: Lady Redding's. And then it was right there, of course. I had it: "To at least attempt to make an effort to climb the ladder!"

"Oh," he said. Then he sighed. "That..."

"Yes, that! That is what is called being an adult—a responsible, realistic, rational adult."

I stopped to look at him. His head bowed. He looked like he might break down and cry. "Look," I snapped, "she can't even afford to take care of herself. She can't even make enough money to buy the medications that help her to breathe."

"Maybe that's not her fault."

"Yes, it is!"

I hadn't meant to yell. I looked down at Gabriel's arm.

The moonlight just happened to beam down on his tattoo.

"What does that mean, anyway?" I said.

He opened his mouth, like he was going to tell me, but then he changed his mind. He covered it with his hand. Quickly, he got up from the grass. "I'm sorry. My intention was not to upset you. I'll leave you alone now."

I was furious that he wouldn't tell me what it meant.

He stood there for a moment, looking up at the stars. Then he looked down at me.

"What?" I wanted to know. The venom was still there—even worse than before.

I saw him hesitate, afraid to speak, yet knowing that what he had to say was important. "Your mother told me one time that she thought her daughter was kind. Not just kind, but the kindest person she'd ever known. That's what she said about you, Mercy."

"Well, maybe she was wrong."

"No," he said. "I don't think she was..."

But I thought I saw doubt in his eyes.

# FRIDAY

$L$ooking through the reflector telescope would get me away from all of this, I thought to myself on Friday morning as I packed a backpack with an extra change of clothes, my hairbrush and a toothbrush to spend the night at Valerie's house. It would take me somewhere else—to a better place, to faraway space—where there were no people or anything that had to do with their problems. If Gabriel, with his sad and haunted eyes, was right about how people needed to find something to give them a sense of hope, a sense of admiration, and love too, something that didn't have anything to do with themselves, then that was my place, not here in the apartment, or at Valerie's house, or Heritage Shopping Mall, or the art museum looking at *Sky Above Clouds IV*, or the back room of Stella's and Apollo's, sitting next to Robin in the dark and looking up at projected stars in a makeshift planetarium. The room, the shop, and the mall wouldn't even exist soon. Just like the supernova Betelgeuse with the rainbow nebula around it, everything in my here and now was dying.

It caught me off guard when I found Mom sitting on a chair at the kitchen table, drinking a cup of coffee and looking through the newspaper. "You're awake," I said.

She looked up at me, then down at my wrist with the bracelet still on it, then at the backpack over my shoulder. Her voice wheezed and whistled as she spoke. "You're leaving?"

"I already told you that I was going to spend the night at Valerie's house."

"Oh." Another whistle escaped from her lips. "I forgot."

"Write down her number and put it in your pocket in case you need to call me."

"Okay, Mercy."

She didn't look well. Even though she was sitting, she looked completely out of breath. "What are you doing?" I asked her.

"Looking through the want ads," she wheezed.

I looked down at the paper and saw that she'd circled three ads. "You circled a secretarial position at a law firm?" I said, frowning, and pointed at one of the ads.

"I thought it might be a good change."

"Except you don't know how to type..."

"I know, but what's the harm in applying for it? Maybe it doesn't matter that I don't know how to type. Maybe they'd be patient with me; maybe they'd teach me how to type."

I looked at her skeptically. She bit her lip.

I continued to look at the paper, my eyes moving to the next circled ad: "A dog groomer?" I said. "You can't be serious."

"It's at a veterinary clinic within walking distance of our apartment."

"What makes you think that they'd hire you? You've never even owned a dog."

I waited for her to stop coughing.

"I know, but it's within walking distance of our—"

More coughing...

At last I said: "Aren't there any waitressing jobs?"

She sat up straight in the chair. "Yes, a couple. But they're all miles away from here. And anyway, I wanted to try to find something else."

"Why?"

"Because, I was thinking, maybe BONANZA BURGER closing next week really isn't such a bad thing. Maybe losing my job there will help me find a better job." She looked up at me, hopefully.

"Except you don't know how to type, and you don't know how to groom a dog." I looked at the paper again: "Flight attendant?" I couldn't help laughing. "You've got to be kidding."

"Please, don't laugh at me when I'm trying to—" The coughing attack was worse this time.

"You should just stick to what you know," I told her after it was over.

She stared down at the paper, gulping for air. I started to make my way to the door.

"Wait a minute!" she said, gasping. I turned to look at her. "Are you? What about? Do you think?"

"What, Mom? Are you asking if I've changed my mind about not going next week?" She nodded her head yes.

In response I held up my wrist and showed her the bracelet. "Take a good look at it," I told her, "because it's the last time you're going to see it."

Her eyes filled with tears. She looked down at the paper, then back at me, then down at the paper again. "Okay," she said finally, "if that's what you really want to do, if trading the bracelet for a telescope and not going next week is really what you want to do, then okay."

"Thanks very much for your permission." I was being sarcastic.

She took a big gulp of air. "Mercy, I love you. If that's what you really want to do, then it's okay with me because I love you."

I started to turn toward the door.

"I'm sorry," she said. She waited for me to look at her again.

"Sorry about what?" I wanted to know.

"About how you feel..."

I felt my blood boil. "That's what you're sorry about—the way *I* feel? Shouldn't you be sorry about the way *you* feel, Mom?"

"I—"

"Shouldn't you feel sorry about lying to me about where you got the money to buy the bracelet? Or about buying the bracelet in the first place?"

"No," she said. "I'll never be sorry that I stopped buying my asthma medications to buy you the bracelet. I just can't be sorry about that."

My expression turned hard as stone. "I'll see you tomorrow."

"I love you." I turned toward the door. "I love you," she said again.

"Nothing here is based on love!" I shouted, my hand clutching the doorknob. "It's based on something else—like self-gratification, like getting what you can no matter what the price, and trying to find love in it but not finding it, and not knowing where to find it even though it's so simple if you'd just look in the right place!"

I heard her behind me, wheezing and whistling and gasping for air. I could feel her holding out her hand to me, wanting me to turn back, wanting me to tell her that I loved her too—no matter what she had done, no matter what the cost.

*I* marched in the direction of Heritage Mall, my mind made up to trade in the bracelet for the telescope. Afterwards I'd take the escalator to the Home Gardening Center to show it to Ms. Starburn. I'd show her that she'd been wrong about me, that I wasn't dumb and dreamy and doped on movie stars, that I wasn't a prime example of what was wrong with my generation. And that I wasn't going to spend a week with Fiona Wonder!

Three big red signs had been taped to the doors of Coleanne's: *60%—70% Off Everything*, one read; *Huge Clearance*, read another. The biggest sign read: *Everything Must Go!*

Inside the department store the escalator had been turned off, a piece of yellow tape barring entrance onto the motionless mechanical stairs. Next to the escalator and the mannequin on the pedestal was a red lawnmower, a box of American Country Style dishes, and two La-Z-Boy chairs. Peering down the escalator I saw flashes of white hot light, the sound of a blowtorch, and a man walking around in a yellow hard hat.

"Can I help you?" It was the sales lady with the salt and pepper hair and gold hoop earrings. She wore a blue pantsuit. The frown on her face was the size of Texas.

"How come those things are up here in the women's department?" I asked and pointed at the lawnmower, the set of dishes and the chairs.

"Because that's all that's left. Everything else was taken away last night."

I looked from the lawnmower back to the escalator. "Is Ms. Starburn still down there?"

"Who?"

"She works in the Home and Gardening Center. She used to be a teacher."

"You mean Sybil?" I thought about Ms. Starburn taking her shirt with the nametag pinned to it and thrusting it out to me. *I'm not your teacher anymore*, she had said. *I'm this!* "She's not down there," the sales lady told me, the frown on her face growing bigger by the second. "She's gone, just like everybody else that used to work down there. The only ones down there now are those men from that company—" She stopped to try to remember the name: "Hardman's Dem. Co. That's because next week the mall is going to—"

but her voice trailed off when the sound of the blow torch started up again in the basement. "Those men from Hardman's," she said, "I thought they were here to make improvements on the mall, not tear it down, but that's exactly what they're going to do. They're going to tear down the entire mall as soon as all the shops clear out. In the meantime, they're doing inspections. They're trying to figure out where to put the explosives."

I looked at her, bewildered.

"For when they tear it down," she told me. "They're going to blow it up from the inside out."

"Just like Betelgeuse," I said. I hadn't actually meant to say it out loud.

The sales lady started to turn away from me to go back to her clean-up work, but for some reason she changed her mind. She told me: "I've worked here for twenty-five years. I'm fifty-five years old. After Coleanne's closes next week, who's going to hire me? My husband died last year. I'm all alone. How am I going to make my house payment? And with all those people in government talking about getting rid of Social Security and Medicare, what am I going to do? What's any of us going to do? It's enough to make you go crazy, just like that woman, Sybil."

That shocked me. "What do you mean crazy? Ms. Starburn went crazy?"

"You know what she told me yesterday in the office when she was collecting her last paycheck and turning in her nametag?" I just stood there, my heart racing, waiting for her to tell me. "She told me that she'd had enough. I mean of America. She said she couldn't take it anymore. She told me she was going to leave the country. Can you imagine?"

"She ran away?"

"That's exactly right; she ran away. Now can you think of a crazier thing than that? She said she was going to move to Europe and try to work in a school over there, teaching English. *But aren't you going to miss home?* I asked her. *Miss what?* she came back to me. *Dead malls and half-empty strip malls and another minimum wage job and thousands of foreclosed homes and never-ending cars on never-ending freeways and shit food and unaffordable healthcare and a total lack of concern for the arts and educating our youth and the psychotic obsession with all these endless wars and*—Well, by the end of her little speech I could tell that she'd gone a bit loopy and, you know, like *Socialist.*" Then she just stood there, staring at me. "You look familiar," she said at last, still frowning. "I think I've seen your face before in the paper."

I took a step away from her.

"Wait a minute. You're that girl who won a week with Fiona Wonder."

I took another step away, turning toward the exit.

"Wait a minute! I want your autograph. I want an autograph from the girl who's going to spend a week with Fiona Wonder, the movie star."

I felt like running.

"You're a prime example of all the great things that can still happen in this country of ours. You're the reason why I know it's going to be okay, because the most amazing thing, like winning a week with a real live movie star, can still happen to any of us. That's why Sybil is crazy for leaving. Doesn't she know that this is still the greatest country on Earth? Hey, where are you going? Don't go. What about the autograph?"


*E*ven though it was already past three in the afternoon, Valerie still had on her pajamas—a white T-shirt and plaid boxer shorts—when she swung open the front door of her house. I could see the outline of her extended stomach and big breasts.

For a moment we just stood there, staring at each other. I had been wondering what she would say to me after our telephone conversation yesterday—I mean telling her the truth about Robin and how he'd asked me to

Junior Prom. I thought maybe as soon as she saw me she'd do something drastic, like get a mug from the kitchen and fill it with hot water and throw it at me. "Is that all brought with you?" she said to me at last. She looked at the backpack that I held in my right hand.

"Yes."

"Well, don't just stand there; come inside."

Wordlessly, I followed her as she started to walk up the stairs to her bedroom. The house felt quiet, big and empty, full of unsaid thoughts. Everything was beautiful as always—big and spacious, perfectly in order. It felt clean, but in a bad way: too sterile. Like an operating room. I stopped walking as the realization hit me that the suffering of others had paid for all this stuff.

At the end of the long hallway the white double doors that led to her parents' master bedroom were closed. When Valerie reached the door to her bedroom, she turned back to look at me. "How come you're just standing there?"

"Can we go back downstairs to the kitchen? I didn't have any breakfast and I don't feel so well. I think I need to eat something."

She screwed up her face at me: "I just ate."

As usual, her room was a mess. The air smelled slightly rank. A big pile of dirty clothes lay in the corner near her unmade bed, the floor littered with old school papers, opened teen magazines, empty candy bar wrappers, potato chip bags, an empty cheeseburger box, and our junior year high school yearbook. I looked down at the yearbook, then quickly away. She had opened it to page 123, the sports section, and more specifically to the picture of the JV baseball team. I followed her gaze to the bathroom connected to her room. The light was on, the door ajar. I saw it—the iridescent orange dress with the threads of smoky gray and black—hanging on a hanger attached to the shower rod.

"Hey, Val, about our conversation on the phone

221

yesterday..."

"I don't want to talk about that!" she said as she picked up a pair of jeans and a T-shirt from the floor, stormed into the bathroom and slammed the door behind her. When she came out ten minutes later she had changed clothes. She sat on her bed. There was no place for me to sit down, so I just stood there watching her bite at a fingernail.

"So what do you want to do?" she said finally.

I felt my stomach rumble.

"Nobody's home," she said.

I placed my backpack on the floor.

"What'd you bring to wear tonight for Gretchen's party?" she wanted to know.

"What I'm wearing now."

"Oh."

I saw her eyes move toward the bathroom and the dress hanging on the hanger. "You want to go to the mall?"

"No."

"You want to look through the yearbook and—"

"No."

She stood up. "This is boring. We've got to do something. Let's go downstairs and play some pinball and—"

That's when we heard the sound of an engine. Both Valerie and I looked out her bedroom window to see a big white truck with chrome wheels and a sound system pounding out music pull into the driveway. Turning away from the window, Valerie said, "It's just my brother and what's-his-name. The pitcher. You know, Randy. Come on, let's go see what they're doing." I didn't move a muscle. Her face turned red with anger. "I said *come on*!" she yelled at me.

We found them in the basement, sitting together on the sofa watching a boxing match on television. The sling still cradled Jeremy's arm, and Randy wore the same shiny silver knee-length shorts he was wearing on Tuesday.

"Who is it?" Jeremy wanted to know.

Randy turned to look at us. "It's just your sister," he answered, "and her friend—the one whose mom works at BONANZA BURGER."

"You mean *used* to work there," Jeremy said. "The restaurant's closing."

"No, it's not. Who told you that?"

"I heard it from Ally, who heard it from Gretchen, who heard it from Courtney."

"You mean Chicken Livers?"

Jeremy nodded.

"You knew about this?" Randy said, looking at me. When I did not respond he just shrugged and turned back toward the TV and the boxers in the ring.

"It doesn't matter to me if the restaurant closes," he said at last. "I'm still young and have my future in front of me." He looked back and smiled. He waited for me to respond. But when I didn't he got bored and turned back to the television screen and asked Jeremy if he wanted to watch a baseball game.

"Whatever," Jeremy replied, still facing forward. "Who's playing?"

"No, I mean at Chesterfield Park. I was asked to umpire some of the little league games this summer, but I told them no way, because it would take up too much of my time. Rob did it though."

"You mean Robin?" Valerie chimed in.

"Yeah," Randy said, not looking back at her.

"Let's go," she said.

Jeremy groaned, still facing forward. "Um, excuse me. Who says you're invited?"

"Oh, come on. I'm bored. Please!"

Randy turned round to look at her again.

"Please, can we go?" Valerie said again.

His eyes went from her to me then back to her.

"Yeah," he decided, "you can go."

*W*e were packed like sardines into the cab of Randy's white pickup—Randy in the driver's seat, of course, Jeremy next to Randy, then me because both brother and sister stated clearly their disdain to sit next to one another, and Valerie in the window seat. The music pounded out of the stereo system. When "Love the Way you Lie" started to play on the radio Valerie screamed out the lyrics. My head started to pound from the loud music. I felt a little sick. I wasn't sure if it was the music, or Valerie screaming next to me, or the fact that I hadn't eaten since Nikki had made those ham and cheese sandwiches the night before, but my stomach was rolling and my head was throbbing.

"Valerie, shut up!" Jeremy screamed at her, but she just kept singing.

Randy did not drive us to the park as he said he would. Instead he drove into the mall parking lot. There were no cars. He hit the gas hard and cut a cookie. Valerie held onto the roll bar and shrieked and squealed with approval.

"You like that, huh?" Randy said. He grinned with his tongue sticking out of his mouth. His eyes flashed as he kept turning the wheel, guiding the truck in tighter and tighter circles.

"This is boring," he announced suddenly. "We need more action. There's nothing to hit here."

He veered the truck toward Coleanne's parking lot. There were still cars parked there—cars and people. Just as he hit the gas again, the truck barreling headlong toward the doors of the department store, I saw the sales lady in the blue pantsuit make her way from the entrance to her car. I remembered that she had looked at me scornfully when I'd told her to forget about my autograph, because she had it all wrong: I wasn't going anywhere next week.

"Careful!" Jeremy shouted and pointed at her.

Randy laughed. "Maybe I ought to flatten that ugly old bitch!"

She looked like a deer caught in the headlights. The tires screeched, stopping the truck just in time. She looked back at us, her hand over her heart, open-mouthed, terrified.

Randy couldn't stop laughing. "Stupid old bitch!" he shouted through the open window.

I closed my eyes and tried to picture my teacher, Sybil Starburn, on a plane leaving the country. She wasn't the crazy one, I had told the sales lady. *We* were the ones that were insane.

Randy drove the truck onto the highway, hit the gas to accelerate. "Faster!" Valerie told him. She looked like she was having the time of her life. "Let's cut more cookies. Let's do it in Dad's office parking lot!" she screamed at the top of her lungs.

"No way!" Jeremy screamed back at her.

"Turn right, Randy. Go for it!"

He jerked the steering wheel over three lanes and onto the familiar off ramp that led to Dr. Redding's office. A few minutes later we were in the parking lot. Randy began to rev the engine.

"Louder," Valerie said. "Louder!" she screamed.

"Hey, you two, cut it out!" Jeremy said. He readjusted his arm in the sling. He looked really annoyed now—and also a little scared. "What happens if Jeannette comes out here and sees us? And what about Dad?"

I thought of Dr. Redding last night—the way he'd looked as he came out of his office, as if something were seriously wrong. Like he had just gotten the news that he needed surgery and that it was going to cost him a fortune.

It was Jeremy who convinced Randy to leave the parking lot. Because he didn't know where to go next, he ended up driving down the same road that Kurt had driven Mom and Nikki and Gabriel and me down to watch the drive-in movie from afar. He swerved the truck onto the unpaved road and it wasn't long before the chain link fence appeared. After the movie had ended last night, Kurt had driven slowly down the hill, reopened the gate, got back into the truck, drove through it, then got out again and pushed it closed. Of course he couldn't re-lock the lock that he had broken with the wire cutters.

"Turn around," I said.

Randy shot me a look. "Did you say something? Did the mouse actually speak?" He looked at me murderously: "I mean *squeak*."

He put his foot on the gas and plowed through the gate at top speed, mangling it.

Valerie peeled with laughter.

I saw the oak trees then the willow tree where I'd sat the night before, where Gabriel had come to talk to me, to ask me why I was so angry. Randy drove past it, the tires spinning and kicking up grass and mud. The truck worked its way up the hill. Any minute now we'd be at the top. We would see the blank white screen of the outdoor movie theater where last night Fiona Wonder's face had shown as big and bright as a planet.

"I said turn around. Don't go up there!" I screamed.

Randy's foot tapped hard on the brake. "All right," he said. It came out more as a growl.

I should have closed my eyes. If I had closed my eyes, then I would not have seen the truck reach the crest of the hill. I would not have seen the movie screen—except I did. A couple of seconds later Randy spun the wheel and began to work the truck back down the hill. I slumped down in my seat.

"I'm hungry!" Valerie announced.

"Big surprise," Jeremy said underneath his breath. We stopped at Big Burgers.

"Everybody is paying for their own food," Randy announced as we pulled up to the drive through. The ordering commenced. Randy and Valerie wanted the same thing: the number three combo meal—a bacon double cheeseburger, an extra large order of French fries and a soda. Jeremy wanted a fish sandwich, taters and a chocolate milkshake. Randy looked at me. "What about you?"

I dug into my pocket and retrieved a handful of loose change. In total I had thirty-two cents. I craned my neck and looked at the prices of the items on the Value Meal menu. I didn't even have enough money to buy a plain hamburger or a small order of fries. "Well?" Randy said, looking at me impatiently.

I put the loose change back in my pocket. "Nothing," I said.

"*Nothing*," he mimicked me underneath his breath. Looking out the passenger window, Valerie snickered. All three of them dove into their food as soon as he had parked the truck.

"Are you going to Gretchen's party tonight?" Randy asked Jeremy. He took a huge bite of the bacon double cheeseburger.

"Probably not... I have to get up early tomorrow for Dad's office barbeque."

"You like college?" Randy asked him.

Jeremy just shrugged.

"I bet the parties are great."

"They're okay."

"The girls, too?"

"They're okay."

"Better than high school, I'll bet. I mean the parties and the girls."

"High school's not so bad. I sort of miss it," Jeremy said. He looked down, studied the uneaten fish sandwich in the wrapper on top of his lap.

"You're pre-med, right?" Randy asked him.

"Yeah..." He took the uneaten fish sandwich and stuffed it back inside the grease-soaked paper bag that the woman at the drive-thru had handed to Randy.

"Are you going to be a pulmonologist, like your dad?"

"Yeah," Jeremy said, unblinking, and stared out the truck's front window.

Randy stuffed the last of the burger in his mouth. "That's cool. There's good money in that. As for me, I'm majoring in business. One day," he said, "I'm going to own a string of chain restaurants. That is, if I don't make it as a pitcher in the majors."

Nobody said anything for a few minutes.

"You should give Mercy your number," Valerie said at last.

"You're talking to me?" Randy said.

"Yes."

"Why would I do that? You think I want to date her?"

"No, of course not; I know you don't."

"Then why would I give her my number?"

"In case you don't make it to the majors and end up owning those restaurants," Valerie told him. "Then you can give her a job when she becomes a waitress just like her mother."

Randy laughed: "That's harsh."

"I'm just telling the truth."

"That's the way she talks about her friends? Your sister is a real bitch," Randy said, still laughing, to Jeremy.

Jeremy just sat there, staring straight ahead. He shrugged.

Valerie finished eating. Without looking at me, she passed the empty burger box, French fry container and soda to Jeremy, who stuffed it inside the paper bag with his uneaten fish sandwich. He took the container of uneaten taters and his half-finished milkshake and put it in the bag too. Then he passed it to Randy, who stuffed his trash inside it before throwing it out the window. It landed in a bush. Valerie snorted: "Pig!"

We were off, back on the highway, past CostMart and Patriot Plaza. The driving, as usual, was reckless, out of control, manic. Randy drove the truck off the highway and onto a road that led into a residential community. About fifteen minutes later we ended up at breakneck speed inside the parking lot at Chesterfield Park.

Valerie had to stop, bend down and place both her hands on her stomach as soon as we got out of the truck. She belched, loudly. She said that she felt like barfing. Ahead of her Randy and her brother Jeremy did not wait. They walked in the direction of the baseball field. She came close to upchucking but was able to hold it down, barely.

"Are you sure you're okay?" I asked as we started to walk again toward the field.

"Just don't talk to me!"

It was not difficult to honor her request. After a good amount of searching we found her brother and Randy sitting about halfway up on the bleachers behind home plate. By then it was dusk, and the dirt on the baseball field looked yellow. I took in a big breath and smelled the cut grass. The backstop behind home plate looked twenty-feet-tall. There were parents down there, clinging onto the fence, some shouting encouragement to the kids from the two little league teams playing each other on the field. The players looked like they were around age eight. The team on the field wore red shirts with stark white letters. They were called the Bulls. The other team, the one at bat, had on sky blue shirts with dark blue letters. They were called the Astros.

"There's Robin," Valerie said, sounding a little out of breath. She pointed at the umpire standing behind the catcher at home plate.

The scoreboard tallied the Bulls winning by three runs. It was the beginning of the ninth inning and the losing Astros were coming up for their last turn at bat. The first batter struck out. The second batter struck out. The third batter was hit by a pitch. Randy seemed to like it when that happened. The fourth walked. The fifth reached first base by catcher interference. The sixth batter, number 8, walked to the plate as a chorus of groans and moans escaped from the stands.

The kid was short and scrawny, all bony knees and

elbows. The helmet he wore was too big for him. His sleeves went down below his elbows. One of his shoes was untied. He swung twice and missed twice. It looked like he was shaking.

Someone booed, then another. I heard one man say to another, "Well, it's over now that that kid is up." The other man agreed and said, "Yep. There's no way that we're going to win with him at bat."

Dressed entirely in black, Robin stood slightly crouched with the umpire's mask over his face. Randy screamed at the pitcher: "Strike him out!" The ball flew. The bat connected. We could actually hear the sound, "whack"!

For a minute the boy just stood there, looking up at the ball, amazed. That's when Robin touched the boy's shoulder to give him a nudge of encouragement, and the kid started running. The ball landed between two outfielders and continued to roll. The kid on third base scored easily, as the kid who had been on second rounded third and kept running. He, too, made it to home plate. The kid who had been on first ran like the wind. Without much of an effort at all he made it to home plate, and the game was tied. One more run and the Astros would win the game. By then number 8, the boy who had hit the unlikely line drive, had gotten to third base. One of the coaches motioned with his arm, swinging it forward, and yelled, "Keep going! Slide at home plate. Slide!"

"There's going to be a collision!" Randy exclaimed. He looked excited now, standing up and waiting expectantly for the impact between the runner and the catcher. The kid was running as fast as he could, while at the same time the ball was relayed to the catcher. Behind home plate Robin crouched down low. The kid slid into home plate with his tongue hanging out of his mouth and a fierce look of anticipation, and terror too, on his face. Poor Number 8, an outcast right fielder, a pinch hitter, was scrawny and pathetic as a ball player, yet he wanted so badly to win the game for his team—at least that's the way I saw it. Did Robin see that too?

As he slid into home plate at the same time the ball arrived in the catcher's glove the dust rose then settled. It was only a second—although it felt like eternity—before Robin drew his hands as flat as the horizon and called out so that everyone could hear, "SAFE!"

The crowd erupted: relieved, surprised, joyful. Number 8 looked up at Robin as though he couldn't believe it. All the other kids from the Astros ran toward the boy. They lifted him above their shoulders and carried him off the field.

Randy looked angry. He crossed his arms over his chest. He let out a big wad of spit from his mouth onto the bleachers in front of him. "Nice call, Rob," he said under his breath.

I watched Robin take the mask off his face. I saw him look over at the child—neither smiling nor frowning, but knowingly. Instantly, I knew what he had done and why he had done it.

"Come on, let's go," said Randy, sounding disgusted. His eyes met mine and held my gaze. "What?" he wanted to know.

"You were telling the truth about my mom waiting on you at Waffle Falafel on the night of Junior Prom."

He paused a moment, then said, "So?"

"I just wanted to tell you that I know now that you were telling the truth."

He didn't say anything.

"Did you throw something at her, Randy?" He looked surprised but remained mute. "Did you throw a bottle of ketchup at my mother?"

"What if I did?" he said at last. "If I told you I did, then what would you do about it?"

"I wouldn't do anything," I whispered. "I just want to know."

He paused. He looked at Robin, who was watching the

boy that had just won the ball game. "Yes, I did," he said, turning back to me. "But it wasn't my fault. I mean about the ketchup getting all over her. I didn't know that the cap wasn't screwed on tight. I didn't know it was going to fly all over the front of her when it hit her. It was really her fault, not mine. I mean she could have caught it. You know what I mean?"

Back inside the truck, Randy started the engine and drove us back to the Redding's house in silence.

$M$rs. Redding sat alone with a glass of white wine at the dining room table, looking down at her hands, her face expressionless, when Valerie, Jeremy and I came into the house.

"Hey, Mom," said Jeremy.

She looked up at him: "Oh, Hello."

"You okay, Mom?"

She straightened in her chair, picked up her glass and took a sip of wine. That's when Dr. Redding came out of the kitchen, holding a big drink in his hand.

"Hey, Dad," Jeremy said.

"Son," Dr. Redding said.

"Kids..." Mrs. Redding started to say.

"Don't," he stopped her.

She took a gulp of wine, her hands clearly shaking, and then set the glass down on the table. "Yes, you're right. I'm sorry."

"Your mother and I are just having a little conversation," Dr. Redding said.

"Got it," Jeremy said and made his way downstairs.

"Valerie," Dr. Redding said, "your mother ordered you and your friend a pizza for dinner. It should be here in a minute. There's money for the delivery boy on the table in the foyer."

"What are you talking about?" Valerie wanted to know. That's when the doorbell rang for the pizza.

Inside Valerie's bedroom we ate the pizza. It wasn't very good and I started to gag—I couldn't eat another bite. "What's wrong with you?" she demanded.

I set down the slice of pizza. "I just can't finish," I said.

Sitting cross-legged next to me on the floor, she went back to eating and told me, her mouth full of food, that she was going to start getting ready for the party.

That's when we heard them. They were still downstairs so their voices were muffled. It was real low at first, then louder and louder, then a bit frantic. I always wondered what it would be like to hear them fight. When Nikki and Kurt fought it was a knock-down, drag-out war: it was passionate. Not the Reddings! I'd seen them fight once— the night that Dr. Redding had told Lady that he didn't like the dress that she had chosen for the art museum's annual Christmas party. I'd seen how he dominated her so easily, and how she allowed it to happen.

Then we heard them coming up the stairs—Mrs. Redding calling after Dr. Redding.

Valerie got up as quickly as possible from the floor and announced that she was going to take a shower. She told me that I should listen to some music or watch a movie or do something, she didn't care: she'd be out in half an hour. She closed the door to the bathroom behind her. A moment late I heard the water running in the shower.

I got up from the floor, went to the bedroom door, and opened it just a crack. There they were on the landing near the double doors to their bedroom.

"Wait a minute, Rob," she said.

"Do I have to explain it all over again, Lady?"

"I just don't understand..."

"You don't understand what? The fact that it's over, finished." He sighed heavily. Placing both his hands on the railing he looked down at the great room. "Look," he said, his voice sounding hard and disciplined, "the accountant has been over it a million times. We've simply reached a point of insolvency. The cost of drugs has skyrocketed, the insurance companies won't pay what they owe us on time, there are more and more people coming in who don't even have insurance and—"

"But Rob, it just can't be."

"And those investments!" he said. "They've all gone south. I knew that I shouldn't have listened to those gamblers—"

"But what does it mean?" Desperation filled her voice.

"It means, goddamn it, that we're going to have to close the practice."

"Oh, my God," she said.

"It means that we're bankrupt. It means, probably, that we're going to have to sell this house, or at least try to sell it, and after that, if we're lucky, we're going to have to downsize our entire life. Jeremy might have to quit school. Valerie won't go at all. I'll start applying to hospitals as soon as possible, although the competition is fierce, and I don't know how easily I'll be able to find a resident physician position. We might have to move to another state. By the time we get settled again it could take months, or even longer. In the meantime, you'll have to find a job."

"You're not serious," she said.

"We're seriously broke, Lady."

She pinched her forehead with her fingers. "I can't believe it."

"It's not the end of the world." He spat out the words at her.

"Rob, are you sure that there isn't some mistake? Are you sure that this accountant isn't just—I mean—maybe he's wrong. Maybe you need a second opinion. When people go to the doctor and hear a diagnosis that they don't really want to hear, or one they find hard to believe, then they always get a second opinion..."

He spun from the railing to face her: "This is not my fault!"

"I never meant to imply that it—"

"This is what happens in a recession! People lose their

jobs, can't find new jobs, go broke, can't afford health insurance, and can't afford to pay *me*."

"But—"

"If there's one thing that *is* my fault, it's that I let you do whatever you wanted, buy whatever you wanted, allowed you to act like a forty-four-year-old spoiled child, let you just assume that the stream of money was endless, that it grew on the venerable money tree in our back yard. Well, the tree is dead and all the leaves have fallen off. So you're just going to have to get used to it!"

He didn't help her up when she collapsed on her knees to the floor.


*I*t was about forty minutes later when Valerie emerged from the bathroom. I didn't think that she'd heard anything because of the running water and after that the hair dryer. Valerie's hair was up, she was wearing a lot of black eye makeup, and she had on the iridescent orange dress.

"So what do you think?" She actually spun for me. In truth, I thought she looked huge and red and terrifyingly ugly. "I said, what do you think, Swimmer?" Valerie walked to the plastic mirror—the one from Spinner's that made her looked misshapen and contorted. "Jealous?" she said, looking at herself in the mirror.

I looked up at her. "What?"

"You heard me, you're jealous. Don't try to pretend it's not true. You always have been and always will be jealous of me. That's why you lied to me yesterday on the telephone about Robin asking you to Junior Prom."

I stood up from her bed. "Valerie, I did not lie to you."

She refused to turn around and look at me. "Yes, you did. He never would have asked you. No offence or anything. You're just not good enough for him." She looked at her ugly reflection in the mirror one more time, then turned and walked over to me. "The truth hurts, I'm sure. But it's okay; I forgive you."

I opened my mouth but found no words to answer her. "Let's just go to the party," I said to her.

*W*e walked silently through the darkened neighborhood, our entrance fee to the party, a six-pack of Valerie's father's beer, hugged tightly to her chest. Her dress swished back and forth as she walked. She seemed nervous. Her breathing quickened with each step. We walked up a hill, around a bend, down the street with the big yellow speed hump, past a house with a smiling ceramic pig by the front porch, and turned right onto Gretchen's street. When Gretchen's house appeared, the inside lit up with silhouetted bodies moving from window to window, I clutched at the bracelet on my wrist. It was the only thing I had left.

Chad Westerberg, a senior with spiky hair and a lot of acne, spilled beer on my shirt. That's the first thing that happened. It deteriorated quickly from there. When she saw us making our way from the front hall to the kitchen, Gretchen rolled her eyes and made a face at Ally, who stood with Randy in the family room near the stereo system. In the kitchen, Valerie downed a cherry vodka shot, then another. Behind us a girl said, "Nice dress," and the comment was quickly followed by high pitched laughter.

"Come on," she said to me, and huffed out of the kitchen back to the staircase. We walked around, Valerie pretending like she was having a good time, and when that wore off, we walked around looking for someone (I knew who it was we were looking for) and then pretending not to pretend that actually it had been a mistake to come, that nobody wanted to talk to us, that everyone was really hoping that we'd leave soon, especially Valerie, and that that dress looked hideous on her, and what was she thinking, anyway? And, you know, don't say anything to piss her off because look out—she'd find a car to ram into yours, because that was Valerie Redding, a rich, fat nut case for you... Angry fat girl! Angry fat girl! The freak in the dress that made her look like the planet Mars, or the Princess of War.

Valerie was back in the kitchen, doing more vodka shots, when Robin Bell arrived just before midnight. He didn't look like an umpire anymore, I was relieved to see. He had on blue jeans and a blue shirt, tennis shoes and no baseball cap. When he saw me standing alone near the foot of the staircase he waved and started to walk toward me.

"Robin!" Ally screamed and threw her arms around him. "I'm so bored. Come dance with me!"

He looked uncomfortable. He slowly unhooked her arms from his neck. "Maybe later," he said.

"Oh, come on!" Ally said.

"I'll dance with you," said Randy. He had turned up the volume on the stereo so that the song playing, a Nicki Minaj tune, nearly shook the walls.

"Turn that down. I hate her. She's into Satan!" Ally yelled at him.

Randy looked like she had just slapped him in the face. "Bitch!" he said.

She just laughed at him.

"Hey!" Randy yelled and grabbed her arm.

"Let go of me!" Ally screamed back at him.

I couldn't take it anymore. I ran outside to the front lawn. I would have kept running except it was after midnight, Valerie was still inside with the key to her house, and I had nowhere to go. I walked to a tree by the driveway and sat down at its trunk.

I already knew he had followed me outside even before I heard the sound of his voice. "Mercy," Robin said to me, just like Gabriel had said to me last night, "is it okay if I sit down?"

But he didn't wait for me to answer. He just sat next to me, leaning his back against the bark of the tree. A few minutes went by, and then he touched the shooting star bracelet on my wrist. He asked me, softly, "Have you decided yet, Wonder? Whether or not you're going to trade it for a telescope?"

I yanked my hand away. "Don't call me that."

"Sorry," he said.

"Don't call me that ever again."

"I said I was sorry. I won't call you that anymore."

He took a pen out of his pocket. "May I?" he said softly, carefully. He reached again for my hand, careful not to touch the bracelet. I let him take the pen and write something on my arm. I couldn't see what it was because it was too dark.

"Just in case you ever want to talk," he said to me. "Or just in case you ever want to look at stars with me."

I didn't want to think about it. If I thought about it too long, then I might start to cry. Then I didn't feel like I'd cry—I felt anger. Anger at him!

"I saw what you did today," I told him. "At the baseball game..."

"What?" he said, bewildered. "You mean the game that I umpired today? You were there?"

"I was there with Randy and Valerie and Jeremy. We watched the ninth inning. I saw what you did on the last play of the game. I saw that you purposely blew the call. That kid, number 8, he wasn't safe at all. And you knew it. But you felt sorry for him. So you called him 'safe'. I saw it, and I think it was wrong. You can't go around doing things like that—like you're God or something, like you think you know what's best. Because maybe, for all you know, you've actually caused more harm than good. You can't go around trying to make things better when they're not supposed to be better. They're supposed to be the way that they are."

He was listening. I got up.

"Hey, Mercy, wait," he said and got up too.

"You shouldn't have done it," I said again and started to walk away.

That's when I saw Valerie standing at the front door of Gretchen's house, looking drunk and upset. She looked from Robin, to me, then back to Robin, then back to me. "Dirty lying white trash whore!" she screamed at me and came barreling down the steps, across the lawn, in the direction of Robin. It looked like she was going to plow right into him. Robin looked right at her, not moving. He was going to take the hit. If that's what needed to happen, he was going to take it. At the very second she veered off course, decided not to collide. Instead she just kept running, screaming her head off, away from the house, the lawn, the party, and of course, Robin.

"Mercy, wait!" Robin called after me when I went after Valerie.

Up the sidewalk she had stopped running. She bent down, her head almost touching the front lawn of the house with the ceramic pig statue near the front porch, and threw up. I waited. It was late—nearing one in the morning—and dead quiet except for the sound of Valerie retching and the barely noticeable hum of electricity surging through the street lamps.

Valerie stopped throwing up. She straightened, staggered, almost fell down, regained her balance, put the back of her wrist to her mouth and wiped away some of the cherry-red vomit from her lower lip. "I don't want to be friends anymore," she said, her voice barely a whisper.

"That's fine with me," I told her. "I don't want to be friends with you anymore either."

It was settled.

She started to stumble along the sidewalk again, dizzy and out of breath. I thought about walking the other way. I thought about how good it would feel to just disappear into the night. But then I remembered that Robin was back there and how much I didn't want to see him. Or did I? I didn't look down at my arm to see what he had written. Whatever it was, I would wash it off. But first I needed to pick up my backpack from Valerie's house.

"I don't think I can make it back. I think I'll just sleep here on the grass," Valerie moaned. And then in the darkness, walking on the sidewalk, she appeared: Mrs. Redding. She had on a pair of blue jeans and a white T-shirt, her hair tied back with a ribbon, without makeup. Everything about her looked plain and unremarkable. Not beautiful at all. Just fed up, seething mad, ragged and tired.

"Valerie!" she said harshly, walking fast towards us. "Do you know how long I've been looking for you? You need to come home right now!" She drew closer to her daughter, then immediately stepped away. "You smell like throw-up."

"That's because I just threw up, stupid," Valerie slurred at her.

"Are you drunk?"

Valerie started laughing.

"Answer me! Are you drunk?"

Valerie screamed her answer: "Yes!"

Mrs. Redding's face went even whiter than normal. "Come with me!" she said sharply and went to grab Valerie's arm.

"Don't touch me!" Valerie screamed.

"Be quiet!" Mrs. Redding screamed back at her. "You'll wake the entire neighborhood."

"I don't care," Valerie said. Then she screamed it: "I don't fucking care!"

"Valerie, be quiet!"

"No!"

"Yes!"

"I said no!"

Mrs. Redding slapped her, hard, across her face.

She sobered up immediately. For the longest time she just stood there, her hand over her cheek where her mother had struck her.

A high pitched, strange noise came out of Mrs. Redding: "This isn't happening," she squealed. She placed her trembling hands to her chest. She looked crazed.

"None of this is happening. We are not standing here right now. We are not—"

"Mommy, you hurt me," Valerie said, her hand still pressed against her cheek. She started to cry.

"This isn't the way it's supposed to—"

"You hurt me, Mommy!"

"I'm not supposed to be here, Mercy," she said as she turned to look at me. "I want my life back. I want it back! Like those big clouds at the bottom of the Georgia O'Keefe painting. I want to go back to those big white clouds. I want to start over!"

Valerie started screaming.

"I want to start over!"

Valerie couldn't stop screaming. She bent her head down and charged like a wild boar, ramming right into her mother. They landed in the front yard, rolled, and ended up a couple of feet away from the ceramic pig. On top of her mother, Valerie continued to scream. She started clawing at her mother. Then Mrs. Redding started to claw too.

"Get off of me!" I heard Lady Redding scream. "I want it back. Oh, God, help me! I want it back!"

I took one more look at them then started to walk in the direction of Valerie's house.

In the doorframe Dr. Redding's short and chubby body blocked the light as well as my view of the mirror and the vase of flowers on the table in the foyer. He waited to speak until I had walked up the driveway and to the front door. "I just got a phone call," he told me. "You'd better hurry up and get your things together."

# SATURDAY

$\int$he had been taken to the same hospital as before, the one where Nikki and Kurt and I had sat with her in the waiting room for hours and hours, waiting for help, waiting for mercy, but none had come, and she had gotten better on her own. She had been able to muster all her strength and take care of herself. Because that's what she did. That's what she'd always done.

Dr. Redding hadn't seemed to notice his wife and daughter rolling around on the grass of his neighbor's yard, wrestling, screaming and fighting, as he drove away. He didn't notice the shadow of a boy—Robin—standing a few yards away, watching them then turning to watch the car with us inside speeding past him.

On the highway, just past Heritage Mall, Dr. Redding told me what the man on the telephone had told him. My mother had had an asthma attack, collapsed, lost consciousness and stopped breathing during her graveyard shift at Waffle Falafel. The man had called 911. He'd given her CPR. She still had not responded when the paramedics arrived, so they gave her oxygen. Now she was in the

242

hospital. She hadn't woken up. She was in a coma. She wasn't dead, but she wasn't alive either.

Dr. Redding looked at me sideways in the car. "Has your mom suffered from asthma for a long time?" he wanted to know.

I didn't feel like talking to him about her condition. "What was the name of the man on the telephone?" I wanted to know. "Did he say what his name was?"

Dr. Redding had to think about it for a minute. He said, finally, "He said his name but I can't remember it now. He wasn't a doctor or a nurse. He said that he was a friend of your mother's. He said that in your mother's pocket he'd found a piece of paper with our telephone number on it. He said that he'd be there at the hospital when you arrived, and that he'd be waiting for you in the Emergency Room."

Dr. Redding pulled into the hospital parking lot. "I'll come inside with you if you want me to," he said. But he refused to look at me. "I don't know if you know this, but I'm a pulmonologist. I'm a lung specialist. If you'd like, then—"

I got out of the car and slammed the door behind me.

*I* thought maybe it really wasn't happening, that it was all a cruel joke and that when I went through the sliding glass doors that I'd see her there, sitting on a chair, catching her breath, with Kurt and Nikki beside her, because that's what had happened last time.

But there was no Nikki, and no Kurt. There was just Gabriel, sitting with his hands between his legs and his head slightly bowed, waiting for me as he'd told Dr. Redding he would. When he saw me he stood up.

"Where is she?" I wanted to know.

"ICU," he said. "Come on, I'll take you there."

I followed him past the reception desk, down a long white corridor. We stopped at an elevator and waited.

When the doors opened he pushed the button to take us to the eighth floor.

"Tell me what happened," I said.

"I came to see her at Waffle Falafel about half past eleven," he told me. "Nobody else was there. It was just the two of us. I sat down and she got me some coffee and some pistachio ice cream, because that's my favorite. And then we just started talking. She was behind the counter and I was sitting opposite her. It was so nice, Mercy. It was so nice. Nobody else was there. We were just talking, and it felt so good. It felt so peaceful. She was telling me how much she loves you. She was telling me that last night she felt so bad, and about wanting you to be proud of her, and that she couldn't concentrate at all on the movie. And then she unpinned her nametag from her uniform and looked down at it. She asked me if I had noticed that her name was misspelled. And I said, yes, I had noticed. And she said that she wanted to fix it. That she should have fixed it a long time ago. So I said, 'Well, why don't you then?' And she said, 'That's exactly what I'm going to do.' Then she went into the kitchen to get a pen. When she came back, Mercy, she looked so happy. She had a pen with her. And she took the pen, and then—"

He stopped talking when the elevator door opened. I turned right and he turned left. "Her room is this way," he said and held out his hand to me.

I took it and we walked past the nurse's station, down another long white corridor.

"Keep telling me," I whispered. "Don't stop."

He stopped walking and let go of my hand.

"Suddenly she started wheezing. She couldn't stop." His back hit the wall. He closed his eyes. Big teardrops started falling from his closed lids. "She couldn't stop wheezing, and she had this pitcher full of ice water, and then the pitcher just dropped from her hand. The pitcher dropped and shattered. And then she collapsed. I ran behind the counter. She had already started turning blue.

244

And I couldn't do anything. Oh, Jesus! Oh, God! I couldn't do anything for her. So I called 911—immediately! I listened to what the paramedic on the other end said to me. I listened to this woman on the other end of the telephone tell me how to get air into her lungs. And I tried. Mercy, I promise you, I tried! But she just kept turning blue. She just couldn't—"

He couldn't talk anymore. He was crying too much. He turned from the wall, walked across the hallway and opened a door.


*T*hat's where Mom was, alone in a bed, hooked up to a respirator. Her uniform was gone and she was dressed in a hospital gown. They'd taken her ponytail out and her hair was all around her, spreading out like the feathers of a bird. The respirator was the only sound in the room. It made a sucking sound. It sucked in, and Mom's chest expanded; it sucked out and Mom's lungs deflated.

"The doctor," Gabriel told me, "said it was Status Asthma-something. I can't remember now, but both her lungs collapsed. She went into cardiac arrest."

We just stood there, looking at her. Then after a while he got a chair and pushed it up to the bed. "Sit down," he told me.

I went to sit then changed my mind. Suddenly there were other people in the room—Nikki and Kurt. They looked sleep deprived, upset, scared. "Hi, honey," Nikki said to me. She moved to give me a hug. I pushed her away.

Gabriel said to them, "Let's leave them alone for a while, okay? Let's go to the cafeteria and—"

"No, I don't want to be alone with her!" I shouted and ran out of the room.

I paced the hallway outside of Mom's room. I heard Kurt and Nikki and Gabriel talking softly to each other. I heard the respirator sucking in and out. A nurse dressed in pink scrubs went into the room. I heard her tell them that the room was too crowded, that they'd have to clear out. They could come back in half an hour. There was a coffee machine at the end of the hallway near the elevators, she told them, and some chairs where they could wait.

"But I want to be here when she wakes up," I heard Nikki tell the nurse.

The nurse said something back to Nikki that I couldn't hear.

The four of us walked wordlessly down the hallway to the coffee machine and waiting area.

*H*ours passed, the entire night. A nurse came and changed the channel on the television. The local weatherman on channel four said it was six-fifteen in the morning, currently 75 degrees outside, blue skies, no chance of rain, a beautiful Saturday morning. Nikki, who had gone with Kurt to have a cigarette outside, came up to me. "Hey, kiddo, you look tired," she said. "How about I drive you home so you can sleep for a couple of hours?"

I shook my head.

"Are you sure?"

"Yes."

"It's going to be okay, Mercy. She's going to wake up."

I stared at the television screen. "What if she doesn't?"

I could feel her wince. She said, after a long pause, "Listen, baby, I'll ask Kurt to go to your place to get some things for you, like a hairbrush and toothbrush, a change of clothes, some magazines..."

"Okay," I said.

"I'll stay here with you."

"Okay."

"I'm going to find Kurt now, but I'll be right back."

"Okay."

She turned to walk away.

"Nikki?" I said, stopping her.

"What is it?"

"What happens if she doesn't wake up?"

Her face went white. Slowly she walked back to me. She placed her hand softly on my shoulder. "Then you'll come live with Kurt and me."

"You don't have to say that. You don't even like me."

She sat down next to me, put her arms around me and held me tight. "I *do* have to say that. I *do* love you."

"Okay," I said, my head buried on her shoulder. "Okay, okay. Thank you. I love you, too."

When she raised my head I could see that she was crying.

"She's going to wake up, goddamn it," she told me, then marched out of the waiting room.

I found myself nodding off. When I woke up I looked across the room to see Nikki and Kurt sitting side by side on two chairs, a suitcase next to Kurt's legs.

"I didn't have to pack anything," Kurt told me. "When I went to your place I found this by the front door."

I stared at the suitcase, not understanding.

"Your mother must have packed it for you," Nikki told me.

It made sense, suddenly. She had packed the suitcase for my week with Fiona Wonder.

"What time is it?" I wanted to know.

"Just past seven in the morning," Kurt told me.

"I'll get you some orange juice, a donut and a piece of fruit from the cafeteria," Nikki said and got up from her chair.

Kurt got up too; he said he needed a cigarette.

"Did Gabriel leave?" I asked them.

"No," Nikki answered. "He's been here all night. He's sitting with her right now."

"Oh."

"We'll be back in a minute," she told me.

That's when I heard her voice on the television. I looked at the screen to see Fiona Wonder. She was on the

Saturday edition of *Wake Up, America!*

"So something really interesting is happening next week," the interviewer, a very tall and slender woman with blonde hair, said to her.

"Yes, that's right. I am going to spend a week with the girl that won the Shooting Star contest in *Almost There Magazine*."

"And when will she arrive?"

"Tomorrow."

"So how do you feel about it? I mean, are you excited?"

"Oh, yes. But honestly, I'm a little nervous."

"Why is that?"

"Just because—well, I just hope that she likes me."

"I'm sure that she will."

"Thanks. I hope so."

"And what are your plans for the week?"

"To be honest, anything that she wants. If she just wants to hang out at my place, then that's what we'll do."

"And if she wants to do something more extravagant? Like go nightclub hopping, or fly around on your private jet?"

"Oh, no, I hope not. I actually hate nightclubs. And I don't have a private jet. I fly commercial. Always have and always will."

"Is that so?"

"You know what the best thing is about flying?"

"No."

"To me, it's looking out the window at all that sky. And being above the clouds... And seeing all that endless blue sky, and the horizon in front of you... It's awesome!"

"So let's take a look at that bracelet. Show it to the camera." Fiona held up her wrist and the camera zoomed in on it. "That is absolutely gorgeous! You know, I bought one for my daughter as soon as it came out. She also sent in her receipt to *Almost There Magazine*. She was hoping to spend the week with you." Fiona Wonder smiled on cue. The interviewer said: "And the bracelets are still on sale at...?"

"What?" Fiona said, as if she had forgotten where she was. She smiled again and turned to the camera. "Yes, the bracelets are still on sale at all major department stores."

"Time & Luxingham, Pacy's, and Coleanne's?"

"That's right."

"Whatever made you decide to create the bracelet in the first place? Or have you always been interested in jewelry design as well as acting?"

"Actually, my last movie sort of bombed, so my agent thought..."

"Ha-ha-ha," the interviewer cut her off. "So what time does she arrive tomorrow?"

"Who?"

"The girl that won the contest, of course..."

"Early. Seven in the morning."

"I bet she won't sleep at all tonight, thinking about it."

"Neither will I," said Fiona. "But I really am looking forward to meeting her. I have a feeling that we're going to learn a lot from each other."

"Thanks so much for spending some time with us this morning, Fiona. And have a fabulous time next week with your new, lucky friend!" The interviewer smiled brightly into the camera. "Harold, back to you."

"Thanks, Cindy. Next up we meet Jason Hepple, a recently returned solider from Afghanistan who lost both his legs in combat but not his spirit. Now Jason has a half million-dollar contract with Nike. They will feature this amazing American hero wearing their brand new running shoes called, very appropriately, American Spirit. Hear the inspiring story next, and watch Jason test out the shoes on his two new titanium legs, live, on *America, Wake Up!*, right after this commercial break."

Gabriel's huge body suddenly blocked my view of the television screen. "How is she?" I wanted to know.

"You need to spend some time with her."

"I can't," I told him.

"Yes, you can. It's important. It's important just in case—"

"I don't know what to say to her."

"Then don't say anything. Just sit with her."

"But that doesn't feel right."

"Then you've got to figure out what does feel right."

"I'll go as soon as I eat something. Nikki went to the cafeteria to get me—"

"No," he cut me off. "Go now."

I went into her room and sat down on the chair. "Hi, Mom," I said. The respirator went in and out, in and out.

I took the bracelet off my wrist and put it on hers. I stood up, and then sat back down. I must have been crying. I couldn't feel my face, but I was vaguely aware that my cheeks were wet. It was like someone had taken a knife and sliced right through my heart.

"I didn't mean what I said about not going. I'll go. Okay, Mom? I'll go tomorrow. I'll spend a week with Fiona Wonder. I promise. But please, Mom, just wake up! Everything is going to be all right now because I'm going to go. Did you hear me? I'm going to go, because that's what you want. I want to give you what you want. Just wake up. Please, wake up."

I sat there, waiting. I looked down at her wrist with the bracelet on it then looked at my wrist. Then I turned my hand over. Robin had written his phone number in sky blue magic marker, and at the end of the number he'd placed a star.

Back in the waiting room with Gabriel, silence was our solace. I looked down at my wrist, then at his arm. "Will you tell me now what it means?" I asked.

"What, this?" he said.

"Was she a girlfriend?" I said. "Was she your wife? Or a gang that you used to run with? What?"

"Over the years," he told me, "I've seen a lot of bad things. Not just seen them but lived through them, and watched others live through them too. Mostly, people not being kind to one another. It got to the point where it was too much for me to handle—all the cruelty. I couldn't find goodness or kindness or love or hope in the world anymore. I almost decided that I didn't want to live anymore. But before that, I thought, I'm going to give it one more chance. Then I thought of the word. I just like the word," he said, softly. As he had before, he put his hand over the word. "Maravilla— it's the one thing that makes it all worthwhile, I think. So I decided to keep looking for it. I put it there to remind myself to keep looking for it. And I did find it again. I found it in your mother."

"You found *what* in her?"

"Maravilla: she's always had it."

"But what does it mean? Why won't you tell me what it means?"

He took his hand off of his tattoo and held it up to me. "It means, Wonder." And then the saddest eyes that I had ever seen in the entire world filled up with tears. "I just hope she doesn't die."

He got up after that. He had to, because he just couldn't sit there any longer. I watched him walk away, all the way down the long corridor. He turned and disappeared from view.

*T*he hours passed. Noon: Nikki and I shared a turkey sandwich, an orange and a piece of stale cake in the cafeteria. I took the suitcase that Mom had packed for me into the bathroom, unzipped it, found the toiletry bag, found my toothbrush and started to cry. Two: Kurt went to take his kids to the park. Nikki and I stood by Mom's bedside, wordless, while the doctor updated us on her condition. Four: Kurt returned. The three of us watched reruns of *Friends* and *Seinfeld* in the waiting room. Seven: More food: this time meat loaf, mashed potatoes, green beans and gelatin. Afterwards Nikki smoked three cigarettes in succession outside the ER doors. I stood next to her by a trash can, staring at my feet.

Midnight: "Where are you? Are you okay?" It sounded like I'd woken him.

"It's my mom," I told Robin, Nikki's cell phone pressed hard against my ear. "She's in a coma. She won't wake up."

"I'll come right away."

"No, don't."

"Mercy—"

"I'm supposed to go to California tomorrow. My plane leaves at six in the morning. My mom already packed a suitcase for me. This morning on *America, Wake Up!* I watched Fiona Wonder talk about it."

"You don't have to do that. You don't have to go, Mercy."

"Don't I?"

"No."

"But it's what she wants."

"What do *you* want, Wonder?"

I stared down at my feet. "You weren't supposed to call me that anymore, remember?"

"I forgot," he whispered.

"It's okay. I have to go. I'm sorry I woke you. I'm sorry that—"

"Mercy—" he said.

I hung up.


*I* went back to the waiting room with the chairs and the television. I sat down and wept openly, with feeling, while on the television Amber Dawson, a twenty-year-old movie star, made jokes about her love of fast food during her opening monologue on *Saturday Night Live*.

Her brain scan had showed little to no activity, that's what the doctor had said. Did anyone know if she had ever signed a DNR? We had to start preparing ourselves for the inevitable: that she would not wake up and simply pass away.

I slept. I dreamed I was on an airplane on my way to California. I looked out the window and saw Mom. She smiled at me and waved, then flew away toward the setting sun.

Somebody woke me up, shaking me. It was Nikki. She was sitting on one side of me, and Kurt on the other. "Mercy," she said.

Another day had passed. It was early Sunday morning. I knew immediately.

"Oh, baby," Nikki told me, "I'm so sorry. She just wasn't strong enough." Nikki broke down. "Oh God," she said. "You were right! I should have stolen an asthma inhaler. I should have at least tried!"

I got up and ran down the same long corridor that I had watched Gabriel walk down earlier. I turned the corner and saw Robin. I tried to run past him. Then everything got kind of black and fuzzy and something weird happened to my ears. It was like I was losing consciousness. It was a relief, actually.

I woke up in his arms.

"Hi," he said. "You fainted. Out cold. Good thing that I was right here to catch you. You could have hit your head."

"She's dead!" I said.

His entire face changed. He helped me up and looped his arm through my waist and helped me walk back to her room.

They'd already taken her body away. Her personal things, including the Shooting Star Bracelet that I'd placed on her wrist, were now inside a bag on the table by the bed. I took it out of the bag and placed it back on my wrist. With one hand I held onto the bag, with the other my suitcase. "I have to get out of here," I said.

Inside his truck, Robin asked me where I wanted to go. I didn't have an answer.

"I'll take you home," he said at last. But I shook my

head. "Then where," he said, "to the airport?"

I opened the plastic bag and took out Mom's Waffle Falafel nametag. I saw what she had done with a green felt pen. I saw that she had added the one missing letter to her name so that after all these years it finally read right. She was no longer Miram; she was now, finally, Mir-**I**-am.

I looked down at the Shooting Star Bracelet on my wrist. "Don't take me home. And I'm not going to the airport either. Take me to the mall," I told him.

He looked confused.

"I want to go to the astronomy shop. I want to trade the bracelet for a refractor telescope."

I looked out the windshield at sky. I could see it all ahead of me before it happened—my eye to the eyepiece of the refractor telescope. I would watch it all: Mom's funeral, our bare apartment being repainted for a new tenant, Hardman's Dem Co. demolishing Heritage Shopping Mall and the closure of Dr. Redding's private practice. Maybe if I looked hard enough I could see the person on the other end of the plane ride that I wouldn't be taking to California, holding up a sign that read WONDER/SWIMMER. I might see Ms. Starburn going the other direction, on the other side of the ocean, starting over, or Valerie, alone and miserable in her new house, wherever that might be, studying herself in the warped mirror while Randy threw balls at batters and Robin, on some peaceful grassy knoll, looked up at the night sky through his telescope. I saw her face, as big as a planet, winking back at all those who watched her, while Kurt and Nikki, and Dr. Redding and Mrs. Redding too, looked for work, and Gabriel kept searching for maravilla.

"But I thought you'd decided on a reflector," Robin said to me.

I pinned Miriam's nametag to my shirt. "I already have one," I told him.